THE BARON'S KISS

"I was thinking of our conversation that night you danced with me at your coming-out ball," said Julius. "You said then that it was not your company whom your suitors were seeking, but rather the company of my uncle's fortune. And I can readily see how you might think so, but yet it seems hard that you should suspect any man who enjoys your company to be a fortune hunter. Now, however, it is obvious you absolve Lord Steinbridge of such mercenary motives. Otherwise you would not even be considering his offer on a provisional basis."

"True," admitted Elizabeth. She eyed him with mistrust. "But that still does not explain why *you* should be grateful to him for restoring my faith."

"Doesn't it?" said Julius, returning her look steadily.

"No, it doesn't," said Elizabeth. She was almost angry, yet looking into her eyes, Julius had the strangest impression there was an emotion besides anger lying just beneath the surface. It inspired him to sudden recklessness. Bending down, he kissed her full on the lips.

Elizabeth drew back swiftly. "Why did you do that, my lord?"

"Because—" began Julius, then stopped. Why *had* he kissed her? Because he loved her, of course; that was the answer that came promptly to his lips.

It was therefore with a sensation of unreality that Julius heard himself saying, "Because I love you, Elizabeth Watson. And I'd like to marry you myself. . . ."

Books by Joy Reed

Published by Zebra Books

THE BARON
AND THE
BLUESTOCKING

Joy Reed

ZEBRA BOOKS
Kensington Publishing Corp.
http://www.kensingtonbooks.com

ZEBRA BOOKS are published by

Kensington Publishing Corp.
850 Third Avenue
New York, NY 10022

All Kensington titles, imprints, and distributed lines are available at special quantity discounts for bulk purchases for sales promotion, premiums, fund-raising, educational, or institutional use.

Special book excerpts or customized printings can also be created to fit specific needs. For details, write or phone the office of the Kensington Special Sales Manager: Kensington Publishing Corp., 850 Third Avenue, New York, NY 10022. Attn. Special Sales Department. Phone: 1-800-221-2647.

Zebra and the Z logo Reg. U.S. Pat. & TM Off.

First Printing: March 2002
10 9 8 7 6 5 4 3 2 1

Printed in the United States of America

For Mary Jack Wald, with thanks

One

"Why, Mama, what is the matter?" Elizabeth paused in the doorway, regarding her mother with surprise.

Mrs. Watson raised a tearstained face to her elder daughter. "We are ruined, Elizabeth," she said. "Ruined!"

Elizabeth's heart gave a sickening thump at these words. Then common sense reasserted itself. "Surely not," she said. "You know it cannot be as bad as that, Mama. We may not be rich, but the money Papa left you invested in the funds ought to be safe enough, even if you have been outrunning our income. I thought you were being rather extravagant, giving that rout and ordering all those new gowns for Sophia last month."

Tearful or not, Mrs. Watson bristled at these words. "I'm sure I've not been extravagant at all, my dear! No more than any woman with two grown daughters can possibly be. And I'm sure I thought our income was secure enough, but it seems it is *not*. I just got a letter from Mr. Lloyd, and he tells me we have no more money left at all. I don't know how that could be, for I have not spent a penny more than I could help. It was quite necessary to give that rout for Sophia last month, for otherwise she would have had no chance at all of attracting Mr. Lassiter."

"But Mr. Lassiter has been engaged to Anne Bell these

six months," said Elizabeth, regarding her mother with bemusement. "And surely you did not imagine in any case that Sophy would marry *him?* He must be fifty at least and has nothing but fortune and the promise of a baronetcy to recommend him."

Mrs. Watson brushed these words aside with a sweeping gesture. "That's neither here nor there," she said. "I'm sure Mr. Lassiter would have made Sophia an excellent husband if she had happened to take his fancy. As it is, I can't admire his taste in tying himself up with that chit Anne Bell, but one never knows till one tries. Poor Sophia would have had no chance at all with him if I had not given that rout. Even you must see *that,* Elizabeth."

There were many things Elizabeth could have said in reply to this speech, but she knew from experience that none of them were likely to do any good. She contented herself with saying, "Well, I thought it was flying rather high, Mama, for you to be giving a grand party with dancing and a sit-down supper. But even if you have been exceeding your income a bit, you ought to be able to come about easily enough. It's not as though you have been spending your capital. We have only to exercise economy for a few months, and then all will be well again."

"But that's what I have been telling you, my dear. Mr. Lloyd says there is no capital left. I'm sure I don't know what could have happened to it, for as I say, I have not been at all extravagant. Of course I have been obliged to sell out of the funds from time to time, but—"

"Sell out of the funds?" repeated Elizabeth with dismay. "Don't tell me you have been selling out of the funds, Mama! Why, that *is* your capital—the source from which your income is drawn!"

Mrs. Watson's plump, pretty face took on a mulish look. "Don't use that tone with me, Elizabeth," she said. "I'd like to know what else I was to do, if I did *not* sell out of the funds. The trifling little bit we make on the shares is barely enough to feed and house us. And what with Sophy's needing new dresses for the assemblies every month—and of course we cannot do without a carriage here in town, for it would not do to have to walk everywhere or use hired hacks as though we were a parcel of dowdies. And though it may be old-fashioned, I simply cannot feel that any family with pretensions to gentility can exist without at least one manservant. And with coal costing such a lot, and wax candles, too—"

Elizabeth cut through these reflections in a voice sharp with anxiety. "How much is left, Mama?" she said. "Exactly how much have we left in the funds?"

"Why, just what I said before, my dear. It seems we have nothing at all. And what is still worse, Mr. Lloyd tells me that now we haven't any capital, we aren't to get any income, either. I don't understand how that could be, for I am sure that before he died, your papa told me I would have enough to keep me and you girls as long as we lived."

With as much patience as she could muster, Elizabeth explained how her mother's income was directly derived from the capital invested in the funds, and that if the capital ceased to be, then the income must also. It was doubtful if Mrs. Watson understood much of this explanation, but she did seem to grasp its long-term implications. "We are ruined," she repeated, thrusting a sheaf of papers at Elizabeth. "Just look at these bills! And I haven't but five pounds in the house—and the grocer hasn't been paid yet, nor the butcher."

Determined to know the worst, Elizabeth took the sheaf of bills from her mother. Topmost was a dressmaker's bill amounting to several hundred pounds. At the bottom was pointedly written, "Payable on Receipt." She flipped through the rest of the stack, her heart sinking as she saw the extent of their plight. "We *are* in the suds,

Mama," she said with dismay. "I wish I had known before that we were living so far beyond our means. Whatever were you thinking of, charging all these things when you must have known you hadn't money enough to pay for them?"

Mrs. Watson burst into tears once more. "I only wanted what was best for you and Sophy," she wept. "It goes to my heart to see my daughters dwindling into old maids. Oh, I daresay you don't feel it, Elizabeth, for you never cared for pretty things and beaux and parties like an ordinary girl. All you care about are books. But your sister is different. Dear Sophia is such a pretty girl and so very taking in her ways. I'm sure it's only want of being seen in the proper circles that prevents her from making a great match."

Elizabeth merely nodded. She knew well her mother's ambitions for her younger sister. "But you will hardly achieve a great match for Sophia by sending us all to debtors' prison," she pointed out. "And in any case, I don't think my sister really wants a great match. If only poor Mr. Arthur could get a better living, I believe she would be perfectly happy marrying him and settling down as a clergyman's wife."

"A clergyman's wife!" said Mrs. Watson, her eyes flashing. "I will never consent to see Sophia throw herself away upon a penniless curate."

Elizabeth could not help laughing at this, in spite of the gravity of their situation. "But you know, Mama, we are a good deal less than penniless ourselves," she pointed out. "Mr. Arthur may not be wealthy, but at least he hasn't thousands of pounds of bills he can't pay."

This produced a fresh effusion of tears from Mrs. Watson. "You are very unfeeling, Elizabeth," she wept. "I told you before, I did it all for you and Sophia. If you had an ounce of proper gratitude, you would be thanking me rather than reading me a lecture. And I'd like to know what you've ever done to repay all the sacrifices I've made for you," she added, her tears giving way to indignation. "I'm sure I've given you chances enough to meet eligible men, but you won't be friendly and conversable like other girls, and so no man ever looks at you twice. The only thing you've ever done is write a book that no one wants to read and that's hardly brought us a hundred pounds in spite of its taking you the best part of two years to write."

Elizabeth flushed. Her book was a sore point. "I did not write the book for money, Mama," she said. "You know it was Papa's ambition to write a book about the Second Punic War. It was only his dying so suddenly that prevented him from doing it. Since I had been with him to Italy and Spain, and I had all his notes, it seemed the least I could do, to try to fulfill what had been his own lifelong dream."

"Yes, but what good did it do?" demanded Mrs. Watson practically. "No one wants to read about the Second Punic War. At any rate, *I* don't, and neither do any of the other people I know. Not but what I am sure it's a clever enough book in its way. That gentleman in *Blackwood's Magazine* seemed to think a good deal of it, and I overheard Dr. Fischer say the other day that for a girl your age to write such a book is nothing short of remarkable. But if you don't get any money for your work, what is the point of it? You had much better try writing Gothic novels like Mrs. Radcliffe. I'm sure her books are popular enough, and it stands to reason there must be a deal more money writing novels than boring books on history."

Elizabeth sighed. "I am afraid I wouldn't know how to begin writing a Gothic novel, Mama," she said. "Even if I could write one, it wouldn't likely do any good. You know it was almost a year after I sent my other book to the publisher before I got any money for it, and we need money right away."

"Then what are we to do?" wailed Mrs. Watson, breaking out into a fresh influx of tears. "Oh, if only Sophia had married Mr. Lassiter! Then we could all be easy."

Elizabeth forbore to mention that even if Mr. Lassiter had married Sophia, he might have balked at paying several thousand pounds of bills belonging to her family. She stooped to kiss her mother on the brow. "Never mind, Mama," she said. "Let's put away all these bills and get ready for dinner. I will try to think of some way out of this bumble broth."

"If you're imagining that Amelia Reese-Whittington will do anything for us, you are mistaken," said Mrs. Watson dolefully, as she shoved the bills into the pigeonholes of the desk. "One would think, with Amelia being my own cousin, that she would feel more responsibility toward her relations. But when I wrote her last year hinting that she might like to bring Sophy out, she was very disobliging. She said her own expenses were so great that she could hardly afford to live in London herself, let alone sponsor Sophy."

"We won't bother Mrs. Reese-Whittington then," said Elizabeth, mentally crossing this possible solution off her list. "Come, Mama, there's no use worrying any more now. Come upstairs and wash your face and change your dress. Mary Anne has dinner almost ready to serve, and we won't be any better off if we let it go to waste."

Although Elizabeth had tried to speak cheerfully for her mother's sake, her mood was anything but cheerful as she went up the stairs to her own room. The chill that greeted her inside that Spartan chamber did nothing to improve her mood.

There were only two proper bedchambers in the town house the Watsons rented. It had seemed only right to Elizabeth that Sophia and her mother should occupy them. They were feminine creatures who loved pretty things and luxury. She, Elizabeth, was made of sterner stuff.

While Sophia had been embroidering samplers at her mother's knee and studying dancing, deportment, and housekeeping, Elizabeth had been traveling through Italy, Spain, and northern Africa with her father. Mr. Watson had been intent on tracing every movement made by the Carthaginian army during the Second Punic War, and these researches had taken him and his daughter to some out-of-the-way places. Elizabeth had slept in rude lodging houses, in third-rate hostelries, and even in the open air when nothing better was available.

Compared to these accommodations, her present small attic room was a palace of luxury. Yet it seemed a bleak enough place on that cold January evening. Dark and fog shrouded the view from the unshaded windows, and the light of her candle threw into high relief the irregularities of the plank floor and the shabbiness of the patchwork quilt covering the narrow iron bed. The room was cold, too, for it possessed no stove or fireplace. Elizabeth shivered as she unbuttoned her woolen pelisse and the dun-colored stuff gown beneath it. It suddenly occurred to her to wonder why she had chosen to resign all claim to beauty and comfort in her life.

It was certain that her life had little of beauty and comfort about it. If there was a sacrifice to be made in the Watson family, she was always the one to make it. Always the heaviest burdens seemed to fall on her shoulders. It had been so ever since the death of her father. In a way, Elizabeth supposed it was a kind of compliment to her character, and she had often felt a secret pride to be the strong one, the generous one, the capable one. But now, as the Watsons were teetering on the brink of financial ruin and her mother was looking to her for assistance,

Elizabeth felt a surge of rebellion. Why must she be ruined when she had done nothing herself to earn ruination?

She, of all the family, had always had the most uncomfortable rooms, the plainest gowns, the smallest share of spending money. It had never occurred to her to grumble at this. Indeed, it had often been her own suggestion that she take less than the others. As her mother had said, she did not care for pretty things and beaux and parties. Or did she? Elizabeth went over and looked at herself in the glass over her washstand. What she saw was a girl with flaxen hair drawn back into a tight knot at the nape of her neck. The girl's face was pale, but her eyes were dark, and so were her lashes and the level line of her brows. They formed a strong contrast against the pallor of her hair and complexion. Her other features were fine and regular, but still hers could not be called a pretty face, Elizabeth told herself. Instead it was a serious face—the face of a high-minded girl who preferred books to beaux.

Her sister Sophia, on the other hand, was definitely a pretty girl. Sophia's hair was golden blonde instead of flaxen pale, her eyes were a warmer brown that did not contrast so sharply with her complexion, and her face was rounder and rosier than Elizabeth's. Her figure was rounder, too, and not so unfashionably tall. All in all, it was no wonder that Mrs. Watson had chosen to pin her matrimonial hopes on her younger rather than her elder daughter. It might have been thought excessive of her to spend the sum total of the family's capital to show Sophia off to advantage, but there was no doubt that Sophia repaid the investment insofar as any young woman could.

So Elizabeth reminded herself, with sisterly loyalty. Much as she might deplore her mother's folly, she felt no resentment that her future security should have been jeopardized for her younger sister's sake. It was not as though Sophia had personally played any role in jeopardizing it. There was nothing grasping or selfish about Sophia. She was a sweet, sunny-tempered creature, accustomed to yielding to the opinions of those around her. If you told her it was going to rain, she obediently took an umbrella; if you told her the Whigs were progressive while the Tories bade fair to be the ruin of the country, she would obediently parrot the words to everyone she met, until she met a Tory who convinced her it was the other way around.

The only matter in which Sophia had shown any independence of thought was in the matter of choosing a husband. And in this matter she had shown herself independent indeed. She had persisted in preferring the addresses of Mr. Philip Arthur, the curate of the local church, to any other gentleman. Yet even here she had been brought to yield, for Mrs. Watson had spoken so eloquently of the folly of tying herself to a penniless man that Sophia had, in the end, tearfully relinquished her hopes in regard to Mr. Arthur. She continued to cherish a partiality toward him, however, and it was probably this that had kept her a spinster despite the several offers of marriage she had received during the past few years.

Poor Sophy, Elizabeth thought to herself. *It seems hard she may not marry the man she loves. If Philip Arthur had any gumption at all, he would simply marry her out of hand. Sophy was twenty-one last birthday, and there is nothing to keep her from marrying whom she chooses. But being a man of principle, he will not do it unless Mama gives her approval. I can understand his qualms, I suppose. I doubt he earns a hundred pounds a year as curate of St. Sebastian's, and it would be madness to try to support a wife on such a pittance. But still it seems sad that he and Sophy cannot be together, when they care for each other so much.*

In her sympathy for her sister's plight, Elizabeth forgot for a time to grieve over her own. Indeed, as she reminded herself, her own plight was not so bad as Sophia's. She, too, might be a penniless daughter of a bankrupt mother, but there was no beau whom she was barred from marrying because of a want of funds. Her mother was perfectly right in saying that spinsterhood was inevitable for her. What man would want to marry a too-tall, too-pale, too-serious girl who could not make social conversation? A girl who found parties an ordeal and dancing an awkward chore, and preferred to curl up in a corner with a book?

And for that matter, what man would Elizabeth want to marry? She considered the question dispassionately as she stood regarding herself in the glass. In the end, she came to the conclusion that there was none. It was true that when she was younger, she had cherished vague, romantic dreams of a knight in shining armor who would one day arrive to sweep her off her feet. But those were dreams of which she had always been faintly ashamed. They did not seem in keeping with her own sensible, rational nature. And as the years had gone by and she had become better acquainted with men in general, she had come to see more and more how irrational those childish dreams had been. There were agreeable men in the world, of course, and some who were not merely agreeable but also intelligent and right-minded. But for better or worse, she had never met one yet who had tempted her to change her spinster state. And since none had ever seemed inclined to ask her to, this was probably just as well.

With a sigh, Elizabeth turned away from the glass. *I must be mad,* she told herself, *mooning about love and romance, when we are on the verge of bankruptcy! I had better be thinking instead how to get us out of this pickle Mama has got us into.* She suspected that thought on this subject was likely to prove as futile as thoughts of love and romance, but she put the suspicion from her firmly. Futile the situation might be, but she would not accept it as such until she had examined it from every possible angle.

During the next few days, Elizabeth did indeed examine the situation from every possible angle. She demanded a full accounting of her mother's outstanding bills and bravely totaled them to obtain the final, appalling sum of their debts. She then compiled a list of possible sources of funds. Both Sophia and she might find employment; there were a few trifles of furniture that might bring a hundred pounds or so; the finer part of Sophia's wardrobe might be sold secondhand, and there were a few pounds due her by way of royalties for her book, which her publisher had promised to send on to her. But these monies were as a drop of water against the vast ocean of their debts. In the end, Elizabeth came to the conclusion that ruin was inevitable. She was sitting at her mother's desk, wondering whether she might yet venture a last-ditch appeal to Mrs. Reese-Whittington, when Mary Ann, the Watsons' senior maidservant, popped her head around the door.

"There's a gentleman to see you, miss," she said. "A stranger, he is. Gave his name as Mr. Pierce."

Elizabeth started. She had just been thinking that given the extent of her mother's debts, it could not be much longer before the bailiffs came calling. Now, as if on cue, here was a strange gentleman asking to see her. Of course he must be a bailiff, for she was expecting no other callers this morning. She sprang to her feet, her heart in a turmoil of panic.

It was on the tip of her tongue to tell Mary Anne to deny her to the gentleman. That would buy at least a little time in which she might yet think of a way out of their predicament. Then rationality asserted itself. The Watsons' financial predicament was so serious that no amount of time could make much difference. Even if Mrs. Reese-Whittington were willing to help, she could hardly be expected to defray the whole balance of their debts. There would still be creditors to deal with, and she, Elizabeth, might as well deal with them now as later. Perhaps if she dealt civilly with them, they would be disposed to be lenient in their terms.

Elizabeth drew a deep breath. "Tell the gentleman to come in, Mary Anne," she said. She then stood waiting, her heart beating as though she had just run a footrace.

Two

The gentleman came into the room and stood looking around him. He was a jolly looking gentleman of middle age with a round, smiling face. Elizabeth was disposed almost to resent him, his smile was so broad and his good humor so evident.

But of course that was not a rational attitude, as she reminded herself. If one had to deal with bailiffs, it was better to deal with a good-humored one than an ill-humored one. So she forced an answering smile to her lips and said, "Good morning, sir. Please be seated if you will. Mr. Pierce, was it?"

"Yes, Pierce is the name," said the gentleman, smiling more broadly than ever as he seated himself on a shabby chintz sofa. "Jason Pierce, of Pierce and Burton, out of Lincoln's Inn Field."

Elizabeth's smile froze on her lips. The situation was even worse than she had imagined. To have a bailiff calling at the house would have been bad enough, but an attorney seemed a foe even more formidable. "Yes?" she managed to say, through frozen lips.

"Yes, indeed," assented the smiling Mr. Pierce. "I take it you are Miss Watson? Miss *Elizabeth* Watson?"

"Yes," said Elizabeth cautiously. She was a little surprised by the question. Of course her mother had entrusted the settlement of the Watsons' financial affairs to her eldest daughter, but it seemed remarkable that this stranger should know it.

Mr. Pierce's next question was even more unexpected. "Authoress of *A History of the Second Punic War?*" he demanded, surveying Elizabeth shrewdly. "You avow you are that selfsame Elizabeth Watson?"

"Yes, of course," said Elizabeth in bewilderment. She could not imagine what the stranger's questions were tending to. She could only regard him with wide eyes, waiting for him to go on.

Mr. Pierce's smile gave way to a broad grin. "That's all right then," he said. "This was the direction given by your publisher, but I had to make sure. And of course I'll have to have positive proof of identity before the business is settled, but that's only a formality. I don't doubt you are exactly who you say you are, Miss Watson. Though if you don't mind my saying so, you do seem a bit young to have written such a book—such a very *scholarly* book, you know."

There was a pause, during which he seemed to expect Elizabeth to say something. "Thank you," she said faintly.

Mr. Pierce beamed. "You are very welcome, Miss Watson. It's an honor and a privilege to meet such a learned young lady."

Elizabeth felt unequal to answering this and so merely bowed, waiting for Mr. Pierce to go on. This he did after a moment's pause and with an air of recollecting himself. "You will be wondering what this is all about," he told Elizabeth.

"Yes," she agreed fervently.

"The fact is that I have come about a bequest. A most interesting bequest, and of a kind I have never encountered before in my legal career. Were you acquainted with the late Lucius Atwater? The Honorable Mr. Lucius Atwater?"

Mr. Pierce paused again, once more regarding Elizabeth keenly. She racked her brain, but the name was unknown to her. "No, I think I never heard of a Mr. Lucius Atwater," she said

"Well, I hardly expected that you would. He was a very quiet-lived gentleman, for all he was an Atwater. A very old and high-born London family, the Atwaters— very good *ton,* and moving in the best circles." Mr. Pierce smiled at Elizabeth, who was still looking bewildered. "Ah, well! If you don't know Mr. Atwater's name now, you'll have reason to know it in the days ahead—aye, and to bless it, too. What I have to tell you will likely come as very welcome news to you, Miss Watson." Mr. Pierce's eyes wandered around the parlor, dwelling thoughtfully on the scorch mark in front of the hearth rug and the shabby chintz of the furniture.

Elizabeth's mind was working rapidly. The word "bequest," together with various other of Mr. Pierce's words, had aroused certain possibilities in her mind. Still, she could hardly believe financial rescue could have come as opportunely as this. "Do you mean that Mr. Atwater has left me a bequest?" she said cautiously.

"That's exactly what I do mean," said Mr. Pierce, beaming at her. "A very handsome bequest, Miss Watson. When word gets out, you will be a much-envied young lady."

At these wonderful words, Elizabeth knew an impulse to throw her arms around Mr. Pierce and kiss him. She was almost afraid to ask any more questions, lest her good fortune evaporate on examination. But reluctant as she was to look a gift horse in the mouth, she could not resist the urge to question Mr. Pierce further.

"But why?" she asked. "Why should Mr. Atwater leave me a bequest? As I told you just now, I have never heard of the man before. And it's not as though we were any relation to each other. Mama would have mentioned it before now if we were," she added dryly. A connection to one of the great families of London, however slight, was not a card the socially ambitious Mrs. Watson would have neglected to play.

"Why did Mr. Atwater leave you his fortune? Why, because of your book," said Mr. Pierce, as though this were an obvious conclusion. "He had read it, d'ye see, and admired it very much. It just so happens that Mr. Atwater was by way of being a scholar himself, and the Punic Wars were an area of particular interest to him. He told me so himself a year ago when he called me in to make his will. 'Jacob, I've never read a better book on the subject,' he said. 'The lady has done a first-class job. That kind of scholarship ought to be encouraged, and it seems to me it's my duty to encourage it the only way I can. I'm dashed if I won't make her my heir.' And that's just what he did," finished Mr. Pierce, beaming again at Elizabeth.

"I see," said Elizabeth. Although she thought it rather eccentric of Mr. Atwater to choose his heir in such a fashion, she could only bless such convenient eccentricity. In a voice that she strove to keep casual, she asked, "This bequest of which you speak, Mr. Pierce—will it be a long time in coming to me?"

Mr. Pierce smiled indulgently. "A natural question, Miss Watson—a very natural question," he said. "However, I'm afraid I can't answer it at present. An estate like Mr. Atwater's isn't settled all in a day, you know. There's a deal of formalities to go through before we'll know exactly where we stand. Why, I can't even tell you the exact amount of the bequest until I've had a chance to look into things a little."

"Would it be"—Elizabeth's voice shook slightly— "would it be as much as three thousand pounds?" Three thousand pounds was the amount of her mother's debt, give or take a few pounds, and Elizabeth felt that if her bequest amounted to so much, all her prayers would have been answered.

"Three thousand pounds!" said Mr. Pierce, and he burst into merry laughter. "My dear Miss Watson, I would be much surprised if it were not at least *three hundred thousand* pounds. Indeed, I think I may say with assurance that it will be considerably more than that."

Elizabeth felt dizzy. She sat looking at Mr. Pierce, and he sat looking back at her, his smile as bright as ever. "Do you mean to say," she said at last, in a carefully measured voice, "that Mr. Atwater has left me several hundred thousand pounds for no better reason than that he admired my book?"

"That's exactly what I do mean to say," said Mr. Pierce. "But there, I'm forgetting." His face sobered, and he leaned forward, addressing Elizabeth with unwonted earnestness. "I wouldn't want to mislead you, Miss Watson. The bequest does not come totally without conditions."

Elizabeth felt almost relieved. The idea that someone could leave her such a fortune for such a trifling reason was preposterous. No doubt there would be some impossible condition attached to the bequest that would put it beyond her reach. "What is the condition?" she asked as calmly as she could between the alternations of hope and fear in her heart.

"Oh, well, I wouldn't call it a condition exactly, Miss Watson. It's more what you might call a suggestion. Not to put too fine a point on it, it was Mr. Atwater's hope, in leaving you his money, that you might be enabled to research and write a book on all of the Punic Wars. Apparently nobody's ever done that, or at least not in a manner Mr. Atwater approved of. He felt you'd done such a masterly job looking into the second one that you might be able to do the same thing with all of 'em, dealing with the subject in what you might call a comprehensive manner."

"Oh!" said Elizabeth, a slow smile spreading across her face. "Oh, I could do that, Mr. Pierce! If I had three hundred thousand pounds, I am sure I could write such a book. I could visit Sicily—and investigate the sites of Messana and Depranum. . . ."

Mr. Pierce regarded her benevolently while she enumerated the various places she would want to visit. "That's the ticket," he said. "Mr. Atwater was sure you could do it, only the means might be wanting. Well, now you've got the means—or will have them once the estate is settled. As I say, that may be a while yet, but I hope not too long." He gave Elizabeth a searching look. "You seem like a sensible young lady, Miss Watson, and there's no doubt you're a clever one. On the whole, I'm tempted to deal frankly with you."

"Yes?" said Elizabeth absently, her thoughts still bent on foreign itineraries. "By all means deal frankly with me, Mr. Pierce. What is it you wish to tell me?"

"Why, only this. You will understand that a bequest of this size from a man in Mr. Atwater's position is likely to cause a certain amount of—well, what you might call contention. Indeed, there's already been some contention on the part of certain relations of Mr. Atwater's. It's possible they may cause a bit of—ahem—unpleasantness for you, in the settling of the estate."

These words rolled across the landscape of Elizabeth's rosy dreams like a splash of India ink. She regarded Mr. Pierce blankly. "Relations?" she said. "Had Mr. Atwater close relations, then? I had assumed he did not, or he would have left his money to them instead of me."

"Why, it depends what you call close, Miss Watson. Mr. Lucius had none of what you might call direct descendants, being a lifelong bachelor. But he did have a couple of brothers, both of whom married and produced sons. It is from that quarter that I would expect most of the opposition."

"Go on," said Elizabeth, as Mr. Pierce paused. "Mr. Atwater's nephews think the estate should go to them rather than to me?"

"One of them seems to think so, at least. I have heard no word of opposition from Julius. That is the present Lord Atwater, the son of Mr. Lucius's elder brother. Julius is a very wealthy man in his own right, and though Mr. Lucius was fond of him, he didn't hold with piling fortune on fortune when he thought the money would do more good elsewhere. He did leave a few of his personal things to Julius—a valuable painting, and some family heirlooms—but that was all. And he didn't leave so much as a scrap to Mr. Gilbert Atwater, his other nephew. That was the son of his younger brother Thomas, and I must say that Gilbert hasn't taken it well at all. Nor has his mother, Mrs. Thomas Atwater. She's what the French call a *femme formidable* in any case, and both she and Gilbert feel strongly that he ought to have his uncle's money instead of you. But that's all nonsense, of course, and quite contrary to Mr. Lucius's expressed wishes. They haven't a hope of upsetting the will, but there may be some unpleasantness before it's all over, and I thought you ought to be prepared for it."

Elizabeth was silent. Mr. Pierce looked at her searchingly. "I hope you won't let it disturb you, Miss Watson," he said. "There's no doubt that the estate belongs to you in every legal sense. Mr. Lucius was of perfectly sound mind when he made his will, and there are plenty of people willing to attest to it if necessary. But I do feel we should lose no time settling the estate, so you may take possession as soon as possible. That will make your position even more secure, for possession is nine-tenths of the law, you know."

Elizabeth was silent a moment longer. At last she spoke, pronouncing the words with difficulty. "You say the bequest is legally mine, Mr. Pierce," she said. "But

I am afraid that morally it is not. I was a stranger to Mr. Atwater, and I did nothing to deserve his estate. It seems to me that it would more properly belong to his family."

Mr. Pierce stared at her. "You don't mean that you would refuse the bequest on that account?" he asked.

"I'm afraid I do, Mr. Pierce. It's not that I do not want it, you understand. On the contrary, I want it very much indeed, but I don't feel that I am morally entitled to it. Don't you understand?"

It was obvious that Mr. Pierce did not understand. He shook his head slowly. "And here I thought you were a sensible young lady," he said sadly. "Didn't you hear what I just told you? Mr. Lucius wanted you to have his estate. He left it to you very explicitly and in a manner that makes certain no one can seriously dispute his judgment in so doing. You need have no qualms about accepting his bequest."

"But I do have qualms," said Elizabeth. She knew herself for a quixotic fool, but she also knew her own conscience. She was sure she could never enjoy a fortune gained in such an equivocal manner. "I can't—I simply can't accept three hundred thousand pounds from a perfect stranger when there are relatives who have a more natural claim on it. A smaller bequest, perhaps—a matter of a few thousand pounds—I would gladly accept, but not a fortune of this size. If you would kindly talk it over with the Atwaters . . ."

Mr. Pierce regarded her a moment longer, then shook his head. "It's the shock," he said, speaking as if to himself. "Of course she's not feeling entirely rational. Not that any woman is ever entirely rational; it's not in their natures, bless their hearts."

"I *am* rational!" said Elizabeth, whose pride was stung by these words. "I am perfectly rational! It would be far more irrational of me to accept a fortune I have no right to."

"Of course you are entitled to your own opinion," said Mr. Pierce, with an air of humoring feminine irrationality. Elizabeth was nettled anew, but before she could speak again, he rose to his feet. "I'll tell you what, Miss Watson. I've given you a deal to digest this morning, and it's not to be expected you'll do it all in a minute. Take a day or two to think it over—or no, better yet, take a week. Think it over for a week, and at the end of that time you can let me know what you intend to do about the bequest."

"I already know what I intend to do," said Elizabeth. "I tell you, I cannot accept this bequest, Mr. Pierce!"

"That's right. That's right. I'm sure your scruples are very much to be admired, Miss Watson. But just you think it over, that's all. I'll call again in a week's time with some papers for you to sign, and you can give me your decision then."

Mr. Pierce spoke these words with the same air of humoring feminine irrationality that had irritated Elizabeth before. He remained steadfastly deaf to her assertions that she knew very well her own mind. Wishing her a good morning, he reassumed his hat and took himself off.

After he had gone, Sophia peeped cautiously around the parlor door. "Who was that, Elizabeth?" she asked. "I heard voices, but didn't like to interrupt."

"Oh, Sophy, you will never guess what has happened," said Elizabeth, collapsing on the sofa. "Come in, and I'll tell you about it. But order us some tea first, if you please. I declare, I'm actually shaking all over."

Sophia obediently ordered the tea, then seated herself on the sofa, spreading her rose-pink muslin skirts neatly around her. She listened in astonishment as Elizabeth described the reason for Mr. Pierce's call. "Did you ever hear of such a thing?" demanded Elizabeth. "It's like something out of a fairy tale. To think someone would leave me a fortune for such a reason!"

"And must you truly refuse it?" said Sophia, sounding a trifle wistful. "It would be a great thing for you to have some money of your own, Elizabeth. I often feel you don't get nearly your share, for Mama will insist on spending three times as much on me as on you. I have told her many times it isn't fair, but she insists on doing it, and you always back her up."

Elizabeth regarded her sister affectionately. "Sophia, you are a darling," she said. "There never was such a sweet, unselfish girl. Just between you and me, I will admit that I wouldn't mind having a little money of my own. Mama has been going it at such a great rate that we haven't two pennies left to rub together."

Sophia looked dismayed but unsurprised by these words. "I was afraid of that," she said. "She *will* insist on buying dresses at Madame LeGrande's, though they are so dreadfully expensive. I often tell her I wouldn't mind making my own dresses, but she won't hear of it. Oh, Elizabeth, if what you say is really true, then don't you think—not that I wish to make light of your scruples—but don't you think, perhaps, that this legacy is a kind of Providence? I do not speak for myself, you understand. *I* can always marry Philip, and I am sure we could manage on his salary very well, no matter what Mama says. But you and Mama—"

"I understand," said Elizabeth, breaking in upon her sister's speech with an understanding smile. "It does seem quite providential, the inheritance coming at such a critical time. I thought so at first myself, but now I suspect it's more in the nature of a moral test or temptation. You must see I can't accept such a fortune under such circumstances, Sophy. Not when there are other people whose claim is so much better than my own. My conscience would never give me a minute's rest if I did."

Sophia, being well acquainted with her sister's conscience, gave a resigned sigh. "It does seem too bad, having to refuse a fortune when we could use the money so badly," she said. "But of course you cannot do anything that is contrary to your conscience, Elizabeth."

"No," agreed Elizabeth. She hesitated a moment, then went on in a diffident voice. "I did think perhaps—of course I cannot rely on it, but I did hope that if I give the money back to the Atwaters, they might make me a gift, a smaller legacy, you understand, that I might accept in good conscience. But of course I could make no such condition in giving the money back," she added proudly. "It would be entirely up to them whether they gave me anything or not."

"Well, I think it is the least they could do, if you are generous enough to return to them the whole amount," said Sophia. "Three hundred thousand pounds! Are you going to tell, Mama, Elizabeth?"

"Are you going to tell me what?" demanded a voice from the doorway. "And what's this about three hundred thousand pounds?"

Both Sophia and Elizabeth looked around with a guilty start. Mrs. Watson was standing in the doorway, regarding them with a look of suspicion. "What's this about three hundred thousand pounds?" she repeated.

Ever since Mr. Pierce had left, Elizabeth had been debating whether or not to tell her mother about her bequest. She had a shrewd idea that Mrs. Watson would not be so understanding as Sophia about her scruples in refusing Mr. Atwater's estate. But now her hand was forced. It would clearly be necessary to tell her mother something in explanation of the words she had overheard, and Elizabeth felt she might as well make a clean breast of the situation as not. Bidding her mother to sit down, she set about describing for a second time all that had passed between her and Mr. Pierce.

Mrs. Watson listened to the account, her eyes growing wider and wider. When Elizabeth first mentioned the staggering amount of Lucius Atwater's estate, she could contain herself no longer.

"Darling, darling Elizabeth," she cried, jumping up and embracing her eldest daughter. "I always knew you were a clever girl, but I never imagined your cleverness would bring you a fortune. Three hundred thousand pounds, and very likely more! Why, you will be rich as a queen!"

"But I can't accept the money, Mama," said Elizabeth. "Sit down and let me explain. Mr. Atwater had relatives, a couple of nephews—"

As Elizabeth had expected, Mrs. Watson was not impressed by the claims of Mr. Atwater's nephews. "You don't mean you are fool enough to think of refusing a fortune on their account!" she cried. "One of these young men is a lord, and rich enough to buy an abbey already, very likely. And the other is very likely rich, too."

"It's not a question of their being rich," said Elizabeth repressively. "It's a question of right and wrong."

"And what can be wrong about accepting this money when we need it so badly? If you ask me, it is wicked to talk about giving it away. It's obvious the money came to you just now on purpose, to help us out of our difficulties. Indeed, you put me out of patience with your scruples, Elizabeth. Thank heaven this Mr. Pierce was sensible enough to make you wait a week before he would accept your decision. Of course you will take the money."

"No, I will not!" said Elizabeth. "You may say what you like about my scruples, Mama, but two wrongs don't make a right. Even if you have brought us to the brink of bankruptcy with your extravagance, I am not obliged to rescue us by accepting a bequest to which I am not entitled."

This, of course, resulted in a storm of tears and recriminations. "You always were an unnatural girl, Elizabeth," wept Mrs. Watson. "A very hard and unfeeling girl. Throwing my errors in my face, when I have only done what I thought was for the best! And now you have a chance to make things easy for all of us, and you insist on turning your back on it."

This was Mrs. Watson's recurring theme during the days that followed. She reproached Elizabeth for her perversity, wept over her ingratitude, and demanded to know what would become of them all when they were sent off to debtor's prison. These reproaches were very hard for Elizabeth to bear, not least because she felt a secret fear that her mother might be right. Perhaps her scruples *were* foolish. Yet she knew she could not accept Mr. Atwater's bequest and keep a clear conscience. She argued it over with herself countless times, but always came to the same conclusion. Still, it was terrible to know she possessed the means of staving off imminent ruin and was barred from using them.

Sophia did her best to comfort her sister during this difficult time, but in a way her kindness was only another reproach to Elizabeth. Elizabeth knew that if she accepted Mr. Atwater's fortune, she would be able to dower Sophia and enable her to marry Mr. Arthur without further delay. Of course Sophia never pointed this out or even showed any sign that she was thinking it, but her reticence only made Elizabeth feel worse. She knew that it was only her scruples that were keeping her sister apart from the man she loved. Elizabeth was willing to suffer herself for principle, but it was quite another thing to make her sister suffer along with her.

Nonetheless, Elizabeth held firm to her resolution as the week allotted for her reflection slowly passed. When, shortly before noon on the day Mr. Pierce was due, Mary Anne came to Elizabeth's room and told her she had a caller waiting for her in the parlor, Elizabeth never doubted that it was he. Neither did she doubt that she would renounce claim to her fortune, difficult as it might be. Praying silently that she might be firm in the face of temptation, she rose and went down to the parlor.

Three

"It's infamous!" said Mrs. Atwater. "Utterly infamous!"

She was standing in the drawing room of Atwater House, in front of the celebrated portrait of the first Lady Atwater. Julius, her nephew, regarded her through half-closed eyes as he lounged upon a nearby sofa. He was thinking to himself what a contrast there was between his aunt and his pictured ancestress. The first baroness had been a woman of uncommon elegance, dark haired, blue eyed, and strikingly lovely even in the stiff-boned bodice and absurd farthingale that had been the height of fashion in the court of Good Queen Bess. There was a hint of mischief about the baroness's painted eyes and a quirk of humor about her painted mouth that made her a real and endearing personality even now, when she had been dead the best part of two hundred years.

Mrs. Thomas Atwater, on the other hand, was a large, solid-looking woman in her fifties. It was possible to concede her handsome, but nothing about her suggested the adjective "endearing." Lines of obstinacy creased her rouged and powdered face, and her succession of chins quivered as she spoke in an impassioned voice. "It's infamous," she said. "Something must be done! I will not stand by and see Gilbert cheated out of his rights. And it is you who ought to do something in the matter, Julius. You are head of the family, after all."

"Aye, you might think of someone else for a change, Julius," said Gilbert. His peevish face beneath its cockscomb of sandy hair looked more peevish than ever as he regarded his cousin resentfully. "Not everybody's got a fortune like you."

Julius glanced from his cousin to his aunt, then raised his shoulders a fraction of an inch. "What would you have me do?" he said. "Lucius's will appears to be quite in order. I will agree it was a trifle unconventional for him to leave his fortune as he did, but—"

"Unconventional!" repeated Mrs. Atwater in a throbbing voice. "To leave his whole fortune to a woman of whom no one has ever heard! Passing over his own flesh and blood to enrich a scheming hussy who is, no doubt, no better than she should be!"

Julius waited until his aunt was done speaking, then patiently resumed his speech. "I will agree it was a trifle unconventional of my uncle to leave his fortune as he did, but it was *his* fortune, after all. There was no question of his being of unsound mind. I dined with him a week before he died, and he was as sharp mentally as he ever was, though it was clear his health was failing."

Mrs. Atwater dismissed these words with a sniff. "Say what you like, he *must* have been of unsound mind," she said. "To have left his fortune to a perfect stranger! Who is this Elizabeth Watson, after all? No one has ever heard of her until now."

"I had heard of her," said Julius mildly. "Her book was very well reviewed in *Blackwood's Magazine* a year or two ago. Lucius called my attention to it at the time, and later he loaned me her book so I might read it for myself."

Mrs. Atwater gave another sniff. "For myself, I am inclined to suspect this book that everyone makes such a fuss about," she said darkly. "What woman would write a book about war and history? It's perfectly nonsensical."

"On the contrary," said Julius. "It was a very well-written book, insofar as I am competent to judge it."

"Then depend on it that Miss Watson did not write it! I am sure there must be double-dealing somewhere. I daresay the book is a forgery, and the will, too. It was all a plot to steal Lucius's fortune."

Julius regarded his aunt with amusement. "If the will was a forgery, then why bother to forge the book?" he asked. "I think you will have to limit yourself to one forgery or the other, Aunt Jane. Besides, whether or not Miss Watson wrote the book is entirely beside the point. Lucius left his fortune to her in a perfectly legal and straightforward manner, and it would be wrong to interfere with what were his own expressed wishes."

"Wrong!" ejaculated Mrs. Atwater. "It was a thousand times more wrong to see his own nephew passed over in favor of a scheming hussy. A Woman of the Town, no doubt, who took advantage of Lucius's being in his dotage!"

Julius sighed. "You know that is not true, Aunt Jane. Lucius was far from being in his dotage. And as for Miss Watson being a Woman of the Town, I had that matter fully investigated at your own urging. It appears that this Miss Watson is a young lady of perfectly respectable character."

"Young, is she?" repeated Gilbert, with a certain amount of interest. "I wouldn't have thought it. I supposed she was some dried-up old schoolmistress. Still, she must be pretty blue to write a book on the Second Punic War, and I've never been able to abide bluestockings."

"In any event, I cannot imagine what Lucius was thinking, to leave his fortune to her," said Mrs. Atwater. "Gilbert would have been a much more natural choice."

"Perhaps, but you know my uncle had the greatest respect for scholarship in all its forms. And though I don't wish to sound critical, it's pretty well known that Gilbert has never shown himself much interested in—er—scholarly pursuits."

"Well, I like that!" said Gilbert indignantly. "I attended Oxford for nearly two terms, y'know."

"And were gated repeatedly for drunkenness, and finally sent down altogether for trying to smuggle a lightskirt into your room," said Julius dryly. "I am afraid that incident did not prepossess our uncle in your favor, Gilbert."

Both Mrs. Atwater and her son began to talk in a confused babble. Julius raised a hand to stop them. "It doesn't matter what I believe," he said. "What matters is that Lucius believed Miss Watson was a more deserving recipient of his fortune than anyone else. I don't know whether he was right or wrong, but as I see it, it's none of my business to interfere with his testamentary dispositions. Especially since it wouldn't be likely to do any good anyway."

Mrs. Atwater's bosom swelled with emotion. "You refuse, then, to lift a finger to help your cousin?" she demanded.

Julius regarded her steadily. "I have helped my cousin countless times during his lifetime, ma'am. If you will cast your memory back, you will recall there was an incident only last year in which I was obliged to pay his debts to the tune of several thousand pounds."

"Oh, that! But that only came about because he is so chronically short of funds. If he had Lucius's fortune, then he would be fixed for life and need not depend on you again to assist him." Mrs. Atwater came a step closer, her hands clasped in supplication. "Please, Julius! I know you swore last year that you would do no more for Gilbert, but this is different. It is not your money we need now, but your name and influence. This Miss Watson might be brought to relinquish her ill-gotten gains if she knew the head of the house of Atwater was taking a hand in the matter."

"I'm sorry, but in this matter the head of the house of Atwater prefers to remain neutral," said Julius. He began to rise from his seat. "If you will please excuse me—"

"But if you would only *see* this Miss Watson, and represent to her the impropriety of Lucius's fortune going out of the Atwater family—"

"No," said Julius with finality. "I would not dream of doing such a thing. You will have to accept that in this case, your idea of impropriety and mine differ radically, ma'am."

Mrs. Atwater regarded her nephew with frustration. He looked back at her with something almost like a twinkle in his blue eyes. That was the most annoying thing about Julius, she reflected with resentment. He was incapable of taking any issue seriously, even an issue that was of lifelong importance to his cousin.

Indeed, when one considered it, there was something offensively frivolous about the whole appearance of the present Lord Atwater. It was nothing one could really put one's finger on. His coat of blue broadcloth and fawn-colored pantaloons were irreproachable in cut and color, and neither was there anything amiss about the tall, lean figure they clothed. His dark hair was neatly combed back in the Windswept style, and his neck cloth was knotted with unobtrusive precision. Yet for all that, there was something not quite orthodox about his appearance— something irreverent and even whimsical. Mrs. Atwater did not analyze it, but she felt it, and the awareness only increased her exasperation.

"Very well," she snapped. "If you will do nothing in this matter, Julius, then I will be forced to act myself."

Her nephew bowed. "You must do as you see fit, ma'am," he said cheerfully.

"Believe me, I will," said Mrs. Atwater, eyeing him with renewed dislike. "I intend to call upon this Miss Watson myself and make her see reason. Come along, Gilbert. I must begin preparing at once to make the journey to Cheltenham, since Julius prefers to ignore his duty." With a last look of dislike at her nephew, she swept out of the room.

Julius stood watching her go, a broad smile curving his lips. Yet in spite of his amusement, he was also conscious of a feeling of compunction. It was not that he regretted declining his aunt's commission, for he felt assured it was a commission as fruitless as it was improper. No, he felt rather compunction for the unknown Miss Watson. Being well acquainted with his aunt, he felt sure Miss Watson would soon be forced to endure a very nasty hour or two at her hands. Almost he considered whether it might not be his duty to warn her of what lay in store for her. But then he dismissed the idea. Miss Watson was a stranger to him, and he owed her nothing, any more than he owed anything to his aunt. Let the two battle it out on their own and the best woman win.

Thus it was that when Elizabeth went down to the parlor that Friday, expecting to see Mr. Pierce's smiling face, it was a very different vision that greeted her. A large middle-aged lady in a formidable bonnet was standing in the center of the room, scornfully regarding the faded and peeling paper that decorated the walls. She swung around as Elizabeth entered and swept her from top to toe with a look as scornful as that with which she had been regarding the wallpaper. "Miss Watson?" she demanded.

"Yes," said Elizabeth, blinking in surprise. "I—er—believe you have the advantage of me, ma'am."

The lady ignored the question in her voice. She went on regarding Elizabeth with the same scornful gaze. "You *are* young," she said. "Younger than I expected."

Elizabeth could only stare at the lady, wondering what her age had to do with anything. The visitor went on, her voice full of suppressed fury. "No doubt you think you have been very clever! But I'm here to tell you that your cleverness will avail you nothing, Miss Watson. There are those with nearer claims than yours on Mr. Atwater's fortune, and we intend to see to it that all your scheming comes to naught!" Comprehension flooded Elizabeth's mind. This lady had clearly come to dispute about Mr. Atwater's legacy. Elizabeth had no idea who the lady was and felt a trifle indignant that she should be attacked in this way, without any attempt being made first to ascertain her own attitude toward the legacy. But she could make allowances for emotion and ignorance, having encountered a plentitude of both in her lifelong dealings with her mother. So she smiled slightly and said, "I believe you are operating under a misapprehension, ma'am. Regarding the money Mr. Atwater left me—"

"It should never have been left to you!" said the lady angrily. "What right had you, a perfect stranger, to receive a penny from my brother-in-law? The money ought to have gone to Mr. Atwater's family, and I intend to see that it does go there, will or no will. What have you to say to that, Miss Watson?"

"Why, only that I agree with you, ma'am. Indeed, when Mr. Atwater's attorney first told me about the bequest, I—"

The lady brushed these words aside, to pounce on Elizabeth's earlier ones. "You agree with me!" she said with triumph. "And yet you have the effrontery to claim this fortune just the same! Let me tell you, young woman, you do not know with whom you are dealing!"

"On the contrary, I think I do know," said Elizabeth. "I expect you are Mrs. Thomas Atwater, the widow of the late Mr. Atwater's younger brother."

"Yes, I am Mrs. Atwater," acknowledged Mrs. Atwater grudgingly. "Though what business it is of yours, I do not know. I suppose you have been making inquiries," she added with a sneer. "No doubt you would like to know how much opposition you are likely to encounter in trying to keep your ill-gotten fortune. Well, I can answer you *that,* Miss Watson. If you do not relinquish claim to Mr. Atwater's estate immediately, you will have *me* to reckon with. And I warn you that I do not deal kindly with thieves and liars!"

Elizabeth was starting to grow angry. She had come downstairs with every intention of relinquishing her claim to Mr. Atwater's estate, but to have it demanded of her in this way, without even giving her credit for her good intentions, roused a devil of obstinacy within her. "You will forgive me if I do not find your threats very frightening, ma'am," she drawled. "Who, after all, are you? And why should your claim on the late Mr. Atwater's estate be so much better than mine?"

Mrs. Atwater drew herself to her full height. "It is not myself, but my son Gilbert who has a claim on my brother-in-law's estate," she said fiercely. "My brother-in-law was excessively fond of Gilbert, from the time he was a child. And if improper pressure had not been brought to bear on him, I have no doubt the estate would have descended to Gilbert in the proper way."

Elizabeth gave Mrs. Atwater a maddening smile. "Well, I don't know what you mean by 'improper pressure,' " she said. "If there was pressure brought to bear upon Mr. Atwater, it was certainly not brought by me. I never exchanged so much as a word with him during his lifetime. Indeed, ma'am, it would appear that Mr. Atwater's fondness for your son was not so great as you would like to suppose."

Mrs. Atwater's eyes flashed. "Hussy!" she hissed. "You would like to have me believe that, wouldn't you? But it's perfectly obvious what you are, Miss Watson. When a young woman receives a legacy from an elderly gentleman who is not her relative, it's clear that her acquaintance with him was of a very particular kind indeed."

Elizabeth was really angry now, and her anger made her reckless. "What are you implying, Mrs. Atwater?" she asked.

"I am implying that you are an unprincipled and immoral young woman who took advantage of an elderly man. No, I will go further than that and state it as a positive fact."

"Then there is no use in our talking further," said Elizabeth. "If I am as unprincipled and immoral as you say, then I would certainly not be willing to relinquish Mr. Atwater's fortune now that I have it fairly in my hands."

She turned and began to walk toward the door. "Oh, if that is your attitude!" sneered Mrs. Atwater. "I had hoped to make you see reason, but I see I might as well have saved my breath."

Elizabeth paused, looking back at her. "Indeed, it would have been well if you had," she agreed. "Believe it or not, ma'am, I had every intention of relinquishing the whole of Mr. Atwater's fortune to his relatives before you came here today. But now that I have seen what his relatives are like, I am convinced he knew exactly what he was doing in leaving his money to me. And I intend to keep it, every penny."

"Of course you do," said Mrs. Atwater scornfully. "Don't expect me to believe that you would ever have given it up unless you were absolutely obliged to. But the time will come when you *will* be obliged to give it up, Miss Watson."

"I've already told you I don't care for your threats, Mrs. Atwater. I'm not the least bit afraid of what you can do."

"Ah!" said Mrs. Atwater significantly. "But it is not only a question of what *I* can do. I am not quite nobody, but there is one behind me whose power and resources are a hundred times greater than my own. And he will see that you regret this day's work."

"Gilbert, I suppose," said Elizabeth with a scornful smile. "I'm not afraid of Gilbert any more than I am of you, ma'am. If he had been a man at all, he would have come here and spoken for himself today, instead of letting his mother attend to it."

Mrs. Atwater colored at this, but replied repressively, "No, I am not speaking of Gilbert. Of course he, too, is not without resources. But it is my nephew, Lord Atwater, of whom I am speaking. You must beware of him if you persevere in your wickedness, Miss Watson. He is a very eminent man who has a great deal of power and influence, and if you do not at once resign this fortune to those who are properly entitled to it, he will use that power and influence to crush you."

Elizabeth stood motionless a moment, then deliberately raised her hand and snapped her fingers beneath Mrs. Atwater's astonished nose. "That for Lord Atwater!" she said, then turned and quickly left the room.

Four

When Mr. Pierce arrived at the Watson home an hour later, he found Elizabeth awaiting him in the parlor. "I have changed my mind," she told him. "I intend to accept Mr. Atwater's bequest. Please see that the proper legal proceedings are begun as soon as possible."

"Ah, I thought you'd be sensible about it, if only you had a chance to think it over," said Mr. Pierce, beaming.

"Thinking it over had nothing to do with it," said Elizabeth coldly. "What changed my mind was making the acquaintance of the Atwater family. Now that I know what they're like, nothing would impel me to assist those people in any way!"

Mr. Pierce regarded her with sympathetic understanding. "Mrs. Atwater came to call on you, did she?" he said. "I rather suspected she would. She called on me, too, trying to convince me that Mr. Atwater's will ought to be set aside. We call her the battle-ax around the office."

"Well, I call her insufferable," said Elizabeth. "And her nephew and son sound just as bad, if not worse. I have no intention of letting them bully me into giving up my legacy." In this mood, she made no objection to signing every paper Mr. Pierce laid before her. "Have you any idea now how long it will be before I receive my monies from the estate?" she asked. "I am in need of a rather large sum of money right away."

Mr. Pierce assured her there would be no difficulty in advancing her a few thousand pounds on her bequest. Reassured, Elizabeth went away to tell her mother and sister the good news.

As might have been expected, both were ecstatic to hear of Elizabeth's change of heart. "Oh, my darling girl!" exclaimed Mrs. Watson, leaping from her chair to embrace her elder daughter. "I knew you must see reason, if I only represented the matter to you in the proper light."

Elizabeth had not planned to tell her mother or sister about Mrs. Atwater's call, but the assumption that it had been Mrs. Watson's specious arguments that changed her mind goaded her into speech. "As a matter of fact, Mama, I still believe the money would more properly have gone to Mr. Atwater's relatives," she said. "And if the Atwater family had not taken such a high-handed attitude about it, I would have been glad to resign my claim in favor of them. But for them to call me immoral and unprincipled and threaten to ruin me if I accepted a legacy that was left to me in a perfectly legal manner—well, that was a bit too much. No one could be expected to bear with such treatment!"

"Did they indeed say all that?" said Sophia, wide-eyed. "Oh, Elizabeth! I don't wonder you were angry."

"I was angry. I *am* angry," said Elizabeth, her eyes flashing at the recollection of Mrs. Atwater's insults. "I have never been so furious in my life!"

"Well, never mind being furious now, dear," said Mrs. Watson soothingly. "The thing is that we have all this delightful money now, and we must decide what to do with it."

Elizabeth eyed her mother with misgiving. "You know we don't have it yet, Mama," she said. "It will be weeks, perhaps even months, before the estate is settled. Mr.

Pierce has promised to advance me enough to pay your debts and meet our immediate needs, but we must not be extravagant."

These words fell on deaf ears, however. "London," said Mrs. Watson, her eyes shining. "We can go to London now! And Sophia can be presented, and we can give her a ball, and I don't doubt she will end by becoming at least a marchioness!"

Both Elizabeth and Sophia regarded their mother in dismay. "But, Mama!" said Elizabeth. "You are forgetting that Sophia wants to marry Mr. Arthur."

" 'Marry Mr. Arthur!' " repeated Mrs. Watson. "I should think not indeed! Marry Mr. Arthur, when she might have her pick of any man in the four kingdoms!"

"But Sophia doesn't want any man in the four kingdoms, Mama," said Elizabeth. "She only wants Mr. Arthur. Don't you, Sophia?"

Sophia blushed at this direct appeal, but said with resolution, "Yes, I do."

"There you are, then, Mama. And there is no reason why Sophy cannot marry Mr. Arthur now I have money— or will have it. I will settle a handsome dowry on her, and she can marry her curate as soon as she pleases."

"Indeed she shall not!" said Mrs. Watson passionately. "I will not hear of it, Elizabeth! For Sophy to throw herself away on a penniless curate, when this wonderful chance has come her way! It's too much—too much— simply too much to bear. It's as the Bible says: 'How sharper than a serpent's tooth is a thankless child!' "

"Mama, be sensible," begged Elizabeth. "What does it matter whom Sophy marries? We have money now, as much as we could ever use. And I thought that was the whole reason for your wishing her to make a great match."

These arguments had no effect on Mrs. Watson, however. She continued to lament that Sophia would be throwing herself away if she married anything less than a marquess.

"Never mind, Sophy," Elizabeth told her sister privately, later that afternoon. "Mama will come around in time. There's not a reason in the world why you shouldn't marry Mr. Arthur now we have the money to dower you."

Sophia shook her head slowly. "Oh, Elizabeth, I know you mean well. And indeed, you are the best and most generous of sisters to talk of dowering me. But the more I think of it, the more I believe it will not answer. I should not like to be beholden to you in such a way, and I know Philip would not either. He may be poor, but he is very proud, Elizabeth. It would fret him for the rest of his life to think he owed a debt he couldn't repay. And then, too, there is Mama. Of course it's all nonsense about my marrying a marquess, but it would grieve her if I were to marry Philip now. Later, perhaps, once she has grown more used to the idea, and after Philip has obtained preferment—then we'll see."

Elizabeth did not like the idea of temporizing with her mother's prejudices. She had looked forward to settling matters between Sophia and Mr. Arthur, and it went against the grain to see their happiness once more postponed. But this appeared to be one of the rare issues on which Sophia was able to be firm, and at last Elizabeth agreed to let matters stand as they were for the present.

"Still, you know Mama, Sophy," she warned. *"She* will never be content to let matters stand. She has her heart set on taking you to London and marrying you off to a lord."

Sophia smiled. "Well, she might achieve her first purpose, but she'll never achieve the second! If I don't marry Philip, I won't marry anyone."

She spoke with such perfect assurance that Elizabeth's curiosity was piqued. "You seem so sure," she commented. "So certain that Mr. Arthur is the man you want to marry."

"He is," said Sophia firmly. "There is no man for me but Philip."

"But how can you know that?" said Elizabeth. She did not doubt her sister's feelings, but they appeared to her quite irrational. After all, the world was full of men, and Sophia had only met a small proportion of them. For her to prefer one above the others seemed a capricious proceeding, to say the least.

"I just know," said Sophia. "I knew Philip was the man for me as soon as I met him."

This, of course, did not satisfy Elizabeth's rational mind. "But do you not think—not that I mean to denigrate your feelings for Mr. Arthur, Sophy—but if you did go to London and went into society and met other men, don't you think it possible you might meet one you liked better?"

"No," said Sophia. She looked hard at her sister. "Elizabeth, if I didn't know better, I would think you agreed with Mama! You don't want to marry me off to a marquess, do you?"

"No, I don't," Elizabeth assured her. "It's only that I don't quite understand why you feel as you do. Why would you want to marry at all, now that we have money? And why Mr. Arthur?"

Sophia smiled, and it struck Elizabeth that there was something almost pitying in her smile. "Oh, Elizabeth, if you had ever been in love, you would understand," she said. "I love Philip, and he loves me. You can take me all over the world and introduce me to every man in existence, but it won't make the slightest bit of difference in my feelings. As far as I'm concerned, Philip and I *belong* together. We will be married someday, God willing, but in the meantime we belong to each other just as much as if we were already married."

"I suppose I must believe you, since you say so," said Elizabeth dubiously. "But it sounds a most uncomfortable state of affairs. I don't believe I would care to be in love myself. Not that it's in the least likely that I ever will be. I'm twenty-six years old, and still heart-whole." Dismissing the subject, she added, "I wish Mama would be more reasonable about this business of our going to London. Not that we can't afford to go now, but I don't see any use in it."

To her surprise, Sophia did not concur in her view. "It might not do any harm if we went to London for a short visit, Elizabeth," she said. "If we humor Mama in this, she might not be so unreasonable in other things. Like my marrying a marquess," she added with a rueful smile.

"But she wants to enter society!" said Elizabeth. "You must see how ridiculous that is, Sophy. Our family isn't a noble one. How in the world could she expect us to be taken into the bosom of the Upper Ten Thousand, just like that?"

"Well, you know, Elizabeth, our name may not be a noble one, but it's at least as respectable as Mrs. Reese-Whittington's. And *she* moves in the best circles by all accounts. Besides, you have just inherited a large sum of money. I wouldn't be surprised if that didn't give you the *entrée* to more places than you imagine."

"Why, Sophia, I never expected to hear such cynicism from you!" said Elizabeth, laughing. "I daresay money *would* go a long way toward making us welcome in London. But no, I'm forgetting. The Atwaters are among the leading lights of London society, and they've made it clear they regard me as a thief and adventuress." Her eyes kindled. "If you had only heard Mrs. Atwater this afternoon! Talking about my ill-gotten gains and how her nephew, Lord Atwater, would crush me with all his power and influence."

"Oh!" said Sophia, shrinking back. "Did Mrs. Atwater

really say that? Perhaps we had not better go to London, then. It sounds as though the Atwaters could make life very unpleasant for us there."

Elizabeth's eyes had grown dangerously bright. "Do you think so?" she said. "And yet I have a perfect right to go to London if I like. Why should I let a few threats from an arrogant family of aristocrats stop me? Upon my word, it would give me a great deal of satisfaction to flaunt myself and my 'ill-gotten fortune' in their faces."

Sophia looked doubtful. "But this Lord Atwater you speak of," she said. "If he really is a lord, no doubt he does have a certain amount of power and influence. You would not want to make an enemy of such a man."

"I already *have* made an enemy of him," said Elizabeth. "His aunt told me so this afternoon. She delivered me a declaration of war on behalf of the whole Atwater family." She laughed suddenly. "No doubt they imagine I am all atremble with fear at the prospect of their wrath! But they are about to learn otherwise. Because I *am* going to London, Sophia. I am going to carry the battle into the Atwaters' own territory. Why, it will be just like Hannibal crossing the Alps into Italy!"

Seeing that Sophia looked a little blank at this remark, Elizabeth went on to explain its relevancy to her sister. "The Romans never expected Hannibal would invade Italy itself," she said. "They were lazy and arrogant, supposing no foreigner would dare challenge them on their own ground. Just like the Atwaters! Well, I will show them as Hannibal showed the Romans. They'll find they have an enemy who is worthy of their steel."

Sophia, who had listened politely and a little uncomprehendingly to this speech, now spoke in a hesitating voice. "Of course I will support you in whatever you choose to do, Elizabeth," she said. "But it sounds a difficult business. How exactly do you intend to challenge the Atwaters?"

"To begin with, I shall let them think I am cowed by their threats. The element of surprise is essential to any successful military campaign. I will refuse to see them if they call here again and hold no communication whatever with them. Meanwhile, we will be arranging matters so we can burst upon London society like a Conger's rocket."

Sophia was looking doubtful again. "But that will be difficult, won't it?" she asked. "After all, we must first find a house in London, and furnish it, and—"

"No, there will be no difficulty about that. Mr. Atwater owned a house in a very good quarter of London, and now it belongs to me. Mr. Pierce thought I might like to sell or lease it, but if we are going to London it will serve nicely as our campaign headquarters. We can have it refurnished and put in order before we arrive, and if the Atwaters hear of it, they will merely think I am getting it ready to sell."

Sophia nodded, looking relieved. "That seems simple enough," she said. "Although I still imagine it will be a bit awkward, refurnishing a house in London while we are living here."

"Yes, I will need an agent in London to act for me, someone I can trust. It ought to be someone with an *entrée* to society, for there are details in my campaign I can't settle without knowing more about the lay of the land. I have been wondering if I ought not to write to Mama's cousin, Mrs. Reese-Whittington."

"But she has never shown the least interest in helping us," protested Sophia. "Mama has written her many times to ask for assistance with one thing and another, but she has always been too busy, or too low of funds, or simply unwilling."

"She may have been unwilling before, when we were only poor relatives. But I suspect she will be much more willing now we have a handsome fortune to draw on," prophesied Elizabeth with a cynical smile.

Her prophecy proved perfectly correct. Mrs. Reese-Whittington was delighted to assist the Watsons when the situation had been explained to her. She was a little puzzled at Elizabeth's insistence on secrecy, but agreed that the Watsons would make all the greater splash when they finally did burst upon the social scene if they were kept under wraps beforehand. *Although you must know that a girl with a fortune such as yours is guaranteed to make a splash no matter how she manages her entrance to society,* she wrote Elizabeth in her broad, dashing handwriting. *Dearest Elizabeth, I look forward to seeing you, your sister, and your dear mama (who was ever my dearest friend, as well as my favorite cousin).*

With Elizabeth's fortune to oil the way, matters were arranged in a remarkably short time. It was early March when Mrs. Reese-Whittington wrote to announce that Mr. Atwater's town house was ready to receive the Watsons. "I have the servants all engaged, and I have instructed my own dressmaker to hold herself in readiness," she wrote. "No doubt you will all require a good deal in the way of gowns and millinery before you are fit to be seen abroad. Still, I doubt not we will have you ready to make your entrance into the *ton* by the time the Season properly starts."

Elizabeth frowned a little over this letter. She had given almost no thought to the question of dress. Of course Mrs. Watson had been babbling about court dresses and fashion plates ever since she had learned they were definitely to go to London, but Elizabeth had paid little heed to her mother's chatter. Now she perceived she would have to give it some heed, or else leave the matter entirely in her mother's hands. Her experience with matters left entirely in her mother's hands had not been such as to encourage her to repeat the experiment.

"Bother," said Elizabeth aloud. "I suppose I shall have to look into getting some new dresses. I hadn't thought of it before, but it stands to reason it wouldn't do to let the Atwaters see me like this." She looked down at her well-worn stuff gown.

"I should think not, indeed!" said Sophy, looking shocked. "Of course you must have new dresses, Elizabeth. You need new things much worse than Mama and I do."

"Yes, but I doubt I will be going into company as much as you and Mama. Only enough to annoy the Atwaters." Elizabeth smiled with satisfaction at the thought. "I'll get some new things, but not too many. I think Mama has already gone a great way to dissipate my fortune, and it won't do if two of us are extravagant."

It could not be denied that Mrs. Watson had made some extravagant purchases in the last few weeks. She had bought herself a set of rubies, an ermine cape for Sophia, and a handsomely bound set of Lord Byron's poems for Elizabeth—"Because I know you love books more than anything else, dear." But in truth, Elizabeth was not greatly worried about these extravagances. Now that the estate was legally hers, and Mr. Pierce had explained to her the full extent of her holdings in funds, mines, and property, Elizabeth felt assured that even Mrs. Watson would have difficulty outrunning her income.

So she set herself to making preparations for their move to London. As she confided to Sophia, there were really some amazing resemblances between the Watsons' journey and Hannibal's historic trip over the Alps. The Watsons might not be encumbered with real elephants, but they had plenty of the white variety, for in spite of the fact that Mrs. Watson had been bemoaning the dowdiness of their furnishings for the past fifteen years, she suddenly discovered on the verge of their departure any number of objects that were full of sentimental value and could not on any account be left behind. Since some of these objects were of considerable bulk—the dining room sideboard, for instance, and Sophia's piano—arranging for their transport to London was a task that would have taxed the ingenuity even of a Hannibal.

There were the servants, too, to consider. Elizabeth had offered to pension off the more elderly of their staff as soon as she had come into her fortune, but the idea of moving to London and participating in a new and fashionable existence was so enticing that every one of them elected to go, even the coachman who was well along in his eighties. Elizabeth had been secretly looking forward to hiring a new coachman, and not, as might have been supposed, because old age had rendered John staid and slow. On the contrary, he had become so increasingly reckless that most people around Cheltenham had their own coachmen pull to the side of the road when they saw the Watsons' carriage coming. This was a mortification Elizabeth felt she could do without in London, but she knew it would hurt John's feelings to be retired in favor of a younger man, so she accepted his decision with as much resignation as she could muster.

"You can put another coachman under him, and perhaps get a little phaeton and pony of your own to drive part of the time, and then it will not matter so much," said Sophia consolingly.

"That's true. I *could* get a carriage to drive myself," said Elizabeth, and straightway added this to the list of purchases she wished to make.

It still seemed marvelous to her that wealth could conquer so many obstacles. But she reminded herself that London itself was still unconquered, and it was yet to be proved whether wealth alone would conquer it. After all, her enemies the Atwaters would be arrayed against her there, and Lord Atwater had as much wealth as she did— perhaps even greater wealth.

"But that doesn't matter," Elizabeth assured herself. "Hannibal had far less men and resources than the Romans, yet he got the best of them for nearly twenty years, and in their own country, too." And sustained by this thought, she went off to finish the last of her packing for the trip.

Five

Mrs. Atwater had come away from the Watsons' house in a state of high indignation. Her indignation lasted during the day and a half it took her to travel back to London, so that when she burst in upon her nephew Saturday evening, it was to pour forth her story in a manner more impassioned than coherent.

"The impudence of her! Oh, if you had been there, Julius, you must have seen how impossible it is that Lucius's fortune should ever go to such a person. She was thoroughly vulgar—a hussy through and through."

"Ought to have the law down on her," said Gilbert, who had accompanied his mother to Julius's house and was now engaged in sampling his port. "Ought to be whipped at the cart's tail, by Jove."

Julius quirked an eyebrow at him. "I fail to see how the law should be expected to interfere with what was, after all, a perfectly legal bequest," he said.

"It may be legal, but it's still intolerable," snapped Mrs. Atwater. "Something must be done, Julius. That young woman must not be allowed to think she has got the best of us. You would think something must be done, too, if you had heard the way she talked to me."

Julius regarded his aunt with amusement. "But how did you talk to her?" he asked. "Knowing you, Aunt Jane,

I'd guess you opened the conversation by demanding she sign Lucius's fortune over to you straightaway."

"Certainly not, Julius. I merely told her that the money ought to be Gilbert's, and that if she did not relinquish her claim to him I would see something was done about it."

Julius grinned, but forbore to comment. Mrs. Atwater took up the thread of her narrative again, her indignation mounting as she developed her theme. "She is a perfectly impossible person, Julius, worse even than I imagined. The most impertinent of manners, and a nasty, sneering way of talking. She told me several palpable falsehoods, too. Why, she even tried to convince me she had been planning to give back Lucius's money, and that it was only my own conduct that dissuaded her! As if I could be taken in by such talk. Of course she had no intention of giving back the money, then or later."

Julius raised his eyebrows. "Did she indeed say she had been planning to give back the money?" he asked.

"That was what she *said,* Julius. But of course it was a lie. One need only look at her to know she lies as easily as breathing."

In spite of himself, Julius found himself growing intrigued by the character of the unknown Miss Watson. "What does she look like?" he asked.

"Like a hussy," said Mrs. Atwater roundly. "Oh, she had made an effort to look respectable, skinning back her hair and wearing a dress she probably borrowed from one of the maidservants. But I wasn't deceived for an instant."

"But what does she look like?" repeated Julius. "Is she tall or short, dark or fair?"

Mrs. Atwater was loath to commit to any more specific description than that Elizabeth was a hussy. After repeated questioning, however, she was brought to admit that she was tall rather than short and fair rather than dark. "Though I am sure that hair of hers cannot be natural. A low-bred hussy with dyed blonde hair, that's what she is. Some people might call her attractive, but for myself I saw nothing to admire."

Gilbert pricked up his ears at this and said he wouldn't mind getting a look at Miss Watson himself, by Jove. Julius was surprised to find himself sharing this inclination. Despite his aunt's criticisms, or perhaps even because of them, he had conceived a strong desire to meet Miss Watson. She sounded a woman with an original mind, and he thought he would like to make her acquaintance.

Mrs. Atwater had gone on talking, meanwhile, still criticizing Elizabeth's manners and appearance. Julius was too busy with his own thoughts to pay much attention to this diatribe, but presently certain of her words caught his ears. "And it was not only toward me that she was disrespectful. If you could have heard the way she spoke of you, Julius! Why, she actually snapped her fingers and said, 'That for Lord Atwater!'" Mrs. Atwater repeated the gesture, her face full of indignation. "So you see, it really behooves you to do something about this young woman. You cannot like to see her insult you, whatever you may say!"

Julius regarded his aunt in amazement. "You say this Miss Watson spoke against me?" he said.

"Yes, she did," said Mrs. Watson. "And snapped her fingers, just like that." Again she repeated the gesture.

"But how did my name come into the conversation at all?" said Julius. "You did not happen to bring it up yourself, did you, Aunt Jane?"

Mrs. Atwater had the grace to look self-conscious. "I might have done so," she said. "I believe I did just mention that you agreed with me in thinking it wrong for Lucius's fortune to go out of the family. But—"

"But I don't agree with you," said Julius. "I don't

agree with you at all. You have been putting words in my mouth, Aunt Jane, and I resent it very much."

There was a tone in his voice that Mrs. Atwater had never heard before. She regarded him with astonishment, and even Gilbert looked up from his port with an arrested expression. "I am sure I am very sorry if I spoke amiss, Julius," said Mrs. Atwater, after a minute's pause. "But if you had seen Miss Watson for yourself, you would agree she was a perfectly impossible person."

"I prefer to make that judgment for myself," said Julius. "And I shall look forward to meeting her, in order that I may."

"Oh, but you won't be meeting her, Julius—not unless you're willing to go to Cheltenham, anyway. And that would be ridiculous. Why should you travel all the way to Cheltenham to make the acquaintance of a young woman of her sort?"

It did seem a ridiculous thing to do, as Julius was obliged to admit. He put the idea out of his mind, but it kept recurring to him in the weeks that followed, in spite of his better judgment. There also remained in his mind a rankling resentment toward his aunt, and a lingering pique toward Miss Watson, who had snapped her fingers and said, "That for Lord Atwater!"

If he had only known it, the object of his thoughts was much closer than he imagined. Despite countless difficulties, Elizabeth had finally gotten herself, her family, and her household goods installed in the late Lucius Atwater's handsome town house. She had purchased a phaeton and pony, and had also been brought to buy a new town carriage and a team of match-bays, Mrs. Reese-Whittington declaring that the Watsons' present carriage and horses were quite unsuited to the social circles they intended to enter. She had also, in company with her mother and sister, visited numerous dressmakers, glove-makers, shoemakers, and milliners in search of those items that constituted the wardrobe of a lady of fashion.

Elizabeth had supposed she would only need a minimal wardrobe, for she had no mind to subscribe to the full round of social activities that Mrs. Watson and Mrs. Reese-Whittington were planning. But she soon found she would not be allowed to play a background role in London as she had in Cheltenham. "My dear, it is *you* the Queen will be most eager to meet," Mrs. Reese-Whittington told Elizabeth, when she spoke of excusing herself from making her bows. "Her Majesty is a serious and well-educated woman and has the greatest admiration for persons of a scholarly mind. Besides, you are the heiress of the family, and it would look very odd if you sat at home while your sister makes her bows. No, you must be presented, too, and we must see you have the clothes to take your proper place in society."

It seemed to Elizabeth that this process required a truly astounding amount of clothing. "Morning dresses, carriage dresses, riding dresses, afternoon dresses, dinner dresses," she told Sophia with a disbelieving shake of her head. "Evening dresses, ball dresses, opera dresses, court dresses! I see clearly I shall spend all day changing my clothing, and never get out of the house at all."

Sophia, who was perched on the bed turning over the leaves of a fashion magazine, laughed. "It won't be so bad as all that, Elizabeth," she said. "I must say, it is delightful to be able to order whatever one wants without regard for price."

"Not quite without regard for price. You will remember I refused the diamond buttons Mama wanted put on my court dress. It's quite gaudy enough without those."

"I think it's a beautiful dress," said Sophia loyally. "And you look beautiful in it, Elizabeth."

Elizabeth snorted. "Nobody could look beautiful in such a foolish rig out," she said. "I least of all."

"You're wrong," said Sophia. She put down her magazine to regard her sister searchingly. "Indeed, Elizabeth, I always thought you were a handsome girl. Now that you've begun wearing your hair in a more becoming way and have the proper dresses to set you off, I do not think it would be too much to say you are beautiful."

"Flummery," said Elizabeth, in a rallying tone. "You're the beauty of the family, Sophy. I could never hope to compete, even if I wanted to."

Yet though Elizabeth spoke disparagingly, she was obliged to admit that proper clothing and hairdressing had made a difference in her appearance. If she did not look actually beautiful, she did at least look fashionable and—yes, there could be no doubt of it—even attractive. Mrs. Reese-Whittington had bullied her into seeing a hairdresser soon after the Watsons had arrived in London, and though Elizabeth had protested that she had no time for fancy hairdressing, her protests had been overruled. She had put herself into the hairdresser's hands most unwillingly, but when she first beheld herself with her back hair twisted into a low chignon at the nape of her neck and her front hair cropped and coaxed into a soft cloud of curls around her face, she was amazed to see how much it did to soften the austerity of her features.

Of course it was ridiculous to talk of her being a beauty. She could never be a beauty when her face was so colorless and the contrast between her eyes and complexion so marked. Oddly enough, however, this very contrast had been praised by the fashionable Frenchwoman who had made up her dresses.

"Mademoiselle has countenance *très épatant*—most striking and most unusual," had said the modiste, eyeing Elizabeth with professional enthusiasm. "The extreme fairness of the hair and the extreme darkness of the eyes—it is a combination one does not often see."

"Yes, she's got her father's eyes," Mrs. Watson had

replied, with a shake of her head. "But of course he had dark hair and a dark complexion, too, so dark eyes didn't look so queer on him."

"Queer, you say? But I should rather call it striking. And such a figure, too—and such features! Mademoiselle will be able to wear any color, any style, and look superb."

Mrs. Watson and Elizabeth had both gaped at the modiste. The Frenchwoman had nodded with positive assurance. "But yes! I have no doubt mademoiselle will be much admired when we have her properly gowned. This *eau de Nil* lutestring, for instance—and the celestial blue, and of course the lilac pink. A trying color, the lilac pink, but I tell you in confidence that it is going to be very fashionable this year among the young ladies. Mademoiselle can wear it better than most."

"But I'm not a young lady!" exclaimed Elizabeth. "I'm twenty-six years old. Won't I look ridiculous trying to ape the latest fashions when I am already as good as on the shelf?"

The modiste regarded her sternly. "You English, you talk nonsense with this business of being 'on the shelf,' " she said. "If a woman looks well, she need never be on the shelf, and so I tell you. Just you remember that, mademoiselle, and do not be so quick to suppose yourself past the age of finding a husband."

Elizabeth, recalling these words, knew an urge to blush. Of course she had no desire to find a husband, now or ever, as she assured herself. It was enough that she should appear well in public and not put her mother and Sophia to shame.

Besides, if I ever do find a man who wants to marry me, it's a hundred to one he will simply be after my money, she told herself cynically. Mrs. Reese-Whittington had already cautioned her against fortune hunters, saying her inheritance would be sure to draw a flock of undesirable suitors who must be weeded out from the more eligible ones. Elizabeth, however, felt this discrimination was hardly necessary. In all her twenty-six years, she had never met a gentleman she wished to marry, eligible or otherwise, and it wasn't at all likely she would meet one now.

And it was at that moment that Mrs. Reese-Whittington burst into the room.

"My dear Elizabeth," she exclaimed. "We are quite undone! Indeed, I cannot imagine how the secret got out."

Elizabeth looked up, instantly alert. "Secret?" she asked. "What secret, Amelia?"

Mrs. Reese-Whittington's sharp-featured face wore a look of despair. "Indeed, my dear, I give you my word I have been the soul of discretion," she said. "I engaged all the servants in my own name, and I never breathed a word of your coming even to my closest friends. But now it seems word must have gotten out in spite of all my care."

Elizabeth relaxed a little at these words. "Is that all?" she said. "It was bound to happen sooner or later, Amelia. Probably the servants have talked, or some of the tradespeople we have dealt with. Of course I would rather news of our arrival had not gotten out for another week or two, but though this forces our hand a bit, it won't make any real difference."

Mrs. Reese-Whittington was shaking her head. "But he's here!" she said. "Downstairs in the drawing room, this very minute!"

Elizabeth drew her dark brows together. " 'He?' " she repeated. "Who is 'he?' "

"Lord Atwater!" said Mrs. Reese-Whittington, and she collapsed onto the bed beside Sophia.

Sophia let out a gasp and dropped her magazine. Elizabeth, however, turned back to her dressing table to adjust a wayward curl. "Oh, yes?" she said indifferently.

Both Sophia and Mrs. Reese-Whittington stared at her. "You sound quite calm!" said Mrs. Reese-Whittington resentfully. "I supposed you would be more disturbed. After all, I have heard you say a thousand times that the Atwaters are your enemies. You're always comparing them to that outlandish family in your book who did all manner of disreputable things—"

"The Scipios," supplied Elizabeth. "They were a Roman family, and Hannibal's chief enemies during the Second Punic War."

"If you say so, dear—though how they could be like the Atwaters, who are English and very good *ton,* I do not know. But that's neither here nor there, of course. What matters is that you have been telling me all along that the Atwaters must not on any account know you are in London. Now it appears that they do know, for otherwise why would Lord Atwater be downstairs?"

Elizabeth nodded thoughtfully. "I suppose I must see him," she said.

"Oh, Elizabeth, no!" cried Sophia. "Have the servants tell him you are not at home. There is no need for you to see him."

Elizabeth smiled at her sister. "But indeed, Sophy, I am quite eager to see him," she said. "It is not every day that one encounters such a paragon of conceit and egoism as Lord Atwater must be. Besides, we will have to meet sooner or later, you know, and now will be as good a time as any."

"Then I'll go with you," said Sophia resolutely. "If you must meet with that dreadful man, at least you need not do it alone."

"Thank you, Sophy, but I think I should prefer to meet him alone. Lord Atwater asked for me alone, did he not?" said Elizabeth, turning to Mrs. Reese-Whittington.

Mrs. Reese-Whittington nodded. "I was sitting in the drawing room when the butler announced him, and he came in cool as you please and asked for Miss Watson. I was so taken aback I just said, 'I'll get her, my lord,' and ran up to your room straightaway. Oh, Elizabeth, I do apologize. If my wits had not gone a-begging, I would simply have denied you were here and tried to throw him off the track."

Elizabeth shook her head. "It's no matter," she said. "In fact, I believe I prefer it this way, Amelia. After all, Lord Atwater must have pretty accurate information about my whereabouts to come and ask for me like this. If you had denied I was here, it would have looked as though I were afraid to see him, and I'm *not* afraid, not afraid in the least."

Notwithstanding these brave words, Elizabeth's heart was beating rather fast as she went downstairs to the drawing room. It was a comfort to remember that her hair was faultlessly coiffed, and that she was wearing a very pretty afternoon dress of lilac pink voile with a wrapping bodice and flounced skirt.

Perhaps I've been wrong to take so little interest in clothes through the years, she told herself. *One does feel more confident when one is wearing attractive garments. If I were meeting Lord Atwater in real battle, now, I would prefer to be wearing armor and a sword—but for this kind of battle, a pink voile dress will do as well.*

The absurdity of going into battle in pink voile made Elizabeth smile, and the smile was still lingering on her lips as she entered the drawing room. "Lord Atwater?" she asked.

Julius, who had been seated on the sofa with his fingers interlaced over his knees, rose and bowed politely. "Miss Watson," he said.

Elizabeth eyed him in a measuring way. The first thing that struck her was his height. She was forced to look up in order to meet his eyes, a thing that was not at all usual with her. This seemed to put her at a disadvantage right from the beginning, and still more disarming was the smile that curved the corners of Lord Atwater's mouth and lit up his clear blue eyes. Looking into those eyes, Elizabeth felt a curious sense of resentment. It was altogether wrong that Lord Atwater should have such a charming smile. If he was her enemy, he ought to act like it, not greet her with smiles as though he were a friend. Why, she was having to stifle an urge to smile back at him this very minute!

"What can I do for you, my lord?" she asked, keeping her face and voice very businesslike.

"Firstly, you can forgive me for calling on you when we haven't been formally introduced," he replied in a deep, pleasant voice. "But you see, I have been wanting to make your acquaintance for some time, Miss Watson."

"Indeed?" said Elizabeth. She was unable to keep a tinge of irony out of her voice. "Well, I am rather busy this afternoon, Lord Atwater, but I can spare you a few minutes." She thought it as well to establish right away that battle would be on her terms, not his.

"Oh, I won't stay if it's inconvenient to you," he said. He looked so genuinely distressed at the idea of putting her out that Elizabeth had to bite her lip to keep from assuring him that he was quite welcome to stay. "As I said, I know I've no business calling on you like this," he went on, gathering up his hat and walking stick and smiling at her apologetically. "But when I ran into Jason Pierce yesterday and he mentioned that you were in town, I couldn't resist the urge to come by and pay my respects."

Elizabeth nodded. Although glad to know the source of his information as to her whereabouts, she mentally cursed Mr. Pierce for his garrulousness. "I see," she said. Then, giving into impulse, she added, "Do sit down, my lord. There is no need for you to go rushing off this way. As I said, I can spare a few minutes."

Julius's face relaxed into a smile once more. Elizabeth felt there was something dangerous about a man who could smile like that. It gave her a curious feeling, almost as though they shared an understanding limited only to the two of them. Yet such an idea was plainly ridiculous. *Why ever did I go and ask him to stay?* Elizabeth demanded of herself, as the two of them sat down, he on the sofa and she on a chair opposite. *It's only letting myself in for unpleasantness. He may smile at me now, but I'll wager within a minute or two he will be abusing me as his aunt did.*

In some indefinable way, Elizabeth felt the interview was slipping out of her control. She made an effort to take command again. "What can I do for you, Lord Atwater?" she asked a second time. "You must have had some reason for calling, besides merely wishing to make my acquaintance."

"No, not really. It was a simple desire to pay my respects to a lady of whom I have heard a great deal. You can call it mere vulgar curiosity, if you like, though it sounds so much better the other way, don't you think?"

These words were accompanied by another smile, but Elizabeth was not going to be taken in this way. *A man may smile and smile, and be a villain,* she reminded herself. Besides, she felt pretty certain it was from Mrs. Atwater that Lord Atwater had heard "a great deal" about her, and the thought did nothing to make her feel more kindly toward him. "Yes," she said in a dry voice. "I made the acquaintance of your aunt a few weeks ago. I suppose she has told you about our conversation."

Julius looked embarrassed. "My Aunt Jane," he said. "I suppose I ought to apologize for that, Miss Watson. I did try to dissuade her from calling on you, but my dissuasions had no effect at all."

"Indeed?" said Elizabeth. She did not bother to keep the skepticism out of her voice.

"Indeed, yes," said Julius earnestly. "I told her she had no business trying to overset Lucius's will. But she is, as you have no doubt gathered, a woman of considerable determination. And when the issue happens to concern her son, Gilbert, her determination is too often untempered by any semblance of judgment."

Elizabeth stared at him. He looked back at her, his expression still serious. "I need hardly say that I do not approve of my aunt's conduct in this matter," he said. "It would be too much to expect her to apologize for it herself, for she prides herself on never swerving from a course of action once she has determined on it. But I apologize for her, insofar as I may."

Elizabeth continued to stare at him. She could not imagine what kind of a strategy this must be. It was ridiculous to suppose Lord Atwater was really glad that she had his uncle's fortune. His aunt had already assured her he was not, and no amount of plausible talking was going to convince her otherwise. Indeed, the very plausibility of Julius's speech inclined her to doubt his motives. Why should he take the time to call on her and pay her compliments and apologize if he had not some larger object in view? Probably he was merely trying a different way of getting her to relinquish his uncle's money. He meant to get her to like him and accept him as a friend, then convince her to sign over her fortune to him.

Elizabeth was horrified to find that this scheme was actually working. She did find herself liking Lord Atwater. He was clearly a more dangerous man than she had imagined, and it behooved her to remove herself from his vicinity as soon as possible. "I'm afraid I must be going," she said, standing up abruptly. "It was kind of you to come and pay your respects, Lord Atwater."

He looked a little startled, but stood up likewise. "Of course. It was very good of you to see me at all, when you are so busy." Glancing around the drawing room, he said, "You have made a charming thing of this room. It is much improved since my uncle's time."

"Thank you, but that is my cousin's doing, not mine," said Elizabeth. She spoke lightly, but was inwardly all alert. The mention of Lucius Atwater had seemed casual, but she did not doubt that it was only the precursor to some further remark Julius might make concerning his uncle's bequest.

But either he was not yet ready to move in for the attack, or he was too wary to take such an obvious bait. "Your cousin?" he repeated. "Would that be Amelia Reese-Whittington? A charming lady. I have known her some years and always admired her, but I did not know until now that you two were related."

Elizabeth pounced triumphantly on this obvious piece of sophistry. "That is hardly surprising, my lord," she said in the sweetest of voices. "After all, you did not know I existed until a few months ago."

"You are mistaken," he said calmly. "I have known of your existence for nearly two years. My uncle first brought you to my attention, praising your book and advising me to read it. He could not say enough about the quality of your scholarship. When I had read your book, I found myself inclined to share his high opinion. I make no claim to be so learned a man as he was, but you have my admiration, for what it's worth." He smiled into Elizabeth's eyes.

The words "hoist with one's own petard" ran inconsequently through Elizabeth's mind. "Indeed," she said faintly. "Well, I thank you very much, my lord."

"You are most welcome," said Julius. He started toward the door, then turned back as though he had suddenly remembered something. Once more Elizabeth was on the alert, and this time she was not disappointed. "Oh, and I meant to ask," he said. "When Pierce told me you were staying here at the house, I thought perhaps you were merely looking through Lucius's things and getting the place ready to sell. But seeing as you've redecorated it and all, it occurred to me to wonder if perhaps you might be planning to stay in town for the Season?"

"Yes, I am," said Elizabeth. The words rang out like a martial challenge. She stood with chin held high, looking at Julius and waiting to hear his reply.

A brilliant smile lit up his face. "Wonderful!" he said. "Then I shall no doubt be seeing a great deal more of you, Miss Watson. I look forward to improving our acquaintance."

Elizabeth was so confused by this unexpected amiability that she actually gave him her hand. He bowed over it, then relinquished it with another smile. Elizabeth gave him a weak smile in return and watched as he turned and left the drawing room.

Six

Julius, as he left his uncle's former house, found himself in a curious state of exaltation.

In all his life, he could not remember being so affected by an encounter with a woman. And such a brief encounter, too—not even the full quarter of an hour that etiquette allotted for a formal call. Yet for all that, his meeting with Elizabeth had seemed curiously fraught with meaning.

He recalled the moment when Elizabeth had first appeared in the drawing room doorway. He didn't know what he had been expecting. He had known, of course, that she was an authoress and scholar, and from that he had vaguely supposed she was a serious sort of woman with no use for frivolity. On the other hand, his aunt had apostrophized her as a hussy and adventuress, terms that would seem to describe a very different type of woman. But the reality of Elizabeth Watson had proven something different from either of these things.

Julius had been prepared to see a pretty woman. Mrs. Atwater had admitted under pressure that some people might think Elizabeth attractive, a grudging admission that made it clear she must be very attractive indeed. Mrs. Atwater would never have damned Elizabeth with even faint praise if justice had not demanded it. But his aunt's words had not prepared Julius for the vision of Elizabeth as she swept through the drawing room door in her flowing robes of lilac pink voile. His aunt had mentioned her height, but she had not mentioned her grace and bearing. Likewise, in describing Elizabeth's coloring as fair, she had somehow failed to remark on the clear translucency of her skin and the wealth of flaxen hair that crowned her head. Fair she might be, and strikingly so, yet no one could have called her pale or colorless. Perhaps it was some trick of reflected light from her rosy draperies, but she had seemed to Julius to glow with the radiance of a pearl.

Indeed, though he was not a poetic man, the words "pearl of womanhood" had sprung into his mind on first seeing her. Then he had looked into her eyes and been struck anew. She had dark eyes, of a hue closer to black than brown and set beneath level dark brows. This would have been striking enough in combination with her flaxen hair and fair skin, but it was not the color of her eyes so much as the fire in their depths that chiefly struck Julius. This was no vapid miss who lived solely to dress, dance, and gossip. A spirit both vital and intelligent lurked in those eyes—a spirit that scintillated like a diamond.

"First she's a pearl and now a diamond," said Julius aloud, with a shake of his head. "I'd better make up my mind." He could not imagine what had inspired him to these flights of fancy. And there was another fancy just as unlikely that had taken possession of him during his conversation with Elizabeth. All the while he had been speaking to her, he had had the distinct impression that she was laboring under some strong emotion.

But that's ridiculous, Julius told himself. Elizabeth had spoken little and smiled scarcely at all during the few minutes they had been together. The only emotion she had shown was an eagerness to bring the interview to a close. Probably there was some urgent duty absorbing her thoughts to which she was eager to return. There was certainly no reason to suppose her emotion had anything to do with him.

Though you'd like to think so, wouldn't you? he told himself with a wry smile. *Conceited ass!*

The truth was that he would have been glad to think he had aroused any kind of emotion in Elizabeth, even a negative one. As it was, he felt he had made no impression on her at all. Those keen dark eyes had swept him a single glance and then dismissed him. Probably she thought he was a mere fashionable fribble with nothing but the cut of his coat to recommend him.

Which isn't surprising, Julius admitted to himself. He had been so taken off guard by the unexpected vision of her that his usual, much-admired sangfroid had deserted him. Likewise, he had shown none of the wit for which he was celebrated among the denizens of the *ton.* He felt dissatisfied now that all the words he had spoken to Elizabeth had been so trite and conventional. Doubtless she would despise him hereafter as a dull, negligible sort of fellow if she thought of him at all, a thing that wasn't likely.

Julius was not accustomed to thinking of himself as dull and negligible. On the contrary, he was in the habit of thinking rather well of himself. It was not merely that he was wealthy, titled, and tolerably good-looking, for those were all accidents of birth and accrued no personal merit to himself, as far as Julius was concerned. But unlike many of his peers, who were content to reap the benefits of their station while ignoring its responsibilities, he had always tried to do his duty by his dependents. He was a good landlord, a kind master, a conscientious member of the House of Lords. In particular did he plume himself on this last achievement, for in all the years since he had ascended to his title, he had not missed a single sitting of parliament. Now he found himself reevaluating himself through the eyes of Elizabeth Watson, and the achievements on which he prided himself suddenly began to seem rather trifling. What was it, after all, to be a good landlord? It wasn't as though he had drained fields or rebuilt cottages with his own hands. All he had done was authorize the expenditure of money—money that might be expected to return him a handsome dividend in time. Likewise, what was it to attend parliament? He had found it rather exciting at first to be playing a part in the processes of government, but of late his attendance had dwindled to a mere habit. It was several years since he had bothered to raise his voice on any issue.

But that's easily enough remedied, he vowed. *I'll make a speech tomorrow. I'll talk about Catholic Emancipation.*

Hastening home, he shut himself in his study and spent the whole evening drafting a powerful and moving speech. When he went to bed that night, he had the comfortable sense of having done something that even Miss Elizabeth Watson must acknowledge as worthwhile.

Elizabeth, reading the speech in the paper a few days later, never imagined she had been the inspiration for those polished periods and eloquent arguments. Sophia had drawn it to her attention, saying shyly that though she knew little about politics, it appeared to be rather clever.

"Yes, it's clever enough," agreed Elizabeth grimly. "There's no doubt Lord Atwater is a clever man. If you had seen the way he tried to cozen me when he was here a few days ago, Sophy, you wouldn't be inclined to underestimate him. Pretending to be so friendly and solicitous, and even going so far as to say he admired my book! But I wasn't taken in for a minute. He came to spy out our weaknesses, to find out where best to strike us when he is ready to make his attack."

Sophia shivered. "Oh, Elizabeth, do you really think so?" she asked.

"Yes, but he'll find himself out in his reckoning," said Elizabeth with vengeful satisfaction. "We will not wait for him to make the first move; we shall rather make it ourselves. Tomorrow night is the opera, and I intend that we shall go. Amelia has hired a box and has promised to introduce us to everyone she knows. Of course the Season has not yet officially begun, so there won't likely be a great many people for us to meet, but we should be able to gain some foothold in society. The sooner we start, the more ground we can gain, and by the time the Queen's drawing room comes around I trust we shall be so firmly entrenched that even Lord Atwater will find us difficult to dislodge."

Accordingly, the Watson family appeared at the opera the following night, an event that marked their first public London appearance. Elizabeth had recklessly decided that no expense should be spared for this important occasion, and money had been poured out in quantities that satisfied even Mrs. Watson. The box Mrs. Reese-Whittington had engaged was the largest and finest in the house, apart from that reserved for royalty. The ladies' toilettes were the height of fashion, their hairdressing faultless, and their jewelry frankly dazzling. Mrs. Watson wore scarlet silk and her new rubies; Sophia was a vision in white lace and a double string of pearls, and Elizabeth wore silver-spangled gauze with a diamond necklace and tiara.

Mrs. Reese-Whittington and Sophia had both praised Elizabeth's appearance in this toilette, saying she looked like a princess. Even Mrs. Watson had conceded that she looked uncommonly well. Elizabeth, however, was by no means sure this was the case. The tiara made her feel awkward and self-conscious, while her low-necked and heavily trimmed dress made her feel exposed and overdressed at the same time. At the last moment she had thrown a scarf over her shoulders in an effort to conceal those parts of her body that usually remained decently covered, but Mrs. Reese-Whittington had wrenched it away from her, saying sternly that she would look like a Quaker and a dowd if she did not bare her bosom like a Christian.

Elizabeth had been too distracted at the time to point out the contradictions in this speech. Now, as she looked around the crowded opera house at the throngs of men and women in full evening dress, she realized her cousin had been right. Compared to the lavish displays of décolletage on some of the women around her, her own dress was quite modest. There were several other tiaras to be seen as well, which also made her feel less conspicuous, but as she sat surveying the grand spectacle in which she was taking part, it began to be borne in upon her what a reckless thing she had done. She had come to London, expecting to cut a dash in society, but how could she ever hope to make an impression on these people? They were used to living in an atmosphere of jewels and silks and gilded splendor. Besides, there were so many of them! To Elizabeth's inexperienced eyes, it appeared that the entire rank of the Upper Ten Thousand were in the opera house that evening.

This thought had no more than crossed her mind when Mrs. Reese-Whittington leaned over to whisper, "London is still sadly thin of company, I fear. There are very few persons of note here tonight."

Elizabeth looked at Mrs. Reese-Whittington in amazement. She seemed to be perfectly serious. "Truly?" she whispered back. "I made sure the whole of London society must be here."

"Oh, no," said Mrs. Reese-Whittington, shaking her plumed head vigorously. "Why, there is scarcely anybody who is anybody. I see the Randalls and Mr. Thierry, but that is all." She smiled and nodded to a couple in the box next to them, and to a single gentleman seated with some others across the way.

"But surely those ladies there must be somebody," said Elizabeth, indicating a couple of richly dressed women in a nearby box. "Their dresses—and their jewels—"

"Their dresses and jewels are all well enough, but they aren't ladies," said Mrs. Reese-Whittington repressively. "Do not seem to be noticing them, Elizabeth, dear. It's a scandal that such creatures are allowed to mingle with their social betters, but so it is. You must learn that not everyone who dresses like a fine lady is one, nor is every man who wears a well-tailored coat a gentleman."

Before the evening was over, Elizabeth felt she had mastered this valuable lesson. She had learned that a lord might wear a snuff-stained shirt and a wig dating from two decades before, while the young men parading the pit in exquisite topcoats and wonderful neck cloths were dismissed by Mrs. Reese-Whittington as the merest of cits. She had learned that a countess might be sheathed in transparent gauze, rouged to the eyebrows, and smell of brandy and patchouli, while a demimondaine might appear as neat and demure as a nun. She had seen Mrs. Reese-Whittington hail one wildly dressed freak of an old gentleman as "dearest Mr. Evers," while another nearly identical one was rejected as "that old quiz Barnabas Potts."

In the course of the evening, Elizabeth learned several other valuable lessons as well. It was not, she discovered, at all the thing to listen to the music at the opera. People came to talk rather than listen, and to see and be seen. There was a constant stream of visitors in and out of the Watsons' box. They came ostensibly to greet Mrs. Reese-Whittington, but the looks they cast at the Watsons made it clear that their real incentive in coming was curiosity about these newcomers. Mrs. Reese-Whittington, fully aware of this curiosity, introduced them all as a matter of course. "These are my cousins, who are staying with me for the Season," she told the inquisitive visitors. "I must make you known to them, for you will be seeing them again soon, I hope. I am giving them a ball in a few weeks, and of course you will receive a card. I do hope you will be able to come. Mrs. Watson, Miss Watson, Miss Sophia Watson."

Sometimes this simple introduction sufficed. The lady or gentleman would bow and say "How do you do?" and after a little more polite conversation would return to his or her seat. But more often than not the visitors remained to ask questions. Sometimes their questions were addressed to the Watsons, but the majority were addressed to Mrs. Reese-Whittington in a low-toned voice. More often than not, Mrs. Reese-Whittington would laugh and respond, "Oh, yes! Very well-off indeed. As a matter of fact, Miss Watson is a considerable heiress. Her sister will have something, too, I believe, though I am not sure of the exact amount. Oh, yes, they are both charming girls. I am sure they will make a great sensation when they are presented."

Elizabeth could not help hearing a great deal of this conversation. To some extent it amused her, but mainly it evoked in her a sense of cringing embarrassment. It was clear that to the majority of these people, her money was the most important thing about her, if not the *only* important thing. She could see it in their manner, in the looks of mingled respect and appraisal they gave her when Mrs. Reese-Whittington mentioned she was an heiress. Sophia, by contrast, received little notice, though one or two people kindly remarked that she was a pretty girl.

Praising her to her face, just as if she were a puppy or kitten! thought Elizabeth indignantly. Being used to hearing her sister admired, it seemed all wrong that Sophia should be slighted while she received the lion's share of attention.

But Mrs. Reese-Whittington clearly felt the evening was going just as it ought. "Oh, my dears, let us rejoice! We have your Almack's vouchers secure," she announced in a jubilant whisper, after one lofty dame had bowed herself out of the box. "You must know the patronesses at Almack's are very exclusive. Quite a dozen people are turned away for every one who is accepted. Of course Maria Sefton is a particular friend of mine, and I am on good terms with Sally Jersey, too, so I was sure we would get them one way or another, but it is as well to have the matter settled early on."

Elizabeth, who had been in London long enough to know that Almack's Assembly Rooms were the *ne plus ultra* of fashionable society, nodded politely. Her cousin went on, addressing her in a confidential voice. "Elizabeth, I hope you do not mind, but I have thought it better not to tell anyone about your book. I have no doubt it is a very fine book in its way, and of course it's greatly to your credit that you should have written it, but we would not want people to think you are *blue*. There is a great prejudice against bluestockings just now, and it's not as though you look the part. I'm sure no one looking at you tonight would ever suspect you have a brain in your head."

Elizabeth was amused by this backhanded compliment, but a little piqued by it, too. Somehow it seemed to emphasize how foolish and superficial was the world in which she was moving. This impression was intensified by their next visitor, a dandyish-looking gentleman named Mr. Casswell. After being introduced to Elizabeth, he lingered by her side, paying her extravagant compliments. "I do hope I shall see more of you, Miss Watson," he told her when he rose at last to leave. "Would you care to go driving in the park tomorrow? I would be proud to be seen with such an Incomparable by my side."

Mrs. Reese-Whittington nodded vigorously, indicating that Elizabeth should accept this invitation. Elizabeth, however, felt less than enthusiastic at the prospect of an afternoon spent in Mr. Casswell's company. As she hesitated, a knock sounded on the door to the box. "Come in!" cried Mrs. Reese-Whittington gaily. The door opened, and Julius Atwater stepped into the box.

Elizabeth felt as though someone had hit her in the stomach. Her lips parted, then closed again. Julius regarded her, his expression smiling but a little uncertain. "Good evening, Miss Watson," he said. "And good evening to you, too, Mrs. Reese-Whittington." He favored both ladies with a low bow.

Sophia and Mrs. Watson had grasped from Mrs. Reese-Whittington's expression that this was no ordinary visitor. But in spite of the fact that Julius had greeted Elizabeth as a previous acquaintance, neither had as yet grasped who he was. They looked expectantly at Mrs. Reese-Whittington, supposing she would introduce this pleasant-looking gentleman to them as she had the other visitors to their box. But it was Elizabeth who made the introductions. "Lord Atwater," she said, her voice cold as ice, "this *is* a surprise."

"A pleasant one, I hope," he said.

There was a question in his voice that was not lost on Elizabeth. Secretly, she wondered at it. *Of course he must know his being here is not a pleasant surprise to me!* she told herself. *How could it be otherwise, when we are enemies?* But in spite of the enmity between her and Julius, she found herself feeling almost guilty for speaking to him so coldly. That, of course, was foolish, for this was merely another of his deep strategies—a way of making her look rude and uncivil in front of other people, probably. So she forced a smile to her lips and said, "To be sure a pleasant surprise, my lord! That goes without saying. Allow me to introduce you to my mother and sister. Mama, Sophia, this is Lord Atwater; Lord Atwater, this is my mother, Mrs. Watson, and my sister Miss Sophia Watson."

Sophia blanched a little at the dread name of Lord Atwater, but managed to return a creditable greeting. Mrs. Atwater was less successful at disguising her feelings. "Lord Atwater, is it?" she said, giving him a hard look. "I have heard about you, my lord. I suppose you are here tonight with your aunt?"

She spoke the word "aunt" with heavy significance. Once again, Elizabeth noted that Julius looked discomposed. "Er—not exactly," he said. "I was sitting in the pit with a friend, as a matter of fact. It was my aunt who—er—pointed you out to me, however. I came up to speak to her a moment between the acts, and she told me you were here."

As he spoke, his eyes flitted to a box across the way. Elizabeth followed his gaze and saw Mrs. Atwater glaring at her through a quizzing glass. Elizabeth stared back at her for a moment, then smiled and nodded graciously as if to a friendly acquaintance. She was pleased to see Mrs. Atwater drop her quizzing glass and grow red with indignation.

There was a gentleman seated next to Mrs. Atwater, a pale, irritable-looking youth with a shock of hair hanging over his face. He, too, was staring at Elizabeth, but his gaze was one of lascivious interest. "Gilbert," said Elizabeth with conviction.

"Yes, that is my cousin Gilbert," agreed Julius. Elizabeth fancied he repressed a sigh. She looked at him curiously, but before she could frame a question, Mr. Casswell spoke again.

"Well, how about it, Miss Watson? Like to come driving with me tomorrow?" he asked. As if just noticing Julius (though his eyes had been fixed jealously on him ever since he had entered the box), he added, "Oh, how d'ye do, Atwater? Haven't seen you this age."

" 'Evening, Casswell," said Julius, returning his bow. "I didn't know you were in town yet."

"Aye, I wasn't planning to come till after Easter, but Fred Finney talked me into coming down early. Talked me into coming to the opera tonight, too. I must say, I'm much obliged to him, for otherwise I wouldn't have met Miss Watson here."

He cast a languishing look at Elizabeth. Embarrassed, she looked at her feet. After a moment, however, she could not resist stealing a glance at Julius. He was regarding her gravely. "Indeed," he said. "You may well be grateful to fate and Mr. Finney. Miss Watson is an exceptional young lady."

"Know each other, do you?" said Mr. Casswell, surveying both him and Elizabeth jealously.

"Not so well as I hope we shall someday," said Julius.

Elizabeth regarded him with open amazement. What could he mean by saying such a thing? Did he think she was encouraging Mr. Casswell to dangle after her, and was he trying to put a spoke in her wheel by implying there was a previous understanding between them? Indignation swelled her breast. She did not know which she resented more, the idea that Julius could suppose her interested in a man like Mr. Casswell, or the idea that he would pretend an interest in her himself, when in reality he detested her.

Looking him straight in the eye, she said, "You do me too much honor, my lord." Turning to Mr. Casswell, she added, "Sir, I shall be very pleased to drive with you tomorrow."

Mr. Casswell beamed and said he was much obliged, by Jove. Julius merely bowed. "Perhaps I shall see the two of you in the park tomorrow," he said. "I often ride there myself." He then excused himself, leaving Elizabeth to ponder his words and wonder if there was a threat in them.

Seven

"He didn't *seem* horrid," said Sophia. "I must say, Elizabeth, I thought him quite pleasant and polite."

"That was only acting," said Elizabeth darkly. "Don't be deceived, Sophia. I'm convinced Lord Atwater is just as much our enemy as his aunt is. It's only that he's more subtle about it—and therefore more dangerous."

She had pondered long over Julius's visit to their opera box the night before. There had been no overt threat in any of his words, but she thought there might have been a covert one in his remark about seeing her in the park with Mr. Casswell. Still, she was not afraid to meet Julius in the park, as she assured herself. The park was a public place, and she would be there with Mr. Casswell, who seemed to hold a place of some importance in the *ton*. He might not have as much influence as a nobleman like Lord Atwater, but still it seemed unlikely that any harm could come to her with such a respectable escort.

Nevertheless, Elizabeth remained uneasy. She was even uneasier when the butler came to her room midmorning to report that she had a caller. *"Not* a gentleman, miss," he said. "In fact, quite a common person. But he says his business with you is urgent, and he begs the privilege of a few minutes' conversation if you can spare him the time. Seeing that he was so insistent, I put him in the small parlor, but I can easily have the footmen put him out if you do not wish to bother with him."

Elizabeth hesitated, then shook her head. "No, I'll see him. In the small parlor, you say?"

"Yes, miss," said the butler. There was disapproval in his manner as he led the way back downstairs.

Elizabeth cared nothing for the butler's disapproval, but she did feel a slight qualm as she went down the stairs. She had been thinking about Julius Atwater only a moment before and speculating about what plots he might be hatching. Now it occurred to her that this strange caller might be part of one of those plots. Perhaps he was a ruffian whom Julius had sent to threaten her, or even a hired assassin. But Elizabeth's common sense soon discounted this idea. A hired assassin would undoubtedly strike at night, and in a place where his victim was vulnerable to attack. He would not force his way boldly into her home in broad daylight when she was surrounded by her family and servants.

Fortified by this thought, Elizabeth entered the parlor and addressed the young man standing by the window. "I am Miss Watson," she said. "You wished to see me?"

"Yes, miss," said the young man. He was tall and splendidly built, with broad shoulders and a pair of notably well-sculpted legs. His voice betrayed a certain lack of culture, but he otherwise appeared perfectly respectable. To Elizabeth's eyes he looked like nothing so much as a well-trained manservant, and this in fact he proved to be. "I don't know what you'll say about my coming to you like this, miss," he went on, looking at her rather shyly. "It's all very irregular, I know, with me being nothing but a footman and out of a position at that."

Elizabeth thought she understood. "Are you looking for a position?" she asked kindly. "I'm afraid we haven't any need of additional servants at present, but—"

The young man was shaking his head. "Oh, no, miss!

Though I don't mind admitting I could use a new position." There was smothered anger in his voice as he went on. "But I don't suppose I'll be able to get one, or at least not in the kind of place I've been accustomed to. The thing is, I couldn't give you a character, for I was turned away from my last post without one. A rotten piece of injustice it was, and that's why I'm here."

Elizabeth could see no possible correlation between these last two statements. "I beg your pardon, but I don't understand," she said. "You say you were turned away from your post, Mr.—Mr.—?"

"Bray's the name—Charles Bray. Aye, turned away I was, and a rotten piece of injustice it was, when everybody knows it was the missus's own son who got Ellen in trouble. I never so much as touched the girl, and there's not a servant in the house who wouldn't say the same. They all know Maria's *my* girl. We're planning to get married next year—or at least we were, but I suppose that's off now, seeing as I've lost my position."

Elizabeth nodded sympathetically, though she was still at sea concerning Charles Bray's reason for calling on her. "I'm sorry your plans have been spoiled," she said. "It does seem too bad. But—you'll pardon me for saying so—but I don't see what you expect me to do about it, Mr. Bray."

"I don't expect you to do anything, miss," he said. "What I'm doing is for my own satisfaction. Before the missus fired me this morning, I heard her going on and on about you, and how she was going to fix it so you was a failure here in London. So I just nipped around to give you a word of warning."

An inkling of the truth was beginning to dawn on Elizabeth. "I see," she said, looking at the young man very hard. "And who is your mistress—or rather who *was* your mistress, as I perhaps should say?"

"Mrs. Thomas Atwater," said the young man. With these words, the whole puzzle fell into place.

"I see," said Elizabeth. "I *see.* So you used to work for Mrs. Atwater, but she fired you because she thought you got one of the female servants in trouble—"

"Which I never did, miss," said the young man warmly. " 'Twas Mr. Gilbert that done it. He goes on something awful with all the female staff, always trying to kiss 'em when he catches them alone. Why, he even offered my Maria a *carte blanche*, but she wasn't having any of it. A proper good girl Maria is, and taking no nonsense from anyone."

"I'm sure she must be a fine girl," said Elizabeth.

She was eager to hear more about Mrs. Atwater's plot, but had first to listen to Charles Bray expand upon the many excellences of his betrothed. "Maria's a good girl, and a clever girl—aye, and a pretty one, too," he told Elizabeth. "I can't think how she ever came to look at me. She's Mrs. Atwater's dressing woman, and I was only the second footman, but still she said she'd rather have me than all the other fellows combined. We agreed we'd be married as soon as we got a bit of money saved between us. But now here I am without a position, and who knows when we'll be able to marry. I tell you, it makes me half crazy, and Maria's mad enough to spit. She says she's going to quit Mrs. Atwater the first chance she can, but of course she'll have to find another position someplace, and it would be best if we could find a place where we could both be together again. But that isn't likely, seeing as I came away without a character."

"Oh, you never know," said Elizabeth noncommittally. "Something might turn up. You say your fiancée is Mrs. Atwater's dressing maid?"

"Aye, that she is, miss."

"And does she know you are here today? She knows you mean to tell me of Mrs. Atwater's plans?"

"Oh, aye, miss; she knows that, all right. In fact, 'twas her idea in the first place. She said it would serve the old beldam right to have her plans thrown all cock-a-hoop, seeing that she'd gone and spoiled ours."

"Well, what *are* Mrs. Atwater's plans? You spoke of her meaning to fix things so I was a failure here in London."

"Oh, aye, I know all about it, miss," said Charles Bray confidently. "It seems somebody told the missus at the opera last night about some party you're giving or having someone give for you. The missus said you had no business appearing in society, and she's planning to fix it so nobody comes to your party. She's going to send out cards for a party the same night—a party that'll put yours all in the shade. She sent one of the other footmen off to the stationer's first thing this morning to have the cards engraved, and she means to send 'em out before the day's over."

A smile spread across Elizabeth's face. "Is that so?" she said. "I am much obliged to you for this information, Mr. Bray. Forewarned is forearmed, you know, and armed with this intelligence I think I can contrive to spoil Mrs. Atwater's plans." She regarded the young man speculatively.

"I'm sure you're welcome, miss," said Charles. "Seemed the least I could do, to do you a good turn while I could."

He began to move toward the door, but Elizabeth laid a hand on his arm to detain him. "Indeed, I am very much obliged to you, Mr. Bray," she said. "Both to you and to Maria. This information will save me a deal of trouble, and it occurs to me I might be able to recompense you in some measure—especially if you were willing to give me more information of the same nature. I don't mind telling you that word of Mrs. Atwater's plans is worth a great deal to me. I would gladly give you em-

ployment in my household, if you would make it a part
of your duties to see Maria often and find out from her
everything you can concerning her mistress's activities.
It would only be for the duration of the Season, but if
you both perform faithfully, I would pay you a sum that
would enable you to marry and perhaps even set up a
business of your own."

Charles Bray stared at Elizabeth as though she were a
fairy that had just granted his dearest wish. "Would you
do that, miss?" he gasped. "Oh, miss, that'd be wonderful, that would. Maria and I've talked it over time and
time again about how we'd like to open our own public
house someday, but we didn't suppose we'd be able to do
it for years yet, if we ever could."

"Well, you speak with Maria and see what she says,"
said Elizabeth. "We shall need her cooperation if the plan
is to succeed. As lady's maid to Mrs. Atwater, she is in
an ideal position to hear all that goes on in the household."

Charles Bray said he was sure Maria would have no
qualms about helping Elizabeth. "Maria's been saying for
years that she'd like to get away from the missus, what
with her temper and her always blaming the staff for
things that are her own fault. She'll jump at the chance
to get back at her, I don't doubt."

"Well, you see her and make sure," said Elizabeth.
Thanking Charles again for calling, she saw him to the
door and bade him return as soon as he had discussed
the matter with his intended.

Thus it was that Charles Bray came to be installed into
the Watson household as Elizabeth's own personal manservant. The butler was inclined at first to take umbrage
at this, for it was properly his task to hire the footmen.
But Elizabeth smoothed things over by terming Charles
her equerry instead.

" 'Equerry' has such a nice lofty sound to it," she told

Sophia with a laugh. "My goodness, I'll be setting up with ladies-in-waiting next!"

"I am sure you could have them if you wanted to," said Sophia. "But I doubt they'd be as useful as Charles Bray seems likely to be. My goodness, what a stroke of luck that he should have come to you as he did."

"Yes, indeed! When I think that we had the cards all ready to send out for our ball, and it was only his coming that saved us from having Mrs. Atwater ruin the whole thing. But instead we will ruin *her* party. We'll give our ball on the night *before* she gives hers—and we'll make sure ours is bigger and better in every way. Of course it means ordering new cards and perhaps a few extra flowers and things, but I'd be willing to do more than that, just to serve that dreadful woman a trick."

From that day forward, Elizabeth took an active interest in the preparations for the Watsons' ball, quite confounding Mrs. Reese-Whittington, who had heretofore found her elder niece wholly disinterested in her plans. Mrs. Watson, however, said many times that she was pleased to see Elizabeth abandoning her foolish and unnecessary ideas of economy. Indeed, under Elizabeth's supervision the plans became more extravagant than even Mrs. Watson had dared envision.

Having learned from Maria via Charles that Mrs. Atwater intended to decorate her ballroom with drifts of spangled gauze and roses suspended on silver wires from the ceiling, Elizabeth gave orders that the Watson ballroom should be decorated with twice as many roses and twice as much gauze. Upon learning from the same source that her rival had hired a certain celebrated orchestra to play music for the dancing, nothing would do except that Elizabeth should hire an even better one. The menu was identical to Mrs. Atwater's, only more sumptuous in its presentation and served as a sit-down supper rather than a standing one. The champagne was of a better vintage and served forth from the bottle in unstinted quantities, whereas Mrs. Atwater had had to be content with serving hers in the form of punch. Elizabeth even had her ballroom chairs covered in the identical green brocade with which Mrs. Atwater had just reupholstered her own.

Overall, Elizabeth felt fairly confident that her party would be a success. Out of the three hundred cards sent, more than two hundred had been returned, a number that Mrs. Reese-Whittington declared flattering in the extreme. "Everyone wants to see and meet you, dearest," she told Elizabeth. "You made such a sensation in the park the other day when you appeared with Mr. Casswell. I have had a dozen people mention it to me at least."

Elizabeth frowned. That day in the park was still clear in her memory, and not because it had been a day of triumph. It ought to have been, for she had attracted a good deal of attention and received many compliments on her dashing military-style pelisse and helmet hat. But then Julius Atwater had turned up, and from that moment on the day had taken an unsettling turn.

"You look charmingly, Miss Watson," he had said, saluting her with a smile from the back of his bay mare. "There is a martial flavor about your attire that seems eminently suitable for a military historian."

Elizabeth had murmured a self-conscious thank-you, while Mr. Casswell had looked confused. "What's that?" he asked. "What d'ye mean, suitable for a military historian, Atwater? Who's a military historian?"

"Why, Miss Watson is," said Julius. He threw a surprised look at Elizabeth. "Has she not told you of her literary achievements? Well, then, it's not for me to trumpet them forth. But I can tell you this: it's no ordinary young lady you are escorting there, Casswell. You ought to be properly cognizant of your good fortune."

He had accompanied these words with a smile toward

Elizabeth—a smile that was almost conspiratorial in nature. But of course they were anything but co-conspirators, as Elizabeth reminded herself. Indeed, it was far more probable that he was conspiring against her rather than with her. Probably he thought mentioning her book a good way to ruin her socially. Mrs. Reese-Whittington had thought it better not to advertise her authorship among the *ton* lest she be labeled with the damning title of bluestocking, but now the cat was out of the bag. Mr. Casswell was so much intrigued by Julius's remarks that he badgered Elizabeth with endless questions, until at last she admitted that she had written and published a book about the Second Punic War.

"Have you, by Jove!" said Mr. Casswell, regarding her with a new respect. "I'll have to order a copy at the bookseller's. What's the title? I'll make a memorandum of it and drive by Hatchard's this very day." He had gone on to make a number of remarks about her book, and about her being brainy as well as beautiful, all of which had made Elizabeth highly self-conscious. And for that, as for so much else, she blamed Julius Atwater.

What was still worse, she was sure the news that she had written a book was all over town by now. It would have been too much to rely on Mr. Casswell's discretion, even if she could have relied on Julius Atwater's. And of course she could not look for discretion from him, seeing that he was her enemy.

As soon as she reached home, Elizabeth had told Mrs. Reese-Whittington what had happened. She had expected that lady to be much dismayed, but on the whole Mrs. Reese-Whittington took the news philosophically. "I'd hoped it wouldn't come out until later in the Season, but never mind, dear," she told Elizabeth. "I don't think it will do you any harm in the long run. As I say, you don't *look* blue. But I do wish you could bring yourself to be a little more gay and sociable. If you would just smile a little more and flirt in a ladylike way, no one would care how many books you had written."

Elizabeth was sure this was sound advice, but she doubted her ability to follow it. Indeed, by the time the day of the ball had rolled around, she had made up her mind that the only thing lacking in the festivities that evening was likely to be herself. "I *can't* flirt," she told herself despairingly as she surveyed her reflection in the glass. "I never learned how when I was younger, and now I'm too old to learn. And as for trying to smile and be gay——" She flashed an artificial smile at the glass, then shuddered at the result. "No, I'd frighten people away if I went about looking like that! I can only smile when I feel like smiling, and I'm not likely to feel that way tonight."

Then it occurred to Elizabeth that she had at least one thing to smile about. Undoubtedly she and her party were going to be a source of great vexation to Mrs. Atwater. Indeed, she knew for a fact that they already were, for Charles had reported that Mrs. Atwater had exploded into fury when she learned the Watsons had changed the date of their ball to the night before her own. "If she hadn't already sent out the cards, miss, she'd have changed hers for certain sure. But it was too late for that, though Maria says she wrote to all her friends and begged them to stay away from your party. Howsomever, she caught cold at that, for it seems everybody's wanting to see you, miss, and also Mr. Lucius's house that you've done over. They all told Mrs. Atwater they'd already sent in their acceptances and couldn't in courtesy stay away. Maria said she stormed around like a wild woman, crying and saying there wasn't any such thing as loyalty in London."

Elizabeth, reflecting on these things, felt a satisfied smile curve the corners of her mouth. "Now that is a genuine smile!" she said aloud, surveying the result in the glass. "If I can only keep that up, Cousin Amelia will have nothing to complain of. And indeed, now I think of it, I have a good deal to smile about. Mrs. Atwater little knows what additional vexation is in store for her. I wonder if people will admire my new dress?"

Looking down at herself, Elizabeth could hardly keep from laughing. The matter of her dress had been her boldest stroke. From Maria, she had learned all the details of Mrs. Atwater's toilette for the following evening, then had them reproduced in her own dress. Mrs. Reese-Whittington had objected to this plan, not so much because she thought it impudent as because she felt dark green velvet rather a matronly costume for a young lady. But when she beheld Elizabeth in her dark green gown with a matching toque atop her flaxen curls, she changed her mind. "It does set off your hair and skin something lovely, my dear. And though I'd rather not see a girl your age in a toque, there's no denying you've got the height to wear one properly. In fact, I wouldn't be surprised if you didn't set a fashion for them."

Elizabeth discounted this extravagant praise, but she was satisfied by her appearance and pleased to think of the trick she was playing on Mrs. Atwater. *Since she won't be here tonight, she won't know that my dress is like hers until she opens her ball tomorrow night,* Elizabeth told herself gleefully, as she gathered up her fan and shawl. *And by then it will be too late. Won't she be furious? My, I wish I could be there to see her reaction.*

This thought brought not merely a smile but a grin to Elizabeth's lips. She cast a satisfied glance at her reflection, then hurried from the room.

In the hall outside, she encountered Charles bearing a sheaf of white roses in his hand. "Oh, dear, *another* bouquet?" she said. She had already received a half-dozen floral bequests from gentlemen she hardly knew. In spite of Mrs. Reese-Whittington's assurances that these were merely a tribute to her charm, Elizabeth was cynically disposed to think them more of a tribute to her fortune—a kind of floral bread sown upon the waters, as it were. It had not escaped her notice that Sophia had received no bouquets, though she had met quite as many gentlemen in London as her elder sister.

So Elizabeth frowned at the flowers and said, "Whom do these come from, Charles?"

"From Lord Atwater," was Charles's surprising answer. " 'Twas his man who delivered them anyway. I knew him by sight, though I don't think he knew me."

"Lord Atwater!" exclaimed Elizabeth. Snatching the square of pasteboard from the bouquet, she read it, then looked up, much shaken. "What does he mean by sending me a bouquet?"

Charles shrugged. "Goodness knows, miss. But they're pretty flowers, ain't they?"

"They *seem* to be," said Elizabeth, scrutinizing them closely. So deeply did she distrust Julius Atwater that she half suspected the roses to conceal some Borgia-like device to injure her. But they appeared to be perfectly innocuous. There wasn't even a thorn to be seen among them, and their perfume was intoxicating. Elizabeth knew a sudden desire to carry them that night. After all, she reasoned, their color would set off her dress to a nicety. Then sanity reasserted itself. She could not possibly carry a bouquet donated by Julius Atwater.

"Take them down to the flower room and leave them there," she told Charles. The roses seemed to regard her with mute appeal as he carried them away. Almost Elizabeth felt they were reproaching her. *Ridiculous,* she told herself. Yet she could not resist adding aloud, "Be sure to put them in water, Charles. They are lovely things, even if Lord Atwater did send them."

Eight

Elizabeth was extremely thoughtful as she continued on her way downstairs. She could not imagine why Julius had sent her flowers. Probably it was merely part of some diabolical scheme, but its nature eluded her. What could he hope to accomplish by behaving as if he admired her?

Elizabeth had little time to ponder this question, for it remained only a few minutes until the ball was to begin. Mrs. Reese-Whittington was bustling about, giving last-minute reminders to the staff, and Mrs. Watson was busy rearranging the garland of roses atop Sophia's golden head. Sophia looked very lovely in a dress of white net over satin, and Elizabeth told her so. "You look lovely, too, Elizabeth," replied Sophia, admiringly surveying her sister's costume. "I'm so nervous! Aren't you nervous, too?"

Elizabeth *was* nervous, but she preferred not to admit it. "There's no point in being nervous now," she told Sophia. "The die is cast. It only remains to be seen whether we have cast it successfully or not."

By eleven o'clock, that question had been definitively answered. There could be no question that the Watsons' ball was a smashing success. The rooms were crammed so full of people that it was nearly impossible to move, and everyone praised the food, the decorations, and the music. There was praise for Elizabeth personally as well, though most of it was not exactly to her taste.

"A handsome gel," Elizabeth overheard one dowager saying to another. "Really, quite *distinguée* in her appearance. And an heiress, too, they say. I believe she would do very well for my Reginald. I'll write him tonight and tell him to come up to town immediately, for if he doesn't hurry some younger son with a title will likely snap her up."

This speech greatly displeased Elizabeth. She had no objection to being called handsome and *distinguée*, but she resented the implication that her fortune made her a commodity subject to the laws of supply and demand. Yet it was very obvious that it did, for she was thronged with would-be partners all evening, as many as six or eight for each dance. Elizabeth found it hard work to choose among so many when most of them were strangers to her. She elected to dance the first dance with Mr. Casswell, because she already knew him slightly and found him inoffensive, but he took it as such a compliment to himself and was so obviously pluming himself on having won the favor of the heiress that Elizabeth had no hesitation about refusing him when he asked her to dance a second time.

She chose to sit the second dance out altogether, thinking to save herself from further such dilemmas, but this made her situation no better. Two gentlemen came close to blows in their eagerness to fetch her a glass of punch and sit with her while she drank it. Elizabeth thought to soothe them by permitting them both to fetch her punch, but then she had to drink both glasses so as to show no favor to either gentleman. Fortunately it was champagne punch rather than straight champagne, but it was still alcoholic enough to have an effect on Elizabeth's head. The evening began to take on a strange, phantasmagoric quality. Everywhere she turned, there seemed to be gentlemen grinning at her, beseeching her to dance, pleading to be allowed to sit with her, fan her, or fetch her refreshments. There was a near riot when she dropped her handkerchief, and an actual fight ensued at the beginning of the third dance when a gentleman claiming Elizabeth had promised to dance with him clashed with another gentleman claiming the same privilege.

Fortunately, this would-be brawl was quickly broken up by a third gentleman, who waded into the fight and quickly reduced both combatants to a more pacific state of mind by banging their heads together. "You're neither of you fit to appear in a lady's company," he said concisely. "Shame to you both for causing such a scene."

Turning to Elizabeth, he then apologized for having forced her to witness such violence. Elizabeth was charmed by his manners, by his efficient method of dealing with the incipient brawl, and by the unmistakably Irish lilt in his voice. When he diffidently suggested that Elizabeth would never care to dance with him now that she had met him in such prejudicial circumstances, she contradicted him with a smile. "Not at all, sir; I would be very pleased to dance with you," she said.

On the dance floor, she learned more about her new partner. His name was Lieutenant Sir Connor O'Connor; he hailed from County Cork, and he had a large estate consisting mostly of farmland and a vast number of debts. All this he revealed quite candidly and with a disarming smile. "For you may as well know the worst of me from the beginning," he told Elizabeth. "There'll be plenty of folk to call me a fortune hunter and hint I'm dangling after your fortune. Well, I don't deny I could use a fortune, and it's commonly understood you've got a very pretty one, but I don't intend to make a nuisance of meself on that account. Mind you, if you *should* happen to fall madly in love with me and wish to become Lady O'Connor, why, that'd be very convenient. But if you don't—well, then, that's all right, too. Call me sentimental, but I'm not after marrying any lass who isn't madly in love with me. It wouldn't be doing meself justice, as I see it."

All this was spoken with such a droll air that Elizabeth could not help laughing. She found Sir Connor's honesty refreshing after the hypocrisy of such gentlemen as Mr. Casswell. "I understand, Sir Connor," she said, smiling. "Let us simply be friends for now, and I shall tell you if I show any signs of falling madly in love with you."

"It's a bargain, then," said Sir Connor promptly. "I'll make a list of me good qualities, and you can study it over in your spare moments."

He continued in this vein throughout the dance. Elizabeth smiled at his sallies and made suitable replies, and as the dance was winding to a close it occurred to her with amazement that she had been flirting. There could be no doubt about it: she, Elizabeth Watson, had flirted with a gentleman and had done it quite successfully, too.

On the whole, Elizabeth suspected the punch had been responsible. But Sir Connor's Irish charm had played a role, too. He had such a winning smile and such winsome blue eyes. Elizabeth thought to herself that they were much like Julius Atwater's eyes. They could sparkle with fun while conveying all the while a world of meaning.

But that's ridiculous, she castigated herself. *It's not fun in Julius Atwater's eyes, it's malice. He hates me and wants to get his uncle's fortune away from me.* It was at that moment she looked up and saw Julius himself regarding her from the edge of the dance floor.

In her consternation, Elizabeth came close to stepping on Sir Connor's elegantly shod feet. Fortunately, she had been so well drilled in the steps of the fashionable dances that instinct took over and carried her through, but Sir Connor had felt her falter. He looked at her curiously. "Is aught amiss, Miss Watson?" he asked.

"Yes—I mean no," said Elizabeth rapidly. "I am feeling a little fatigued, Sir Connor. Now that the dance is over, I believe I would like to sit down for a while."

Sir Connor obligingly led her toward an empty bench. Before she was halfway there, she was surrounded once again by a mob of gentlemen imploring her to dance with them. "No, thank you," she said, over and over. "No, I am not dancing at present. No, thank you, sir; Sir Connor is going to get some punch for me. No, I want nothing more, thank you very much."

Disappointed, the gentlemen drifted away one by one. At last only Sir Connor was left. Having made sure Elizabeth was comfortable, he, too, left, saying he would fetch them something to drink. Elizabeth watched him go, then glanced nervously toward Julius. She fancied she had felt his eyes on her ever since she had left the dance floor. When she looked at him again, she found she was right. He was regarding her with a steady, meditative gaze. On meeting her eyes, he bowed slightly, then began to make his way toward her.

Elizabeth's heart gave a mighty leap. *I mustn't let him make me nervous,* she told herself. *After all, he can do nothing in such a public place.* Yet somehow, the thought did not calm her, and in that moment she began to perceive dimly that it was not what she expected Julius to do that discomposed her; it was the simple fact of his being there.

By now Julius had arrived at her side and was bowing once more. As he straightened, his eyes met hers, and Elizabeth experienced an almost physical shock. *Why, his eyes are not like Sir Connor's at all,* she told herself. She wondered how she could have ever thought they were. Julius's eyes were a deeper blue and deeper set, and there was something besides mere laughter in them. Whether it was malice or not, Elizabeth was not prepared to say; she only knew that it made her feel suddenly breathless.

"Good evening, my lord," she managed to say in a voice that did not sound at all like her own.

"Good evening, Miss Watson," said Julius. He went on looking at her a moment, and Elizabeth had a sudden fancy that he was as nervous as she was. That was plainly ridiculous, of course; Elizabeth told herself he was merely looking for a vulnerable spot to attack. "Your ball appears to be a triumphal success," he said at last. "I have heard nothing but praise since I arrived. And that includes praise for you personally, Miss Watson. Indeed, you look very lovely this evening."

"Thank you," said Elizabeth. She had to fight back an urge to blush and duck her head. Her voice still did not sound like her own, and she was vastly irritated with herself. It was absurd to let Julius Atwater affect her like this. Still more absurd was it to let herself feel gratified by his words. Of course he did not mean what he was saying. The fact that his eyes appeared to be doing her homage as well as his lips meant only that he was an extremely fine actor as well as an extremely dangerous adversary.

Making an effort, Elizabeth went on in a light tone. "I am surprised to see you here this evening, my lord. I would not have expected that you would care to attend our party."

"Why not?" he asked, sounding genuinely puzzled. Elizabeth could not help admiring his ability to dissimulate, even while she deplored it. "I would not have missed it for the world. Did you receive my flowers?"

"Oh, yes," said Elizabeth. "Thank you very much, my lord." She experienced a fresh flush of irritation, finding herself wishing to apologize to him for not carrying his bouquet. Of course no apology was necessary. She had chosen to carry none of the bouquets that had been sent her that evening, reasoning that to do so would only be to encourage their donor to fancy himself favored above her other suitors. Elizabeth was resolved to show favor to no one, and least of all to Julius Atwater. Yet there was something in the power of those deep blue eyes fixed on hers that drew from her more than the simple "thank you" she had intended. "Indeed, they were beautiful roses, my lord. I was sorry not to carry them, but I thought—I did not wish—it seemed cruel to let them wilt in a stuffy ballroom rather than putting them properly in water."

Now what am I doing? she demanded of herself. *Damn Julius Atwater! Not only is he a liar, he is making me one, too!*

She glanced up at Julius and saw he was smiling. As if to further prove his malign powers, she felt her own lips curve into an answering smile. "Well, I must approve your tender heart, Miss Watson, even if I regret not to see you carrying my flowers," he said. "Perhaps you would now indulge your heart toward the donor of the flowers by consenting to dance this next dance with him?"

Of course the proper response to this question was to disclaim any tenderness of heart and put him firmly in his place. Elizabeth knew this, and it was with considerable amazement that she heard herself say, "Thank you, my lord, but I am engaged to sit out this dance with Sir Connor. Perhaps the next dance—"

"Of course," said Julius, bowing. "I shall look forward to it." As though sensing she might take back her acceptance if given any opportunity, he bowed and quickly took himself off.

Elizabeth stared after him, her mind a turmoil of contradictory thoughts. So deep was she in thought that when Sir Connor arrived an instant later with her punch, she jumped. "Here, now, I'm sorry to have startled you, Miss Watson," said Sir Connor penitently. "It's a clumsy creature I am, and no mistake."

Elizabeth could not help laughing in spite of her abstraction. Anything less clumsy than Sir Connor's lithe, well-knit frame could scarcely be imagined. "Nonsense," she said. "You must know, sir, that you have already distinguished yourself on the dance floor for your grace and agility."

Sir Connor smiled modestly. "Ah, it's good of you to say so," he said. "Perhaps I'm not so bad there; it's clumsy in my manners I'm meaning."

"And that is not true, either," said Elizabeth. "Your manners are as adroit as your feet. You have paid me the most outrageous compliments tonight and made me half believe them."

"Well, when I've got you where you believe them complete, I beg you'll let me know," said Sir Connor. "I'm sure I spoke nothing but what 'twas gospel truth." He went on in this vein for some time, but Elizabeth's attention was now distracted, and she heard little of what he said. In a covert manner, she looked around the ballroom for Julius's dark head and tall figure. What was he doing now? Was he dancing with some other lady? Elizabeth told herself it mattered nothing to her whom he danced with. But still she felt an overpowering interest to see who his partner might be—an interest that was all the more overpowering for being completely irrational.

As far as she could tell, however, Julius had not chosen to dance that dance. She caught no glimpse of him until it was nearly time for the fourth dance to begin. Then he suddenly materialized at her side, causing her to blush and start. "Oh! There you are, my lord," she said. "I was looking for you." At these words she blushed deeper, realizing that she had betrayed an unwonted interest in him. It would have been a thousand times better to have acted disinterested when he came to claim her, or even better to have taken the floor with another man and acted as though she had altogether forgotten their engagement.

That would have been a proper set-down for Lord Atwater's conceit!

But it was too late for set-downs now. Julius was saying, "My dance, I believe, Miss Watson?" and the hoard of other would-be partners, hearing these words, fell back and watched disconsolately as Elizabeth rose to her feet and accepted his proffered arm.

As Elizabeth accompanied Julius onto the dance floor, she told herself she was deeply annoyed. Of course it must be annoyance she felt, although the sensation in the pit of her stomach was more reminiscent of fear and excitement. Still, those emotions were justifiable, too. It was possible that this whole business of his asking her to dance might be part of some plot to embarrass her somehow out on the dance floor. Elizabeth told herself she must be very careful, but her mind seemed incapable of concentrating on more than the simple fact that she was dancing with Julius, Lord Atwater.

For a minute or two he did not speak, but merely looked down at her. This gave Elizabeth time to appreciate that he was a very good dancer. He was not, perhaps, so good as Sir Connor, but there was a strength and authority about him that was reassuring. *Reassuring? Are you mad?* Elizabeth demanded of herself in horror, and resolved to open the hostilities without further delay.

"Why did you come tonight, Lord Atwater?" she demanded.

Julius looked at her in puzzlement. "Why, I told you," he said. "I would not have missed this party for the world. Indeed, it promises to be the event of the Season."

Elizabeth smiled cynically. "That remains to be seen," she said. "I understand your aunt is giving a ball of her own tomorrow night."

She watched closely to see if Julius would betray himself at these words. Surely he would show some sign of discomposure at the mention of his aunt's party. But he merely nodded as though the matter were of little moment and said, "Yes, I believe so."

"Of course your aunt will expect you to attend her party," pursued Elizabeth. "What a fortunate thing that her party and ours did not happen to be the same night!"

She had thought that this ought to prod him into a reaction if anything could. But as before, he displayed little interest. "Oh, well, you know it's not an uncommon thing to attend two or three parties a night at the height of the Season," he said. "If worst came to worst, I'd have attended both yours *and* my aunt's. But I'm just as glad not to have to divide my time and attention." He smiled down at Elizabeth.

By making an intense effort, Elizabeth was able to keep from returning the smile. "Indeed," she said. "We are honored to have you here tonight, my lord. Even if you came without a card," she added significantly.

"But I did have a card," said Julius, regarding her with astonishment. "Of course I had a card! I never would have been boorish enough to have come without a proper invitation."

Elizabeth opened her mouth, then closed it again. She was sure he was lying. It was ridiculous to suppose that Mrs. Reese-Whittington would have sent a card to any Atwater, let alone the chief instigator of the family. But she had no means of proving the lie, and in any case she was sure that a man as unprincipled as Lord Atwater was perfectly capable of stealing or forging a card if he so desired. "Indeed," she said indifferently. "I was not aware my cousin had put you on the guest list, but of course it's no matter."

Julius said nothing, and after a moment Elizabeth stole a look at him. There was a line between his brows, and he was looking down at her with a sober expression. "You must have a poor opinion of me," he said. Against her will, Elizabeth found herself protesting. "Not at all," she said.

"Indeed, I have a very high opinion of you, my lord." This was not a lie, as she assured herself. She did have a high opinion of his powers of deception. But Julius was still looking at her, and she felt uncomfortably sure that those clear blue eyes were seeing more than she wanted. To cover her embarrassment, she went on talking, choosing the first subject that came into her head. "There can be no doubt, at least, that you are a gifted orator. I read your speech about Catholic Emancipation that was published in the *Times*. Indeed, I thought it very well done."

At these words, his frown relaxed slightly. "You read that?" he said. "I am honored by your approval, Miss Watson." Regarding her seriously, he added, "I'm afraid I haven't spoken as often as I ought these last few years. But I do endeavor to do my duty in the main, I assure you. I wouldn't want you to think I am a mere fashionable fribble."

Elizabeth regarded him incredulously. What could he mean by saying such things? "I don't think that, my lord," she said, and then fell silent. She could not say what she really thought of him, for in truth she did not know what she really thought of him. She was inclined to both like and distrust him, to admit him as a friend on one hand and hold him at a distance on the other. And that, as she had already assured herself countless times, was perfectly ridiculous.

Fortunately, Julius seemed satisfied by her words, for he let the subject lapse and took up another. "Do you go to St. James's this week?" he asked. "I thought I saw your name on the list of ladies who will be making their bows at the Queen's drawing room."

"Yes, I will be at the Queen's drawing room," said Elizabeth warily. Since this was a matter of public record, she could hardly deny it, but she was on the alert at once, certain that he was gathering intelligence in order to form some kind of malign plan in which she would be the victim.

To her surprise, Julius revealed his plans with apparent candor. "Perhaps I will see you there," he said. "My aunt plans to attend the drawing room also, and it may be that I can accompany her." He grimaced. "Aunt Jane will no doubt cut you, or try to, but I beg you won't pay her any heed. I personally plan to give you my best bow, and I hope you'll be kind enough to return it."

Elizabeth merely nodded in a noncommittal manner. She was busy pondering the meaning of this speech. Was it some kind of trap? Did he mean to trick her into acknowledging him, then cut her in front of the crowd at St. James's? Elizabeth resolved that any sign of recognition must come from him first. She would not be such a ninny as to fall into such an obvious trap.

Julius, meanwhile, had gone on speaking. "I do wish I could bring my aunt to see reason," he said. "As I mentioned before, she is quite irrational on the subject of her son, Gilbert. The thought that Lucius's money went to you rather than him has been a bitter pill for her to swallow, but I have hopes of convincing her in time to take the dose."

Again Elizabeth nodded noncommittally. It was a temptation to believe Julius was speaking the truth, but she reminded herself that he was a clever actor—so clever that she kept having to remind herself to be on guard against him. In this case, however, she was not in much danger of believing him. It was ridiculous to suppose Mrs. Atwater could ever be reconciled to the idea of her keeping Lucius Atwater's fortune.

The dance ended soon after this, much to Elizabeth's relief. It was a great strain to hold out against Julius's friendly manner, and an additional strain to have to remind herself that he was her enemy and she must not trust him on any account. Somehow distrust simply did not come naturally to her where he was concerned.

Elizabeth was puzzling over this fact as she left the dance floor on Julius's arm. She glanced up at him and found he was looking down at her. "An enjoyable dance, Miss Watson," he said. "But over far too soon. Would you consider dancing with me again, later this evening?"

To her annoyance, Elizabeth found the word "yes" rising to her lips. She bit it back, wondering what on earth ailed her. "I don't believe that will be possible, my lord," she said. This was clearly the answer she ought to have made, so why did there have to be so much regret in her voice? Was it possible she really *wanted* to dance with him?

Ridiculous, Elizabeth told herself. *He's not nearly so good a dancer as Sir Connor. Not nearly so entertaining, either. I can't relax for a minute in his company. I'm always afraid he will try to trick me into something I don't mean to say or do.*

Yet in spite of these things, she felt a genuine regret at refusing him. He received the refusal quietly enough, bowing and taking her hand in his for a moment. "I won't pretend I am not disappointed," he told her, "but of course I understand. You are so much sought after this evening that even obtaining a single dance is an inestimable privilege."

"It's not me that's sought after—" began Elizabeth, then stopped.

"Not you?" said Julius, raising his eyebrows. "I beg to differ with you, Miss Watson. Already there are a half-dozen fellows converging on us, and I don't think it's my company they're seeking!"

Elizabeth hesitated, then went on with sudden recklessness. "Neither is it my company they're seeking, my lord. It is rather the company of your uncle's fortune."

Julius's eyebrows shot up. He looked as though he

were going to say something, but the nearest of Elizabeth's suitors had already reached her and was begging her to dance with him. She glanced at Julius, half frightened at having spoken so frankly. Yet she was exhilarated, too. *At any rate, he now knows I am not such an idiot as to suppose I have inspired all this devotion,* she told herself. *If he hopes to cozen me with compliments and invitations to dance, he will see how little such a scheme is likely to succeed.*

By this time there were at least a dozen gentlemen clamoring for Elizabeth to dance with them. She was trying to choose among this multitude when she saw Mrs. Reese-Whittington approaching. Another gentleman was with her—a fair-haired gentleman whose air was notable even in that notable gathering. It was further notable that there was a triumphant smile on Mrs. Reese-Whittington's face.

"Here comes Amelia Reese-Whittington with Steinbridge on her arm," remarked one of Elizabeth's suitors, addressing his neighbor in a low voice. "What odds will you give that she means to tie him up to the heiress?"

"No odds at all," answered the other gentleman with a grimace. "But she'll catch cold at that. Steinbridge is dashed exclusive and rich as Croesus, too. He's no need to go dangling after heiresses."

Elizabeth overheard both these remarks, and they did nothing to reduce the cynicism she felt toward her suitors and her position. Yet she could not help regarding the approaching gentleman with interest. Even without the comments she had overheard, she would have known he was someone important simply by Mrs. Reese-Whittington's manner. "My dear, I have someone I would like to introduce to you," she told Elizabeth. "This is Lord Steinbridge, Marquess of Steinbridge and Earl of Gantley."

Elizabeth curtsied, and Mrs. Reese-Whittington went

on, turning to address the marquess. "My lord, this is my cousin, Miss Watson. The same Miss Watson who wrote the book you so much admired." She smiled significantly at Elizabeth.

Elizabeth blinked. Considering Mrs. Reese-Whittington's previous words on the subject, she had not supposed her authorship was a matter to be mentioned socially. But she hid her surprise as best she could while the marquess returned her curtsy with a bow.

"Indeed, I am greatly honored," he said. "I read your book some months ago, and thought it a most admirable work. Now that I have met its author, I feel doubly honored."

He bowed again, a bow of stiff formality. Looking at him closely, Elizabeth observed that everything about him was stiff and formal, from the fair hair combed straight back from his brow to his rather pedantic way of speaking. Yet there was genuine admiration in his gaze as he regarded Elizabeth, and a smile that did a good deal to soften his somewhat haughty features. "Indeed, I never would have supposed that the lady who could write such a scholarly work was both young and charming."

"Is not that a pretty compliment, my love?" cried Mrs. Reese-Whittington, before Elizabeth could answer. "Lord Steinbridge, you are too kind, I vow and declare. You will be turning my niece's head if you go paying her compliments like that."

"I have no wish to turn her head," said the marquess gravely. "But if she could be persuaded to take a turn on the dance floor with me, I would consider myself greatly privileged."

"Of course she will dance with you, won't you, Elizabeth?" cried Mrs. Reese-Whittington, once more speaking before Elizabeth could open her mouth. "Tell his lordship you are much obliged."

Elizabeth was nettled by her cousin's behavior. She had

never met a marquess before and was secretly rather awed by this one, but still she did not intend to fawn over him. The fact that Julius was still standing by her side further strengthened her resolve. He should see that a title made no impression on her, even a title much greater than his own. "Thank you, my lord, but I am already engaged for this dance," she told the marquess politely.

Mrs. Reese-Whittington's mouth fell open in shock. The marquess looked hardly less shocked; it was evident he was not in the habit of having his invitations declined. Only Julius remained unmoved. Stealing a glance at him, Elizabeth saw he was regarding both her and the marquess with an inscrutable expression.

Although the marquess had been surprised, he made a gallant recovery. "Very well, Miss Watson," he said. "If you are engaged for this set, perhaps you will dance the next one with me? I do hope I have not come too late to engage you at all."

"No, I can give you the next dance, my lord," said Elizabeth. Satisfied at having made her point, she smiled as she spoke, which brought an answering smile to his lips.

"I shall look forward to it, Miss Watson," he said.

In the lull following this speech, the orchestra could be heard striking the opening bars of a rollicking country dance. Elizabeth suddenly realized she was in a quandary. She had just told the marquess she had a partner for the coming dance, but in fact she had no partner. Nor was she in any position to get one, for all her suitors had drifted away at the marquess's approach—all except Julius. With a last vain hope, she looked about for Sir Connor. Of all the men she had met since coming to London, he was the one she would have least minded asking a favor of. But Sir Connor was already out on the dance floor with a pretty brunette, and there was no help to be had from him.

Elizabeth glanced at Julius. His eyes met hers, and she had the oddest impression that he understood her predicament. *Yes, and no doubt he is gloating over it,* she told herself grimly. Nonetheless, she turned to him and spoke in a would-be affable voice. "It looks as though the dance is beginning, my lord. Had we not better be taking our places in the set?"

There was a pause during which Julius appeared to be considering this speech. Elizabeth waited with bated breath. *He will probably deny we are engaged to dance the set,* she told herself bitterly. *That will make me look a fool, having to tell the marquess I have no partner after all.*

But hardly had this thought crossed her mind when Julius spoke. "To be sure, Miss Watson," he said. "We had better be taking our places." He bowed to Mrs. Reese-Whittington and the marquess, then extended his arm to Elizabeth, and together they went onto the dance floor.

Nine

For the first few minutes of the dance, Elizabeth did not speak. Julius did not speak, either, but merely looked at her as they went through the figures together. It seemed to Elizabeth that there was something expectant in his gaze.

No doubt he expects me to thank him for saving my face, she told herself bitterly. *If so, he'll be disappointed. I won't own myself obliged to him—no, not though he saved my life as well as my face!*

But though Elizabeth tried to assure herself that she owed Julius no thanks, her conscience told her otherwise. He might be her enemy, but he had saved her from an awkward situation, and it was only right that she should thank him. So she raised her eyes and said, "I am much obliged to you, my lord."

"For what?" said Julius.

Elizabeth frowned. She had thought a simple word of thanks would do. Now she percei.ed that he was going to force her to spell out exactly what she was grateful to him for. "I am obliged to you for coming to my assistance," she said stiffly. "For agreeing to dance with me, after I had said I would not."

"Oh, that! You owe me no thanks for that. It is rather I who should be grateful to you, for changing your mind and dancing with me."

He spoke the words with apparent sincerity. Elizabeth looked at him narrowly, but his face was as sincere as his voice as he went on speaking. "Indeed, I am honored that you should prefer to dance with me rather than Lord Steinbridge. That's a feather in my cap, and no mistake! Only I can't help fearing you got the worst of the bargain. You must know I can't compare with Steinbridge in either rank, wealth, or consequence."

"I don't care about any of those things," said Elizabeth shortly.

"Well, if you don't, then you are almost unique among the members of the *ton*," said Julius. He continued to look steadily at Elizabeth. "But I think I understand. You did not wish your hand forced by your cousin, did you not? Or perhaps you merely wished to show Lord Steinbridge you were not falling over yourself to win his favor. If so, you did yourself no disservice in his eyes. He is not a man easily impressed, and I could see that he *was* impressed. You are to be congratulated."

Elizabeth looked at him suspiciously. His voice was quite matter-of-fact, but she thought there was a hint of a sting in his words. "You speak as though I set out purposely to impress Lord Steinbridge," she said. "I assure you such was not the case. It is a matter of indifference to me whether I make an impression on him."

"Then I thank you all the more," said Julius gravely.

"For what?" demanded Elizabeth.

"For being slightly less indifferent to me than to Lord Steinbridge."

It was on the tip of Elizabeth's tongue to refute these words, but then she realized they were true. She *had* preferred to dance with him rather than Lord Steinbridge. *But that's only because I told the marquess I was engaged for this dance and then had to make good my words,* she told herself. *In the ordinary way, I would certainly prefer him to Lord Atwater. Lord Steinbridge seems a very sen-*

sible, intelligent sort of man—much more my sort than a scheming rogue like Julius Atwater!

So Elizabeth let the words pass without making any reply. Julius smiled down at her, and though she knew he was a scheming rogue and a thoroughly undesirable character, she found herself smiling back. All in all, it was quite an enjoyable dance, and Elizabeth was almost sorry when it ended. Almost, but not quite, because being a sensible, intelligent girl, she naturally preferred the company of a sensible, intelligent man like Lord Steinbridge.

There could be no doubt that the marquess was a sensible and intelligent man. While he and Elizabeth danced, he discoursed gravely on literature, music, and art, showing an unusual depth and breadth of knowledge. Moreover, he seemed to feel just as he ought on serious matters, having decided opinions on the slavery question and making it clear that he was a moral man as well as a cultured one.

"Much as I may admire Lord Byron's talent, I cannot approve any person whose personal life boasts such irregularities," he told Elizabeth. "The bond of matrimony is to me a most sacred and serious one. Since Byron elected to take a wife, he ought to have looked to his conduct. Instead of which he went on, if anything, more wildly than before his marriage. And now that he is separated from Lady Byron and living on the Continent, he seems to consider himself free to indulge in the most unrestrained license. That being the case, I make it a point to neither read his verse nor recommend it to others. A small gesture, but if others in society would only follow suit, we might soon gain such a power as to cause moral miscreants like Lord Byron to think twice before they strayed from the straight-and-narrow path."

Elizabeth thought these sentiments very admirable, yet even as she admired them, she knew an inexplicable urge to take the opposite side of the question and argue that personal freedom and poetry went hand in hand. There was something so self-satisfied in Lord Steinbridge's attitude, a something almost verging upon smugness. She could not help wondering how he would react to the suggestion that stringent societal repression might very well stamp out vice in its more rampant forms, but was likely to stamp out original thought and creativity as well.

Elizabeth put this thought from her guiltily, however. Of course she did not approve of vice, and therefore, it followed that she must agree with the marquess. *My goodness, you would think I would be glad to find a moral man after dealing with a scoundrel like Julius Atwater,* she told herself reprovingly.

So she kept her thoughts to herself and merely nodded in response to the marquess's comments. He seemed to find this sufficient encouragement, for when the dance ended he promptly invited her to stand up with him for another one. Elizabeth acceded, congratulating herself that by so doing she was not only living up to her principles but enhancing her social reputation. She could see that Lord Steinbridge's distinguishing her in this way had caused no little sensation in the ballroom. There were many jealous stares from other young ladies, many speculative ones from matrons and dowagers, and many disconsolate ones from the gentlemen who had been urging her to dance with them earlier.

Well, it's not as though I am breaking their hearts, Elizabeth assured herself. *They are only pursuing me for my fortune. I am fortunate to be with a man for whom my money holds no attraction.* From the general air and appearance of Lord Steinbridge, as well as from the remarks of other people she had overheard, she had gathered that he was a very wealthy man indeed. Of course Julius Atwater was a wealthy man, too, but he was not a serious and moral man like Lord Steinbridge. His was a

frivolous character as well as an unprincipled one—
though to be sure, he was capable of writing an admirable
speech. But a facility with words was only what one
would expect from an unprincipled scoundrel. How else
to explain why he could hold such enmity for Elizabeth
and yet make it seem he genuinely liked and admired
her?

Fortified by these reflections, Elizabeth made it a point
not to look in Julius's direction the rest of the evening.
Yet she was aware of him nonetheless, as if some inner
sense had been appointed the duty of monitoring his
movements. When he strolled over to talk for a few minutes to a dashing young matron in a yellow dress, she
found herself passionately curious to know what they
were talking about. When he disappeared into the card
room for a time, she could have told to the minute how
long he remained there and at what instant he reappeared.

Elizabeth was annoyed to find herself obsessed in this
manner. Yet she told herself it was not obsession, but
merely a sensible desire to keep track of her enemy's
movements. There was, she reminded herself, a war going
on between her and the Atwaters, and she must not ne-
glect any opportunity to consolidate her position. Accordingly, she allowed the marquess to take her in to supper,
and after supper she carefully divided her time and
dances among her other suitors.

It was sometime in the wee hours of the morning that
the ball began to show signs of winding down. People
began to make their adieux, saying what a lovely party
it had been and how much they had enjoyed it. The marquess and Julius Atwater were among the last to leave.
They both approached Elizabeth at the same moment,
just as she was coming off the floor after an energetic
reel with Sir Connor O'Connor.

The marquess spoke first, in the manner of a man used
to taking the lead. "Good evening, Miss Watson," he said

with a bow. "I wanted to thank you one more time before I took my leave. A most enjoyable party, and I greatly enjoyed our conversation together."

Elizabeth said she had enjoyed it, too, but her eyes kept flickering to Julius. He appeared to be in one of his solemn rather than smiling moods, and she wondered what he was thinking about.

Seeing her eyes upon him, Julius bowed and spoke in his turn. "Good evening, Miss Watson. I have come to make my adieux." He hesitated a moment, then went on rather diffidently. "Perhaps you will think this forward of me, but I wondered if you had an engagement for tomorrow afternoon? I should like to take you driving, if I may."

Elizabeth was caught off guard by this question. Before she could gather wit to answer it, the marquess spoke in a voice of displeasure. "Here now, Atwater, that's not quite fair," he said. "I was just about to ask Miss Watson to come driving with *me* tomorrow." In a jovial voice, he added, "Indeed, I think I must take the precedence of you in this, Atwater. Will you come driving with me tomorrow, Miss Watson?"

Elizabeth looked at him, then at Julius. Julius's expression was as solemn as before, but there was now a dangerous light in his eyes. "Sorry, Steinbridge," he said, "but I believe in this matter *I* have the precedence. I was the first to invite Miss Watson to come driving, and in an affair of this sort title has no weight."

The marquess's brows drew together. He looked as though he were going to say something stringent, but before he could speak Sir Connor stepped in. "Here's a pickle!" he said whimsically. "Two fellows so desperate to take you driving, Miss Watson, that they're ready to fight a duel. And not just plain untitled fellows, either, but a baron and a marquess! It's a great compliment to you, that's what."

"Not as far as I am concerned," said Elizabeth. She had recovered her poise by now, and she managed a smile as she spoke. "Indeed, gentlemen, I am afraid I can drive with neither of you tomorrow. I have already promised to take my sister driving in the park in my own phaeton."

The marquess immediately suggested he might take Elizabeth driving the following day instead. To this suggestion she graciously assented, but she could not help glancing at Julius as she spoke. He was regarding her silently, with an inscrutable expression. He continued silent until the marquess had taken his leave, then told her, "I give you good evening, Miss Watson. I will look forward to seeing you in the park tomorrow, even if I have not the privilege of driving you there." Bowing, he turned and walked away.

Elizabeth was glad to see the situation settled so smoothly. Everything had come out just as she desired. She was engaged to drive out with the marquess and had escaped making any positive engagement with Julius Atwater. Yet she found herself curiously dissatisfied. Surely it could not be that she *wanted* to make an engagement with Julius Atwater? No, for she knew he was a rogue and was determined to avoid him as far as she could. But even so, she found herself resenting that he had made no suggestion to take her driving another day, as the marquess had done. She might not wish to make any engagement with him, but she was offended that he did not seem more eager to make one with her!

"Ridiculous," said Elizabeth aloud. "I am an irrational ninny after all, it seems."

Sir Connor, who was still standing at her side, regarded her quizzically. "That you're not, I'll be bound," he said. "And if all I hear's true, you've the means to prove it. What's all this about a book?"

Elizabeth briefly explained about her book. She felt a little self-conscious talking about it, but since Mrs.

Reese-Whittington had referred to the matter openly in front of the marquess, she presumed she might likewise discuss it.

Sir Connor seemed impressed to learn she was an author. "Though it's a dangerous precedent you've set," he warned her. "I've been in society long enough to tell pretty well who's going to take and who isn't, and it looks to me as though you're likely to be all the crack, Miss Watson. That being the case, we may look to see all the young ladies trying their hand at writing books of history. 'Twill be an awful strain on the publishers, not to mention the reading public."

Elizabeth laughed at this and advised him to stop talking nonsense. "If I do that, I'll have naught to say at all," responded Sir Connor in an injured voice. Then he grinned. "But there, I daresay I've talked your ear off already, and it's time I was taking me leave. So you're driving in the park tomorrow, are you? Perhaps I'll see you there."

Elizabeth said graciously that she hoped she might see him on the morrow. She liked Sir Connor very well—as well as any man she had met in London so far, as she assured herself. Why this should have immediately made her think of Julius Atwater, she could not have said.

She went to her bed that night with the certainty that she had triumphed in the opening battle of her war against the Atwaters. Mrs. Reese-Whittington had confirmed her certainty, rapturously enumerating all the separate and distinct triumphs that had gone into making the evening a triumphant whole.

"If I heard one person praising the decorations, I heard a hundred. And at least as many more praised the champagne. But it was Steinbridge dancing with you that was the greatest triumph of all, Elizabeth. You must know he is very exclusive. Indeed, when I invited him tonight, I had no expectation that he would even come, let alone ask you to dance. I wonder if he will seek you out again, or if it was only a fluke?"

"I am engaged to drive with him the day after tomorrow," offered Elizabeth self-consciously.

Mrs. Reese-Whittington immediately launched into a fresh fit of raptures and swore Elizabeth's success in London was assured. "If Steinbridge takes you up, then you have nothing to fear from the Atwaters!" she exulted. "Though to be sure, it did seem as though even the Atwaters have come around. I did see you dancing with Lord Atwater, did I not?"

"Yes," said Elizabeth briefly. She waited until Mrs. Reese-Whittington had done rapturizing over this fresh instance of triumph, then went on in a diffident voice. "But as regards Lord Atwater, I must say that I was quite surprised to see him here this evening. He claims he had received an invitation, but that hardly seemed possible under the circumstances. You did not send him a card, did you, Amelia?"

"Why, to be sure I did," said Mrs. Reese-Whittington, looking surprised. "As I have told you before, the Atwaters are very good *ton*. I could not omit Lord Atwater's name from the guest list without every one wondering why."

"But he's my enemy!" said Elizabeth. "He and the other Atwaters. Don't tell me you invited Mrs. Atwater and Gilbert, too?"

"Certainly I did, though naturally I did not expect them to come. And of course they did not, even though Lord Atwater did. Very gratifying, that . . . I wonder if he could be developing a *tendre* toward you?"

Elizabeth flushed. "Nonsense," she said. "I am convinced he is as much my enemy as his aunt and cousin."

"Well, perhaps so, my dear. I am afraid there can be

no doubt that Mrs. Atwater is your enemy. Princess Lieven tells me she has been calling you the worst sort of names behind your back. It's very vexatious, but after tonight I think we need not concern ourselves with her any longer. You are so well established now that nothing can shake you, unless you do something really foolish."

Here Mrs. Reese-Whittington cast a sideways glance at Elizabeth. "What is it?" said Elizabeth, who had become well accustomed to her cousin's ways during the past few weeks. "What have I done now?"

"Nothing very bad, my dear. Only, I did not like to see you spending *quite* so much time with Sir Connor O'Connor. That is the kind of acquaintance that can do you no good."

"But why not?" said Elizabeth. "I thought Sir Connor very amusing."

"He's *amusing* enough, I grant you. And of course there's no gentleman in London who is a better dancer. But you must not be thinking he is in any way *eligible*. No doubt he represented himself as a man of property, but—"

"He didn't," interrupted Elizabeth. "He told me he was in debt up to his eyebrows."

Mrs. Reese-Whittington blinked. "Did he indeed? Well, this is frankness, to be sure! But though he appears to have been quite honest about his financial position, still you must see it would not do, Elizabeth. For you, with all your advantages, to throw yourself away on a penniless Irish baronet would be madness—sheer madness. Why, now that Steinbridge seems inclined to dangle after you, who knows? If you play your cards properly, you may even end up a marchioness!"

"Oh, for heaven's sake," said Elizabeth with exasperation. "I think all this is entirely premature, Amelia. I have only just met Lord Steinbridge tonight, and Sir Connor, too. And though they are both agreeable men, I am no more likely to marry one than the other. Indeed, I have no idea of ever marrying anybody."

Mrs. Reese-Whittington regarded her skeptically. "Then it's an idea you had best be considering," she said. "I've no doubt you will be receiving a good many offers in the days ahead. It would be a shame to let the opportunity to make a really good match slip through your fingers."

"You sound like Mama," said Elizabeth dryly.

"Well, I am sure that is nothing to my disadvantage, my dear. Your mother only wants what is best for you. As I do," said Mrs. Reese-Whittington piously. "Just you take my advice and stay away from Sir Connor O'Connor."

Elizabeth thought this advice ridiculous. She was in no danger of marrying Sir Connor, or of even taking his gallantries seriously. In her opinion, it would have been more to the point to warn her to stay away from Julius Atwater.

But Mrs. Reese-Whittington seemed to think Julius was a completely acceptable companion for her. That in spite of the fact that he hated her and coveted her fortune! Elizabeth shook her head over the eccentricities of London society. *At any rate, there can be no objection against Lord Steinbridge,* she told herself. *He is clearly a decent man, and an intelligent one, too.*

The thought of the marquess recalled to her Mrs. Reese-Whittington's suggestion that she might receive an offer of marriage from him if she played her cards aright. Elizabeth could not help laughing at this unlikely scenario. She, plain, bookish Elizabeth Watson, receiving an offer of marriage from a marquess! Of course the idea was nonsensical. It was as nonsensical as her mother's notion of marrying Sophia to Mr. Lassiter back in Cheltenham. *Cut from the same piece of cloth,* Elizabeth told herself. *Only Lord Steinbridge is an even bigger fish than the ones Mama sought to hook for Sophy.* For a moment she felt almost guilty about having usurped her sister's place as belle of the family. *But it's better in a way if I do take her place,* Elizabeth told herself sensibly. *Poor Sophy—all she wants is to marry Mr. Arthur, and Mama still talks of marrying her off to a nobleman! However, she's talked of it much less since I started getting so much attention. I must encourage Mama to concentrate on my marital prospects rather than Sophy's. It won't be pleasant, but at least there's no danger of Mama bullying me into marrying against my will!*

Accordingly, Elizabeth steeled herself to bear the brunt of her mother's attention. There could be no doubt that Mrs. Watson had begun to see her elder daughter in a different light since their arrival in London. Now that an eligible marquess seemed wont to distinguish her, Mrs. Watson could hardly think of anything else.

Her behavior the day after the ball was sufficient proof of this. "You are going driving with Lord Steinbridge today?" she asked for perhaps the twentieth time, as Elizabeth stood smoothing her neat York tan gloves and waiting for the phaeton to make its appearance.

"No, I am driving with Lord Steinbridge *tomorrow,*" said Elizabeth patiently. "Today I am driving myself— and Sophy." She smiled at Sophia, who had just appeared in the drawing room doorway looking lovely in a carriage dress of pale yellow muslin and a wide-brimmed villager hat.

Mrs. Watson gave Sophia a brief glance, then returned her attention to Elizabeth. "But perhaps you will see Lord Steinbridge today, even if you aren't driving with him," she said. "I believe you had better put on something dressier, Elizabeth. That gown is all very well, but you wore it last week when you went to the park."

Fortunately, the phaeton made its appearance at this point. Murmuring a hasty farewell, Elizabeth hustled Sophia out the door and into the phaeton. "Thank heaven," she said with a sigh, accepting her whip from the diminutive groom. "All this fuss about a man I have only danced with twice! I never heard of anything so ridiculous."

"He did seem rather struck with you, Elizabeth," ventured Sophia. "And it doesn't sound as though Lord Steinbridge pays much attention to young ladies in general. No wonder Mama is so set up."

"Yes, but it's only two dances. As well declare Colonel Brant is going to propose to you because *he* danced twice with *you* last night!"

Sophia colored. "Colonel Brant is very nice," she said. "All the gentlemen I danced with last night were nice. But—"

"But they are none of them as nice as Mr. Arthur," suggested Elizabeth, with a smile.

"No, they are not," said Sophia.

Shooting a sideways glance at her sister, Elizabeth thought she looked rather dejected. She decided to risk revealing her own thoughts on the subject. As delicately as she could, she suggested that as long as Mrs. Watson was busy trying to marry her off to a marquess, she would have no time to make matches for Sophia. But Sophia only sighed and shook her head.

"Indeed, I have been hoping the same thing, Elizabeth. But only this morning Mama told me I had better try for Mr. Alton. He was that plump gentleman with the bald head who took me in to supper last night. I explained to Mama that he is a widower with a half-dozen children, but she said he is in line for a baronetcy and a very eligible *parti*."

Sophia looked and sounded so rueful that Elizabeth could not help laughing. "Well, perhaps he is an eligible *parti* for a lady who cares about such things," she said. "But Mama cannot seriously expect you to marry a middle-aged widower. Especially not when you are in love with Philip Arthur. Only be firm, Sophy dear, and I'm sure Mama will eventually agree to your marrying Philip."

Sophia still looked rueful. "I'm beginning to wonder, Elizabeth," she said. "It seems to me that since coming to London, Mama has become convinced that *both* of us can make great marriages. At any rate, she seems more intent than ever on my not marrying Philip."

Elizabeth frowned. "Mama is a fool," she said. "You might do much worse than marry Philip Arthur." She looked suddenly thoughtful. "I wonder?" But she did not tell her sister what she wondered about.

As soon as they reached Hyde Park, the girls' attention was absorbed by other things. It was a beautiful spring day, warm and sunny with a light breeze ruffling the newly budded trees. Every man, woman, and child in the city of London seemed to have come to the park to enjoy it. The carriageway was so choked with traffic that even horseback riders had a difficult time threading their way along, while those in carriages were forced to crawl at a snail's pace. Ladies and gentlemen strolled along the walks in couples, and a group of gentlemen in sporting attire had decided to stage an impromptu footrace.

Into this fray drove Elizabeth and Sophia, and almost immediately became the center of attention. "The Miss Watsons, by Jove!" cried Mr. Casswell, who was among the spectators at the footrace. Carriages halted, heads swung round to look, and before long the phaeton was surrounded by gentlemen both on foot and on horseback, all seeking to be as witty and charming as possible.

"Pretty day, eh, Miss Watson?" remarked one dandyish young gentleman on a chestnut mare. "But not half so pretty as your face, by Jove."

"That was a good party last night," chimed in a short gentleman with a low hat and sporting neck cloth. "Good food, good champagne, and good company, don't you know. I had an excellent time—a really excellent time, upon my word."

"Is it true you've written a book, Miss Watson?" said a third, a serious-looking youth barely out of his teens. "Somebody was saying last night that you'd written a book, but I didn't think it could be true."

"It's true," said Mr. Casswell, taking it upon himself to answer for Elizabeth. "I've just read it myself, and a dashed fine book it is. All about Hannibal and the Romans."

"Hannibal, eh?" said the dandyish gentleman with interest. "How'd you get interested in him, Miss Watson?"

Elizabeth explained about her father's passion for the second Punic War and how she had come to write the book he himself had been prevented from writing. "Well, now, I call that very clever of you," said the sporting gentleman, looking impressed. "I'll have to get a copy of the book and read it for myself."

There were murmurs of agreement from the other gentlemen. "Oh, but you needn't do that!" protested Elizabeth. "I am persuaded it would not interest you. Not unless you happened to be interested in the Second Punic War in the first place, that is."

Her protests went unheeded, however. Mr. Casswell was describing the book to the other gentlemen, who were listening with interest. "Dashed clever fellow, old Hannibal," Mr. Casswell told them. "The way he got his army over the Alps with all those elephants was something ingenious. And then the way he hoodwinked the Romans! Beat them all hollow, he did, right along the line."

"Just as Miss Watson beats every other lady in London hollow," said one gentleman, bowing gallantly to Elizabeth. "My Lady Hannibal!"

This nickname was greeted with cries of acclaim from the other gentlemen. Mr. Casswell looked chagrined that he had not thought of it himself, but did what he could to recover his position by christening Sophia my lady Mago and the gray pony Surus. "Surus was Hannibal's own elephant, y'know," he told the others knowledgeably. "And Mago was his brother—I think—though there seems to have been a deuce of a lot of chaps with the same name back then. Right, Miss Watson?"

With some reserve, Elizabeth admitted the truth of these statements. She did not mind talking about Hannibal; indeed, she much preferred it to making ordinary social small talk. But she was sure her audience was only feigning interest in the subject. As soon as she decently could, she excused herself to her suitors on the pretext that she was blocking the carriageway, and drove on.

Unfortunately, this only rid her of those of her admirers who were on foot. Those on horseback tagged along, including Mr. Casswell. As they drove through the park, others joined with them, until she and Sophia were surrounded by as great a crowd as before. Near the Serpentine they encountered Lord Steinbridge, who was driving a curricle drawn by a handsome pair of bays. He smiled and bowed when he saw Elizabeth.

"Miss Watson," he called. "What a pleasure to see you again!"

He was immediately corrected by the irrepressible Mr. Casswell. "No, m'lord, we're not calling her Miss Watson anymore," he told the marquess. "She's my Lady Hannibal."

"Indeed?" said the marquess, looking amused. "How comes this about?"

Mr. Casswell explained the origin of the nickname, while Elizabeth blushed. "I see," said the marquess, smiling. "I would agree that Miss Watson is a conqueror like Hannibal—but a conqueror of hearts rather than armies."

All this was intensely uncomfortable for Elizabeth. She knew she was no conqueror of hearts. She had never even had a serious suitor before inheriting Lucius Atwater's fortune, so why should she suddenly have become irresistible to the opposite sex? *Because I am rich now, and I was poor before,* Elizabeth told herself, answering her own question. But there seemed no doubt the marquess meant his compliment sincerely, even if it was not to her taste, so she smiled and said aloud, "You are too kind, my lord. Indeed, I am persuaded I bear no resemblance to Hannibal. After all, he got his army and thirty-seven elephants over the Alps, while I cannot even seem to get a single carriage through the park!"

The marquess agreed traffic was very heavy that afternoon, but he remained talking to Elizabeth for several minutes until the press of carriages behind them grew so great that he was forced to drive on. "But I shall come for you tomorrow at three o'clock," he told her, as he whipped up his horses. "You have not forgotten that we are engaged to drive out tomorrow?"

Elizabeth said she had not forgotten. She was feeling a little self-conscious, for it was obvious that the people all around them were straining their ears to catch every word of their conversation. Elizabeth found this annoying, but a moment later something happened that caused her to forget her annoyance for other emotions less easy to classify. "Oh, look!" said Sophia, pointing. "There is Lord Atwater!"

Ten

At the name Lord Atwater, Elizabeth's head whipped around. "Where?" she said sharply. "Where is Lord Atwater?"

"Over there," said Sophia, nodding. Elizabeth looked in the direction of her nod and saw Julius astride his bay mare. He was in conversation with a dark-haired lady who rode beside him on a black gelding.

The conversation seemed to be an absorbing one. Julius's expression was serious and intent as he looked down at his companion. Yet he seemed to become aware of Elizabeth's regard almost at the same moment she was aware of him. He looked up, and his eyes met hers, his face going suddenly blank. The lady, noticing his change of expression, followed his gaze. When she saw Elizabeth, her eyebrows rose. She turned again to Julius and said something with a laugh. He nodded, then bowed to Elizabeth—a deliberate and formal bow that, to her eyes, held something of contempt.

"He's bowing to you," observed Sophia. "Aren't you going to bow back?"

"No, he is bowing to *us*," said Elizabeth. "See, he is looking at you now."

Sophia shook her blonde head. "That's only because he wants to see whom you are with," she said wisely.

Take a Trip Back to the Romantic Regent Era of the Early 1800's with
4 FREE
Zebra Regency Romances!
(A $19.96 VALUE!)
4 FREE books are yours!
PLUS YOU'LL SAVE ALMOST $4.00 EVERY MONTH WITH CONVENIENT FREE HOME DELIVERY!

We'd Like to Invite You to Subscribe to Zebra's Regency Romance Book Club and Give You a Gift of 4 Free Books as Your Introduction! (Worth $19.96!)

If you're a Regency lover, imagine the joy of getting **4 FREE Zebra Regency Romances** and then the chance to have these lovely stories delivered to your home each month at the lowest price available! Well, that's our offer to you and here's how you benefit by becoming a Regency Romance subscriber:

- **4 FREE Introductory Regency Romances are delivered to your doorstep**

- **4 BRAND NEW Regencies are then delivered each month (usually before they're available in bookstores)**

- **Subscribers save almost $4.00 every month**

- **You also receive a FREE monthly newsletter, which features author profiles, discounts, subscriber benefits, book previews and more**

- **No risks or obligations...in other words, you can cancel whenever you wish with no questions asked**

Join the thousands of readers who enjoy the savings and convenience offered to Regency Romance subscribers. After your initial introductory shipment, you receive 4 brand-new Zebra Regency Romances each month to examine for 10 days. Then, if you decide to keep the books, you'll pay the preferred subscriber's price.

It's a no-lose proposition, so return the FREE BOOK CERTIFICATE today!

"The bow was for you, I am sure. Aren't you going to return it?"

"Only if you are," said Elizabeth. Sophia hesitated, then gave Julius a smile and bow. Elizabeth also bowed, but more gravely. She wondered who Julius's companion could be. She was a very lovely lady—quite beautiful, in fact. Her garnet-colored habit clung to her lithe figure like a second skin, and the hair beneath her dashing little jockey cap gleamed like a raven's wing.

The question was answered for her by Mr. Casswell. "Ain't that Mrs. Perry riding with Atwater?" he asked, squinting toward the couple on horseback. "By Jove, I believe it is. Looking very well, too. Last time I saw her was just after Perry's funeral—must have been a year— no, two years ago, more or less. I see she's out of mourning now."

Elizabeth, covertly regarding the dark-haired lady, stored up these words for future consideration. So Mrs. Perry was a widow—a beautiful widow and evidently a society woman, judging by Mr. Casswell's comments. Elizabeth wondered what her connection might be to Julius Atwater. Were they friends, acquaintances, or something more? *Not that it matters to me,* she assured herself. *But I should like to know all the same. Perhaps he will mention it when he comes over to speak to me.*

That Julius would come and speak to her she did not doubt. He had never yet lost an opportunity to talk to her when they met in public. Elizabeth tucked a strand of hair behind her ear and sat up straighter on the phaeton seat. She told herself she would have preferred to avoid Julius, but since they had to maintain a ridiculous pretense of amity around others, she was willing to do her part.

It seemed, however, that on this occasion Julius was not willing to do his. At any rate, he made no move to approach Elizabeth. He merely gave her another nod, then spurred his horse forward and continued down the carriageway with Mrs. Perry.

Elizabeth watched him go with a feeling of blank astonishment. She felt as though she had been snubbed. In truth, there had been nothing snubbing about Julius's bow and nod. Both had been perfectly cordial, and he was, as Elizabeth assured herself, under no obligation to give her anything more by way of greeting. But still she felt offended. How dare he pass her by without a word, when she had already prepared herself to speak to him? It was rude and intolerable behavior, and Elizabeth could not approve it at all.

She fumed silently as she drove along the carriageway. Her annoyance was not wholly directed at Julius, though she certainly assigned him his fair share of blame. Still, she was more annoyed at herself than at him. She had always been a calm, clearheaded woman, capable of thinking rationally even in stressful situations. Now here she was behaving irrationally in the worst traditions of femininity.

Something about Julius Atwater brings out the worst in me, it seems, Elizabeth told herself ruefully. *That being the case, I ought to be glad I was spared speaking to him.* Yet such was her irrationality regarding Julius that she felt not glad at all, but only piqued the more.

Her pique lasted the remainder of the time she was in the park. She paid scant attention to the gentlemen surrounding her phaeton as they chattered and cut capers and tried to attract her attention. If she had been at all observant, she might have seen that a few of them were trying to attract Sophia's attention as well. Colonel Brant, among others, rode up to pay his respects to the blushing Sophia, and so did the widower Mr. Alton.

Sophia looked so uncomfortable when this latter gentleman appeared that her distress penetrated even Elizabeth's self-absorbed mood. She lost no time whisking herself and her sister away from the park, taking such an abrupt leave of Mr. Alton and the other gentlemen that her conduct might have been termed rude in a lady less well dowered.

"But I have no doubt I will be forgiven," Elizabeth told her sister with a grim smile as she drove toward home. "It's appalling how much leniency money can buy. As long as I have Mr. Atwater's fortune, I can be as uncivil as I like, and still gentlemen will call me charming."

"Indeed, Elizabeth, I think you take too cynical a view of it," protested Sophia. "I have no doubt that some of those gentlemen are attracted solely by your money, but I am convinced there are at least as many who are attracted to you for your own sake. Although I doubt if Mr. Alton will ever be one of them!" She gave a gurgle of laughter. "You cut him off in midsentence and left him with his mouth hanging open!"

"Well, I care nothing for Mr. Alton," said Elizabeth. "Besides, we both know it is not me whom he wishes to court."

Sophia sighed, giving a tacit assent to this statement. "If only Mama were more reasonable," she said sadly. "I simply cannot marry Mr. Alton—or, indeed, anybody but Philip. I cannot!"

"You won't have to," promised Elizabeth. "Between us, we'll bring Mama to reason." She smiled. "I have a plan, I think, but certain details still want working out. I shall have to be thinking about them, along with how best I should proceed in my campaign to vex the Atwaters."

The mention of the Atwaters made Elizabeth recall Julius Atwater and the way he had slighted her a short time before. She frowned. *Odious man!* she reflected to herself. *But the gloves are off now. He and his odious family will know after last night that I am not a person to be trifled with. Only the full force of my opening blow*

*won't strike them until tonight, when Mrs. Atwater gives
her own ball. How I wish I could be there to see it!*

Elizabeth would have been gratified indeed if she
could have known how complete was her victory over
Mrs. Atwater.

Mrs. Atwater began her ball that evening with no inkling that anything was amiss. It never crossed her mind
that the original features of her party might have been
discovered and preempted by her rival. She had read in
the paper that morning an account of the Watsons' party,
but had been more interested in the list of friends and
acquaintances who had embraced these social upstarts
than the details of the party itself. Even the description
of Elizabeth's toilette rang no bell of recognition in her
mind. So when the first guests entered her ballroom that
evening, took one look around, and immediately began
whispering among themselves, she took it merely as a
sign that they had been struck by the elegance of her
decor.

"I flatter myself it is quite an original notion," she said,
smiling condescendingly at a certain Mrs. Norton, who
had been gazing wide-eyed at the roses suspended from
the ceiling. She could not in the least understand why
this comment made Mrs. Norton give a catlike smile and
her husband beside her choke back a guffaw.

The sight of her toilette, too, seemed to evoke an odd
reaction in her guests. Several of them complimented her
on her appearance, but there was something about their
compliments that did not ring true. Every time she
walked by, people exchanged smiles, and she kept surprising people staring at her with grins on their faces.
Uneasily she looked down at her dark green velvet dress.
It had seemed very handsome and stylish when she ordered it from the dressmaker, yet people clearly were

finding something humorous about it. In the end she grew
so uneasy that she called Gilbert away from the card room
to ask if there were something wrong in her appearance.

Gilbert, however, professed himself quite ignorant as
to the cause of the guests' amusement. "I don't know
what you mean by calling me away from a game of whist
to ask me such a thing," he said ungraciously. "You're
no beauty, Mama, and never were, but you don't look
any worse than you usually do, as far as I can tell. Now
if you'll excuse me, I'm going back to my game."

By the time Julius arrived at eleven o'clock, Mrs. Atwater was nearly in tears. She hurried over to greet him,
almost breaking into a run in her eagerness to confide
her difficulties to someone. "Julius, I am so glad to see
you," she told him. "Something has gone wrong with my
party tonight. People keep laughing at me, and I don't
have the slightest idea what is amiss."

She paused, for her nephew was regarding her with
the same look of incredulous amusement she had seen
on the face of so many other guests that evening. "What
is it?" she demanded. "Why are you looking at me that
way? For God's sake, tell me what is the matter, Julius!"

Her nephew did not immediately answer. His gaze had
traveled from her to the ballroom, lingering here on the
flowers suspended from the ceiling and there on the
clouds of gauze draping the orchestra pit. "By God!" he
said in voice of deep respect. "That's one up for Miss
Watson, that is! Piqued, repiqued, and capoted, by God."

Mrs. Atwater stiffened. "Julius, I demand that you tell
me instantly what all this is about," she said. "Why does
everyone stand around and whisper, and look at me as
though I had grown three heads? And what do you mean
by referring to that Watson woman? Has she something
to do with it?"

In a voice in which sympathy struggled with laughter,
Julius explained to his aunt the trick that had been per-

petrated upon her. Mrs. Atwater was at first shocked, then furious. "Do you mean to tell me," she demanded, "that Miss Watson wore a dress like mine—exactly like mine—last night? And that her ballroom was decorated like mine—the same flowers and the same gauze—?"

"I am afraid so," said Julius. "Indeed, Aunt Jane, it is a"—his voice quavered—"a most remarkable coincidence."

"It's not a coincidence at all!" said Mrs. Atwater. "It's malice, pure and simple. I thought it was strange she changed the date of her party to the day *before* mine, but I never dreamed that was her purpose. Oh, it's infamous! To think of her making game of me in such a way! And now everyone is laughing at me—jeering at me." She ran her hands angrily over her green velvet–clad figure. "This dreadful dress! I won't wear it a moment longer. I'll go up and change it for something else. And as soon as I come down, I will set about telling everyone what an abominable trick Miss Watson has served me!"

Julius shook his head. "I can understand your being upset, Aunt Jane, but I think you ought to reconsider," he said. "Will that not simply be making it clear to everyone how Miss Watson has hoodwinked you?"

Mrs. Atwater stared at him. "But what else can I do?" she asked. "Surely you don't expect I should allow Miss Watson to make a fool out of me and do nothing about it?"

"Well, it might be better if you did," said Julius. "What I would suggest is that, instead of getting angry, you simply take the matter as a joke. Tell everyone what a remarkable coincidence it is that you and Miss Watson seem to share the same tastes, and make a point of laughing at yourself. After all, it is a pretty funny situation when you think of it."

"It's not funny at all!" said Mrs. Atwater. "It's abominable." Still, it was apparent her nephew's words had given her pause. After a brief internal struggle, she nodded reluctantly. "Yes, I see your point, Julius. Obviously everyone already knows that Miss Watson has made a May-game of me. That's what they've been snickering about all evening, and if I get angry it would only amuse them more. But I must say, I take it very much amiss that no one saw fit to tell me before now what was going on. Not even Aurelia Brocklehurst or Fanny Hartley, and *they* claim to be my friends!"

Julius patted her arm sympathetically and said her friends probably were reluctant to mention the matter, knowing it would upset her. "And so I am upset," said Mrs. Atwater hotly. "That abominable Watson woman! I knew the minute I set eyes on her that she was a wicked, scheming adventuress."

Julius shook his head. "I must say, she does not impress me that way at all," he said. "If I had to guess, I should say she is only getting her own back for the way you have treated *her*. I have heard the way you have been talking about her in public, Aunt Jane. And as for spoiling your ball, it sounds as though you tried to spoil hers first, by giving it the same night as hers. It is only that she got wind of your plans somehow and contrived to turn the tables."

Mrs. Atwater said firmly that it was not at all the same kind of thing. "She has no right to be in society anyway! And I intend to see she goes back where she came from as soon as may be. This business of ruining my party tonight has only made me the more determined."

Julius sighed. "Cannot you let Miss Watson be, Aunt Jane?" he said. "This vendetta you have got up against her is quite ridiculous. Besides, she has already shown that she is more than a match for you," he added, with injudicious candor.

Mrs. Atwater's eyes snapped. "Do you think so?" she said. "I think otherwise, Julius. The quarrel is a personal one now, and I will destroy Miss Watson socially if it is the last thing I do. I wonder—" Mrs. Atwater's expression grew calculating. "Obviously she managed to get wind of my plans tonight, and that was how she was able to spoil my party. I wonder if I might do the same by her? Perhaps one of her servants could be bribed, or some other member of the household. That Reese-Whittington woman, for instance. She has always struck me as being wholly mercenary. Although she is the Watson woman's sponsor and also, I understand, some kind of relation . . . No, I doubt she could be bribed. It will have to be a servant, I suppose."

Julius said nothing, and after a time, Mrs. Atwater became aware of his silence. "You are very quiet, Julius," she said, looking at him challengingly. "I suppose you disapprove of all this?"

"I do," he said quietly. "You know I do, Aunt Jane! As I see it, Miss Watson has done nothing except pay you back in your own coin. If I were you, I would mark the debt paid and move on."

"Never!" said Mrs. Atwater. "I will never rest content until Miss Watson has been driven out of London. And I will do whatever is necessary to achieve that end. It is not merely a whim, Julius, but a matter of conscience with me."

"I see," said her nephew. "Then there is no more to be said, of course. Only I would remind you, Aunt Jane, that I have a conscience, too."

"What is that supposed to mean?" demanded Mrs. Atwater, eyeing him with mistrust. "What are you planning to do, Julius?"

He smiled. "Only whatever is necessary to achieve *my* end," he said, and would say no more. Mrs. Atwater was eventually forced to let him go and turn her attention toward her other guests, in an effort to salvage what honor she could from the disastrous evening.

She spoke to him one last time that evening, however, as he prepared to take his leave of the ball.

"A delightful party, Aunt," he told her politely. "I enjoyed myself extremely."

"No, you didn't," said Mrs. Atwater with a sigh. "It wasn't a delightful party at all. But it's good of you to pretend otherwise."

She gave him her hand, and he bowed over it, then turned to go. Then, as though recollecting something, he turned back. "By the by," he said, "do you go to the Queen's drawing room tomorrow?"

"Yes, I do," said Mrs. Atwater, rather surprised. "Although I am tempted not to, since that Watson woman will be there." Her lips thinned. "It's a scandal she should be allowed to make her bows before the Queen as if she were a respectable woman. I don't like it, but I'm not going to let her drive me away from doing my duty by dear Queen Charlotte."

"Very well," said Julius. "I'll drive you to St. James's, then."

"You will?" said Mrs. Atwater incredulously. "Why, Julius?"

"Don't you want me to?" he asked, evading her question.

"Yes, of course I do. I must say, it's very good of you, Julius." Mrs. Atwater regarded her nephew with a penetrating gaze. "But why this sudden solicitude? You have never accompanied me to a drawing room before."

"Oh, it's been a long time since I was at St. James's," said Julius lightly. "I have a sudden fancy to see the place again—from the outside. Of course I would not be admitted to the drawing room itself. Would I?"

"No," said Mrs. Atwater, still surveying him closely. "It's not the general thing for gentlemen to be present. Although I doubt the queen would mind if you came as far as the door of the audience chamber. I have often seen gentlemen of the Court loitering about there, watching the girls go in and make their bows."

"Very good," said Julius. "I'll do the same. It'll give me a chance to look over the new crop of debutantes."

Mrs. Atwater continued to survey him with bewilderment. "But why?" she repeated. "Why this sudden interest, Julius? What do *you* care about debutantes?"

Julius smiled. "Why, the truth is, I'm thinking of getting married, Aunt Jane. I'm in my thirties now, and everyone keeps telling me I ought to be settling down. I've finally decided to take their advice."

"Nonsense!" said Mrs. Atwater roundly. "I'm sure there is more to it than that." But though she coaxed and questioned, she could get nothing more from Julius than a smiling assertion that he was going to St. James's in search of a wife.

In truth, he had only been joking when he spoke these words to his aunt, but as soon as they were spoken, he had recognized in them a strange inevitability. As he drove away from his aunt's party, he recognized also a truth he had been avoiding for some time, namely, that he was falling in love with Elizabeth Watson.

He had been struck by Elizabeth ever since meeting her—struck by her appearance and her way of speaking and by some quality that set her apart from any other woman he had ever known. Yet that alone had not made him fall in love with her. Looking back, it seemed to him as though he had been in love with her practically from the moment he first saw her, even before he had had any real chance to talk with her and discover the unique cast of her mind and character.

It was a strange and perplexing phenomenon, yet Julius could not doubt that it was real. Ever since he had met Elizabeth, he had felt a yearning to be in her company. It nagged him night and day, driving him to see her and talk with her and find out more about her. It was that yearning that had made him ask her to dance with him twice the night of her cousin's ball and to urge her to drive with him the next day, in spite of the fact that she had given him no encouragement to pursue her. In fact, if he were to be strictly honest with himself, he would have to admit that her behavior was far more discouraging than encouraging. Clearly she did not find him as attractive and interesting as he found her. Indeed, there had been times when he felt as though she would have preferred to cut the acquaintance altogether.

Yet there had been other times when he had sensed something more forthcoming in her manner. When Julius really considered it, however, he could put his finger on nothing to confirm this feeling. She had danced with him twice on the night of her cousin's ball, true, but that had likely only been because she wished to pique the marquess. She had praised the speech he had made about Catholic Emancipation, but that praise had only been drawn from her reluctantly.

I'm a fool, Julius told himself. *She hasn't any use for me at all. She thinks I am a dilettante, a mere fashionable fribble. Naturally she would prefer a man like Steinbridge—a solid, serious fellow with a scholarly reputation.*

He thought back to the day before in the park, when he had seen the marquess talking with Elizabeth. Lord Steinbridge had looked very smitten as he gazed at Elizabeth. Julius told himself savagely that it was enough to make one nauseous, seeing Steinbridge making sheep eyes at Miss Watson, but he knew he was being unjust. The fact was that he was jealous of the marquess—jealous of his position and his character and of the interest Elizabeth seemed to take in him. He had seen her face in the park yesterday when she had been talking to Lord Steinbridge. There had been genuine interest in her eyes and genuine amusement in the smile that had flashed out once or twice during the conversation. She had a lovely and expressive face—lovely and expressive except when he himself was near, when it promptly froze into immobility.

Julius had felt all this at the time, not putting it into words but sensing it on a deeper level. The idea had depressed him profoundly. Much as he would have liked to go speak to Elizabeth, it had seemed suddenly futile to pursue her any longer. Not only had she attracted perhaps the single most eligible gentleman in London, she had made it very clear that she wanted nothing whatever to do with him.

Struck by this sense of futility, Julius had only watched Elizabeth from afar that day without making any attempt to go near her. Even after the marquess had driven away, he had refrained from going to her, although it had been a struggle. Especially when she had finally noticed him and looked right at him over the heads of the pedestrians and passersby. But he had held himself in check and given her only a formal bow by way of recognition. He had then spurred his horse forward, taken himself out of her sight, and had thereafter sought to solace himself with Mrs. Perry's company.

And Mrs. Perry had been nothing loath to solace him. Indeed, it had occurred to Julius once or twice during the course of the afternoon that she might be looking at him in the light of a possible replacement for her late husband.

There had been a time in the not-so-distant past when he would have been flattered by such an idea. Mrs. Perry was a lovely, witty, companionable woman, and he had always admired her. When he had met her that afternoon on one of the park paths, he had fallen in willingly with her suggestion that they ride together. It had seemed to him that her company might give his thoughts a different direction. Even yesterday afternoon, before he had officially admitted his feelings for Elizabeth, he had been aware that his thoughts were inclined to dwell on her to an unhealthy degree. That being the case, he had felt Mrs. Perry might be a good antidote.

But in fact Mrs. Perry had proved no antidote at all. She was as lovely, as charming, and as witty as ever, but she was not Elizabeth. She did not stir his pulse the same way, she did not stimulate his mind in the same manner, and the honeyed mixture of flattery and innuendo that rolled off her tongue seemed cloying after Elizabeth's frank and forthright speech.

Having admitted all this to himself, Julius put away forever any thought of Mrs. Perry. He wanted no woman but Elizabeth, and he wanted her for his wife if that were at all possible. Yet his heart misgave him when he considered the obstacles that lay ahead of him. In the first place, Elizabeth had made it clear she already thought him a negligible character. In the second, his aunt was doing all she could to make her detest the very name of Atwater. And in the third, he had a formidable rival in the form of Lord Steinbridge. What hope had he of prevailing against all these obstacles?

Julius's common sense assured him there could be no hope. Yet when he imagined quitting the field without even trying to win Elizabeth, his heart rose in protest. This was one of the most important things that had ever happened to him in his life—perhaps *the* most important thing. He had fallen in love with a unique and wonderful woman, and it seemed a cowardly thing not to at least make a push to win her, even if his failure was a foregone conclusion.

I shall be like Don Quixote tilting against windmills, he told himself with a whimsical smile. *Not a role I ever fancied, but it does have a certain nobility about it. I'll see her at the drawing room tomorrow and try to get a word or two with her if I possibly can.*

Eleven

As Elizabeth made her preparations for the Queen's drawing room, she had no idea that she was destined to meet Julius that day as well as Queen Charlotte.

It was just as well she did not know, for she was nervous enough as it was. Mrs. Reese-Whittington had talked so much of the protocol involved in making one's bows to the Queen, along with the many pitfalls designed therein to ensnare the unwary, that Elizabeth had come to view the whole process as a hideous ordeal.

It did not help that the ordeal had to be accomplished in the most formal of formal attire. "Hoopskirts!" said Elizabeth incredulously, looking down at the breadth of her violet skirts stretching out to either side. "I haven't seen anyone but old ladies wear hoopskirts for years and years. Was there ever anything so ridiculous?"

"Hoops are *always* worn at court," said Mrs. Reese-Whittington reprovingly. "The Queen insists on it."

"Then she must enjoy making women look like perfect guys," said Elizabeth. "A more foolish combination than hoopskirts with high-waisted dresses was never seen. And all these plumes and ribbons and tags of lace hanging down around my ears! My head feels like a milliner's display window."

"Your head looks very well," said Mrs. Reese-Whittington firmly. "And so does your dress, Elizabeth. I daresay you will be much admired."

Elizabeth smiled incredulously. To her eyes, there was nothing attractive about her full-skirted robe of violet brocade draped over a frilly white satin petticoat, or in the dozen violet plumes that crowned her head, combined with diamonds and lappets and knots of ribbon. Sophy, in a similar toilette of pale pink watered taffeta, managed to look quite fetching; her sweet face and womanly figure seemed more in tune with frills and furbelows. But frills and furbelows were not to Elizabeth's taste, and she felt awkward and ungainly as she followed her cousin, mother, and sister out to the carriages.

They were forced to take two carriages because the width of the ladies' hoopskirts precluded their sitting two to a banquette. This was an additional grievance for Elizabeth. She would have liked to sit with Sophia and perhaps gain some degree of repose from her gentle conversation. Instead, she was shut up alone with her mother, who insisted on telling her over again everything she must not do and say at court and only succeeded in aggravating her already nervous state.

Neither did it help that her carriage was driven by John, the Watsons' elderly coachman. He wended his way recklessly through the crowded streets, scattering pedestrians left and right and drawing shouted imprecations from sedan chairmen and drivers of hackney coaches. When they reached the crush of traffic before St. James's, where rows of carriages waited patiently to discharge their gorgeously dressed occupants, he refused to wait his turn but rather "threaded the needle" between two other carriages, missing both by inches. He then cut off a third carriage whose driver was attempting to maneuver into position by the curb and triumphantly deposited Elizabeth and her mother at the very head of the line. They tottered forth, more dead than alive, to await the arrival of Mrs. Reese-Whittington and Sophia, whose driver had taken a more conservative approach to the palace.

When the four ladies were reunited once more, they proceeded to the audience chamber, led by the knowledgeable Mrs. Reese-Whittington. Along the way that lady delivered a last-minute lecture to the girls on how to smile and how to hold their skirts when they curtsied, and how to back away from the royal presence rather than rudely turning their backs on the Queen. These instructions were reinforced by various persons attached to the royal household, whose task was to lecture the would-be debutantes on royal etiquette. It was all a buzz in Elizabeth's ears, however. She was so nervous that she was literally shaking. Her head felt light, and there was an ominous churning in the pit of her stomach.

I feel as though I'm going to be sick, she told herself. *Only imagine the scandal that would make! I can just see it now, going up to make my bows and being sick before the Queen!*

The idea was a truly horrible one, yet when Elizabeth imagined the furor that would ensue she could not help smiling—a rather tight-lipped smile, it was true, but a smile nonetheless. It was at that moment that she heard her name called behind her.

"Miss Watson?"

Elizabeth turned around. There was Julius, walking toward her. He was wearing a black coat and satin knee breeches, with a *chapeau bras* tucked beneath his arm. He looked very handsome in this attire, but it was not his handsomeness that chiefly struck Elizabeth. It was the expression in his eyes as he looked at her. He was thinking how lovely she looked, and though Elizabeth could not know what he was thinking, she felt it. She found herself more breathless than ever, but in a different way than the nauseated light-headed feeling she had been experiencing a moment before.

"My lord!" she said. "You here?"

She did not mean to smile at him as she spoke; the smile simply broke from her lips of its own accord. An answering smile dawned on Julius's lips. "As you see," he said. "But I have only been admitted on sufferance, on the provision that I keep out of everyone's way. Still, I am glad I came, if only for the privilege of seeing you. You look—beautiful."

Mrs. Reese-Whittington, Sophia, Mrs. Watson, two milliners, and three maidservants had all separately and individually assured Elizabeth that she looked very handsome in her Court dress, and yet she had remained firmly convinced they were none of them speaking the truth. Now, however, when Julius Atwater told her she looked beautiful—the same Julius Atwater she was firmly convinced was a liar and schemer—she found herself not merely believing him but flushing with pleasure at his words.

And in that moment, a miracle occurred. The violet brocade gown that had looked so ridiculous to her before suddenly became the most becoming of garments. The plumes atop her head were converted from a foolish burden to a fascinating adornment. Even the business of making her curtsy to the Queen was no longer an ordeal to be dreaded. What did it matter if she made a good impression on the Queen? She cared nothing for the Queen, except insofar as any loyal subject might care for her sovereign. She was Elizabeth Watson, and Her Majesty might take her as she was, or go hang.

Elizabeth lifted her plumed head and smiled directly into Julius's eyes. "You are too kind, my lord," she said, "but I thank you very much for the compliment."

"You're welcome," said Julius. He continued to look down at her, his eyes admiring—almost reverent. Then his expression changed. "That reminds me," he said, leaning forward to address her confidentially. "There was something I wanted to talk to you about, Miss Watson—a matter of some urgency."

"Yes?" said Elizabeth, a good deal intrigued. Julius glanced around with a furtive air, then bent down and whispered into her ear.

"I wanted to give you a word of warning, Miss Watson. My aunt is very annoyed with you. About what you did the other night, you know—stealing the thunder from her ball! Indeed, the whole trick was very cleverly done." Julius smiled at Elizabeth as he spoke, but his eyes were worried. "Unfortunately my aunt is, as I said, very annoyed. Not to put too fine a point on it, she has sworn to revenge herself upon you. She spoke of bribing some member of your household in order to gain intimate knowledge of your plans. Once that is done, she means to serve the same trick on you, or a worse one if she can manage it. I thought you ought to know, so you can be prepared for it."

Elizabeth gazed at him fixedly. He looked back at her, his expression still anxious. "I thought you ought to know," he repeated. "Perhaps I am speaking out of turn, but it did not seem right to me that you should endure any more persecution from Aunt Jane. Of course, she considers that you merit persecution after making her look a fool the other night, but I know you would never have done what you did if she had not behaved badly toward you in the first place."

"No," agreed Elizabeth faintly. "But do you mean to say you are *warning* me of her plans, my lord?"

"Yes, I thought it only right. I do not approve at all of the way she has been acting. She can be quite amiable on occasion, but—"

Here a voice broke in rudely upon their conversation. "Julius! What are you—I beg your pardon!"

It was Mrs. Atwater. Elizabeth stiffened at her approach, and Mrs. Atwater stiffened, too, as soon as she realized whom her nephew was talking to. "If it isn't Miss Watson!" she said with a mixture of hauteur and hostility in her voice.

Elizabeth smiled coldly and inclined her plumed head very slightly. Julius had turned at his aunt's approach; now he turned back to Elizabeth. "I had better be going," he told her in a low voice. "But I hope you will remember what I have said and be on guard. It was a pleasure seeing you here today, Miss Watson—a very great pleasure."

For answer, Elizabeth merely inclined her head once more. She watched with mixed emotions as Julius went over to join his aunt. Then an attendant came forward and whispered it was time for her and Sophia to make their bows. Elizabeth nodded, squared her shoulders, and went forward to meet her sovereign.

The confidence that had come to her with Julius's compliment stayed with her, so that she sailed through the ordeal of making her bows without the slightest difficulty. She even had the honor of receiving a chilly smile from the Queen. Yet Her Majesty's smile made no great impression on Elizabeth. She was remembering instead Julius's smile and the words he had spoken to her.

Why was he being so nice to her? He had actually warned her against his aunt's machinations and given her some clue as to what direction they would take. Elizabeth could not in the least understand it. Was it some sort of complex plot to lull her into complacency? Perhaps a scheme to make her think she knew what direction the attack was to come from, only to have it come from another direction?

Elizabeth could only suppose this was Julius's purpose. Yet somehow she could hardly believe it of him. He had seemed so sincere in warning her, so earnest in wishing her well. Was it possible that he was really not her enemy at all, but, on the contrary, a friend?

"Ridiculous," said Elizabeth aloud. "Ridiculous!"

"Whatever do you mean, dear?" asked Mrs. Watson. The two of them were in the carriage once more, on their way home from the palace. John was driving at his usual breakneck speed, and both ladies had to hang on to the edges of their seats as he made a sharp turn. "What do you mean by saying ridiculous?" repeated Mrs. Watson, as soon as the carriage had settled back on four wheels again. "I thought everything went very well today."

"Today? Oh, yes, I suppose everything went well enough. I was thinking of the future." Elizabeth frowned, drumming her fingers on the plush upholstery of the banquette. "I must consider what our next step should be. We have made a fair start at routing the Atwaters, but we cannot rest on our laurels yet."

"Amelia was saying we should give a breakfast next, or perhaps a musicale," offered Mrs. Watson.

"Perhaps. I shall have to weigh the options carefully," said Elizabeth. Inwardly, she was resolved to speak to Charles Bray and have him discover through Maria what Mrs. Atwater's plans were before making any of her own. If Julius had been speaking the truth and Mrs. Atwater fancied she could get the best of her by undermining her next social affair, then she obviously merited another dose of her own medicine.

As soon as she was home, Elizabeth lost no time sending for Charles. He in turn lost no time consulting Maria, who reported back that Mrs. Atwater had indeed suborned one of the Watson's household to supply her with word of their plans. "It's Henry, the second footman," Charles told Elizabeth. "And I must say, if anybody but Maria had said so, I wouldn't have believed it. I'd been thinking Henry a very good sort of fellow, the dirty traitor! I've a good mind to find him right now and thrash the life out of him."

"No, you mustn't do that, Charles," said Elizabeth. "Henry mustn't know we suspect him. It does seem rather bad that he would take money to give us away to Mrs. Atwater, but he likely doesn't realize it's important. He never struck me as being a really *bright* young man. Besides, if you think about it, we're doing the same thing to Mrs. Atwater by having Maria report on her plans. All's fair in love and war, you know, and she has made this a war by treating me in such a beastly fashion."

Charles said grudgingly he supposed this was true, though he still seemed inclined to resent Henry's disloyalty. However, he was finally brought to admit that there would be advantages in letting Henry suppose his treachery unsuspected. "If we get rid of him, Mrs. Atwater will only bribe another of the servants, and it might be someone whom we would never suspect," explained Elizabeth. "This way, we know who the spy is. We can keep our eye on him and feed him exactly the information we want to get back to Mrs. Atwater, and it will be very convenient, better even than if there were no spy in the household at all. Besides, there is a delightful justice in using Mrs. Atwater's own weapons against her!"

In addition to the news of Henry's defection, Charles had other information. Mrs. Atwater was planning to give a musicale in a few weeks featuring M. Mauvoisin, the great French tenor who had made such a stir during the last opera season. "He's only to be in London a few days, and Mrs. Atwater wants him so bad she can taste it," said Charles graphically. "Maria says she's already written him, but she took the wrong tack in the beginning by writing as though he were a servant she wanted to engage. Apparently Moosieur Mauvoisin's one of these Republicans like they have over in France, and he wrote back saying he was a free citizen who sang when he pleased

and wasn't for anyone to command. Well, you know Mrs.
Atwater. Instead of trying to soothe him down and humor
him in his fancies, she got up on her high horse and wrote
back saying how well-born her family was and how her
nephew was Lord Atwater and how Moosieur Mauvoisin
ought to be honored to be asked to sing by her. And
Moosieur wrote back saying he hasn't any use for aristocrats and as far as he was concerned she and her
nephew could go the same way as the French king and
queen."

Elizabeth gave a delighted crow of laughter. "Did he
really? Oh, how delightful!"

Charles grinned. "Aye, Maria said it was right funny.
Put Mrs. A in a regular taking, it did, but in the end she
decided to forgive him because it would be such a feather
in her cap to get him to sing at her party. But he hasn't
agreed to it yet and may not, seeing that she made such
a muck of asking him in the first place."

Elizabeth's eyes were glowing. "This is playing into
our hands, Charles! It is a situation made to order. I shall
write to Monsieur Mauvoisin immediately and ask him
to sing at my party instead. And I won't make the mistake
of addressing him as an inferior!"

Within an hour, Elizabeth had drafted a respectful letter to *Citoyen* Jean Mauvoisin, begging him to honor her
gathering with his presence. She was not so crass as to
mention terms, but let it be understood that he might
name his own price and arrange the whole matter as he
chose. This letter was dispatched to France in the care of
a special messenger, and it brought a quick response. M.
Mauvoisin wrote back, saying he would be delighted to
perform at the *Citoyenne* Watson's soiree. Quite an ami-
cable little correspondence ensued, settling the date and
time, and in due course cards were sent out, inviting a
select number of the Watsons' friends and acquaintances

to hear the great M. Mauvoisin sing a few songs at a small evening party.

It was, as Elizabeth explained to Sophia, an even greater triumph than the ball had been. "We have outmaneuvered Mrs. Atwater completely," she said gleefully. "It's much what Hannibal did to the Romans at Lake Cannae. By taking advantage of her weaknesses and our strengths, we have succeeded in utterly annihilating her. She won't hold up her head for a week when she hears of the coup we have brought off."

In truth, Mrs. Atwater was seriously disturbed when she learned of her enemy's triumph. "No!" she exclaimed incredulously. "You cannot mean to say that odious Frenchman has agreed to sing at *Miss Watson's* party? And yet he flatly refused to sing at mine!"

"Aye, so it seems," said Gilbert, with a shrug. "But what does it matter? Musicales are dead bores, and this French fellow sounds a regular rum 'un. Let Miss Watson have him if she wants him."

"But it's infamous, Gilbert! When I tried and tried to get him, and even wrote him a most *civil* letter. And now *she* cuts in and steals him away from me in the most unprincipled fashion! How on earth did she manage it? I believe she must be a witch. It's perfectly eerie how she always spoils my plans."

Gilbert said he didn't suppose there was any witchcraft about it. "Miss Watson probably just offered to pay the French fellow more than you did," he said. "Money talks, y'know, and she's got all Lucius's fortune to back her up."

This statement did nothing to soothe Mrs. Atwater's feelings. "Yes, and that is the most unjust thing of all!" she said. "If Lucius's fortune had come to you instead of Miss Watson, we would never have had any of this to worry about in the first place. But I'll make her sorry yet that she crossed me. I'll crush her so she never lifts up her head again!"

During the weeks that followed, Mrs. Atwater did her best to fulfill this threat. But the same mysterious power that had enabled Elizabeth to spoil her ball and musicale was apparently still working in her favor. Time after time, Mrs. Atwater would devise some clever strategy to revenge herself on Elizabeth, only to see it come to nothing.

Elizabeth, meanwhile, was going from triumph to triumph. The musicale given to feature the talents of M. Mauvoisin was a grand success. The dinner party she held a fortnight later was spoken of for weeks afterward as the height of elegance and lavish hospitality. She was seen everywhere beautifully dressed and surrounded by a troop of admirers. And the chiefest of those admirers was Lord Steinbridge, whom all the gossips whispered was entirely smitten with her.

At last, even Mrs. Atwater had to own herself beaten. It was clear that nothing now could make London society reject Elizabeth Watson; her position was simply too firmly entrenched. Even if it had not been, the plans that Mrs. Atwater had designed to discredit her had an alarming tendency to rebound upon herself. Clearly it was time for a different strategy. Mrs. Atwater bent her brain to this problem and emerged a short time later with a new solution. "Gilbert, you shall have to marry Miss Watson," she told her son. "I have thought it all over very carefully, and it's the only way."

"Marry Miss Watson!" said Gilbert, his eyes bulging. "Why, I thought you hated the gel!"

"I don't *hate* her," said Mrs. Atwater austerely. "To be sure, I still don't feel she has any right to Lucius Atwater's money. But if she marries you, the money will come back into the family anyway, so that will make everything right. You had better start paying your addresses to her immediately. I don't suppose there's anything in these rumors I hear that Steinbridge is making up to her, but it would be as well to get the matter settled as soon as possible."

"But I don't want to get married!" protested Gilbert. "And if I did, I've no mind to take Elizabeth Watson to wife. I'll admit she's a handsome gal, but she's a trifle skinny for my taste, besides being a damned sight too blue. Her sister Sophia, now *she's* a nice, cozy armful—"

"Don't be ridiculous, Gilbert. Sophia will have nothing when she marries, or only what her sister allows her. Elizabeth will have all of Lucius's fortune. If you married her, you would never need to worry about money again."

Gilbert protested a bit more, but it was obvious that the idea of acquiring a fortune through no more work than was entailed by marrying Elizabeth Watson was not disagreeable to him. By dint of much nagging, Mrs. Atwater won from him a reluctant agreement to call upon Elizabeth that afternoon and begin the work of winning her heart.

When the butler told Elizabeth that Gilbert had come to call upon her, she naturally assumed it was part of some plan to discredit her. Accordingly, she refused to see him, sending down word that she was indisposed. But she met him that night at Almack's—a place where Gilbert was rarely seen, given the patronesses' fiat against strong drink and high play. Elizabeth was surprised to see him there, but this was nothing to her surprise at his subsequent conduct. He repeatedly asked her to dance, fetched her several glasses of orgeat that she did not want, and spent the whole evening by her side, trying to make himself agreeable. "It must be some plot," Elizabeth told Sophia. "I'll have Charles ask Maria to keep her ears open to find out what it means."

Maria duly reported back what it meant, much to Elizabeth's incredulity. "So Gilbert is to marry me, just like that?" she exclaimed. "Can Mrs. Atwater honestly think, after all that has passed, that there is any chance of my marrying her odious son? She must be mad!"

"No, but she dotes on Mr. Gilbert that much, she'd suppose any young lady'd jump at the chance to marry him," explained Charles, who was greatly amused by this turn of events. "But she'll find she's out in her reckoning, won't she, miss? I suppose when he comes round here again, you'll send him away with a flea in his ear!"

Elizabeth considered, then shook her head. "No, I don't think I'll do that, Charles," she said.

"But you'll never consider marrying Mr. Gilbert, miss!" urged Charles, looking shocked. "He's a regular loose screw, besides being a shocking gamester."

"Oh, I would never marry him, Charles. Have no fear of that. But it can do no harm to let him hang about. Apparently the Atwaters have decided to be agreeable now instead of disagreeable, and I have a mind to see how far I can make them go in the other direction."

As Elizabeth spoke, she found herself thinking of Julius Atwater. He had already shown himself agreeable, almost from the moment of her arrival in London. Moreover, he still continued to do so, calling on her occasionally, greeting her with apparent pleasure whenever they met, and seeking her out in a quiet yet determined way when they happened to attend the same party. Still, Elizabeth had made up her mind that this friendliness was no more genuine than his cousin's. Both men merely wanted her money, and the only reason Julius had begun to court her first was because he was more intelligent than Gilbert and had realized soonest that this was the best way to achieve his goal.

But I won't be taken in, Elizabeth vowed to herself. *Not by him any more than by Gilbert. I wouldn't trust any Atwater, not as far as I could throw one.*

So she allowed Gilbert to join her court, to dangle after her and send her flowers and bonbons and other pretty trifles. But Julius Atwater she held at a distance, treating him with formality whenever they met and refusing to allow him the place of friendship he was evidently seeking. It was all very well to toy with Gilbert, but Julius was a different kettle of fish, both more fascinating and more dangerous. Elizabeth had no mind to play with fire.

Twelve

Julius soon discerned the fruit of Elizabeth's resolution, though not the cause of it.

He watched with consternation as his cousin Gilbert was admitted into the Watsons' most intimate circle—a circle he longed to join with all his heart. But he would not go where he was not wanted, and he was painfully aware that Elizabeth did not want him. She was always polite when they met and even friendly on occasion, but there was a barrier between them that he could neither surmount nor breach.

There were times when Julius felt it was futile to keep banging his head against that barrier. Clearly Elizabeth did not care about him. Surely he had too much pride to pursue a woman who did not want him—or did he? *Evidently not,* Julius told himself with a touch of humor. He had seen Elizabeth at a party the previous night, during which she had declined to dance with him, refused to sit with him, and spoken only the bare minimum of words to him altogether. Yet he was planning to call on her today just as though she had given him the utmost encouragement. *Of course it's hopeless,* Julius told himself. *But nevertheless I mean to go on trying till there's no use trying any more.*

This was a euphemistic way of saying he would continue to pursue her until she was married to someone else. As things looked now, that time could not be far distant. Lord Steinbridge had continued to court her assiduously in the weeks following the ball, and various bookmakers around London were now offering long odds as to whether he meant to propose to her or not.

If Lord Steinbridge did propose to her, Julius felt certain that Elizabeth would accept him. What woman could resist the temptation to become a marchioness? And even if Elizabeth were the one woman in London capable of resisting that particular temptation, he knew that Steinbridge's proposal would represent various other temptations to her—temptations that might be even greater than his title. Steinbridge was wealthy, he moved in the first circles of society, and he wasn't a bad-looking fellow for all his stiff-necked ways. What was more to the point, he was a scholar like Elizabeth herself. He had taken a double first at Oxford years ago and was still active in literary and academic circles. Altogether, it would not be wonderful if Elizabeth preferred Lord Steinbridge to a man like himself—a man who had been content with a mere second at University and who had never distinguished himself since then for anything much more significant than the cut of his coat.

Julius told himself all this as he drove to Grosvenor Square, and he told it to himself all over again when he saw the marquess's carriage waiting in the street in front of the Watsons' house. He purposely dallied about getting out of his own carriage, hoping the marquess might be leaving by the time he was ready to go in, but after ten minutes he grew too impatient to wait longer and knocked sharply on the door. The butler admitted him, but seemed a little uncertain about whether he might see Elizabeth. "She already has a visitor at present," he explained, adding with heavy significance, "It is Lord Steinbridge, my lord."

"Oh, Steinbridge? He's a friend of mine," said Julius

mendaciously. "He won't mind my joining him with Miss Watson." Not waiting for an answer, he strode over and flung open the drawing room door.

Before him stood a flushed-looking Elizabeth, trying without success to remove her hand from the marquess's. "You do me great honor, my lord," she was saying. "But I must have time to consider."

"To be sure you must," agreed the marquess warmly. "Your scruples do you great credit, Miss Watson. But indeed, if you are concerned about the difference in our stations, I beg you will not let such concerns hinder you. I took the liberty of consulting my mother a week ago, at the time I first formed the resolution of speaking to you. She is of the opinion that your birth need present no hindrance to our union, all other things being equal."

Elizabeth threw him a peculiar look. "Indeed," she said.

"Indeed, no," said the marquess, smiling complacently. "Of course, any understanding between us must be provisional until you have made a visit to Gantley. Mother is very anxious to meet you, and it is her wish that no formal announcement be made until she has become acquainted with you and found out for herself the measure of your merits. Of course I willingly acceded to her request. It was, to my mind, a request both natural and honorable, for you will readily understand how much Mother would dislike to see me make a *mésalliance*. But I am confident that when she has met you and talked with you, she will be as much in favor of our union as I am myself."

"Indeed," said Elizabeth again—rather dryly, Julius thought. She was, he thought, remarkably self-possessed for a young woman who had just received a marriage proposal from an eligible marquess. Then she happened to catch sight of him standing in the doorway, and her self-possession seemed to desert her all at once. Her eyes widened, her mouth fell open, and she yanked her hand away from the marquess as though it had caught on fire. "My lord!" she cried.

"Yes, my dear?" said Lord Steinbridge tenderly. Then he, too, caught sight of Julius in the doorway. His face reddened, but he instantly summoned a stiff smile to his lips. "Ah, Atwater," he said. "You have caught us at a disadvantage."

"So I see," said Julius, in a voice fully as dry as Elizabeth's had been. Again he looked at her, but she immediately dropped her gaze and seemed all at once very interested in a collection of Chinese pots that stood on a nearby table.

The marquess's discomposure was of a less lasting kind. He gave Julius a cautious but friendly smile. "Indeed, Atwater, you have interrupted us at a most interesting moment," he said. "You may have gathered that I have just made Miss Watson an offer of marriage."

"Yes, I gathered as much as that," said Julius, more dryly still. "A *provisional* offer."

The marquess seemed oblivious to the sarcasm in his voice. "That is correct," he agreed. "And seeing that the engagement between us has not as yet been made formal, would it be too much to ask that you refrain from mentioning the matter to anyone? I would take it as a great favor, Atwater—and so, too, I know, would Miss Watson." He threw a tender look at Elizabeth.

"You may rely on my discretion," said Julius shortly. "Be sure I shall mention it to no one."

Elizabeth threw him a fleeting glance, then looked away again. The marquess smiled and clapped him on the shoulder. "You're a good man, Atwater," he said. "In return, I'll make sure you receive an invitation to my house party at Gantley next month." Giving Julius no chance to respond, he turned to Elizabeth, told her he was obliged to leave in order to fulfill another appointment, and wished her a good afternoon. Elizabeth merely nodded in reply. Both she and Julius watched as the marquess left the room.

As soon as the door closed behind him, Julius looked down at Elizabeth. She had become interested in the Chinese pots again and would not meet his gaze. "So," he said, "you have received an offer from Steinbridge."

Elizabeth gave him another fleeting glance, then looked down at the pots again. "Yes," she said. "Only as Lord Steinbridge told you, the matter is not quite settled."

"Yes, I recall him saying it was a provisional arrangement," said Julius. "Contingent upon the approval of the dowager marchioness."

At this, Elizabeth raised her eyes to his face. "And contingent on my approval also, my lord," she said. "It happens that I have not yet given my consent to Lord Steinbridge's very flattering proposal."

Julius raised his eyebrows. "Oh, indeed? I had supposed from the way Steinbridge spoke that your consent was taken as a matter of course."

Elizabeth flushed. "You are being offensive, my lord," she said.

"Perhaps," agreed Julius. "Not very gracious of me, is it? I suppose I ought really to be quite grateful to Steinbridge."

This brought Elizabeth's eyes to his face again in a hurry. "Why?" she said. "Why should you be grateful to Lord Steinbridge?" When Julius did not answer, she repeated the question, drawing a step nearer and even laying a hand on his arm, though she seemed unconscious of the action. "Why should you be grateful to the marquess, my lord?" she demanded. "I don't understand."

"I was thinking of our conversation that night you danced with me at your coming-out ball," said Julius. "You said then that it was not your company whom your suitors were seeking, but rather the company of my uncle's fortune. And I can readily see how you might think so, but yet it seems hard that you should suspect any man who enjoys your company to be a fortune hunter. Now, however, it is obvious you absolve Lord Steinbridge of such mercenary motives. Otherwise you would not even be considering his offer on a provisional basis."

"True," admitted Elizabeth. She eyed him with mistrust. "But that still does not explain why *you* should be grateful to him for restoring my faith."

"Doesn't it?" said Julius, returning her look steadily.

"No, it doesn't," said Elizabeth. She sounded almost angry, yet looking into her eyes, Julius had the strangest impression there was an emotion besides anger lying just beneath the surface. It inspired him to sudden recklessness. Bending down, he kissed her full on the lips.

Elizabeth drew back swiftly. There was no mistaking the emotion in her eyes now; they were literally blazing with anger. When she spoke, however, her voice sounded as though she were struggling with tears. "Why did you do that, my lord?" she demanded.

"Because—" began Julius, then stopped. Why *had* he kissed her? Because he loved her, of course; that was the answer that came promptly to his lips. Yet he could hardly tell Elizabeth he loved her now. She had just received a proposal of marriage from Lord Steinbridge; she was in a highly emotional state, and he had just destroyed any faith she had ever had in his character by taking the unwarrantable liberty of kissing her. All in all, it was a ridiculous moment for a declaration.

It was therefore with a sensation of unreality that Julius heard himself saying, "Because I love you, Elizabeth Watson. And I'd like to marry you myself. And if you can acquit Lord Steinbridge of mercenary motives, then perhaps you can bring yourself to do the same by me."

Elizabeth backed up another step, staring as though her eyes would start from her head. "For you!" she said.

"You want me to—you expect me to—oh, you must be mad!"

"Why?" inquired Julius. "Did you think Steinbridge was mad when he asked you to marry him?"

"No!" said Elizabeth. "Of course not!"

"Then why should you think me mad to do the same?"

"Because—because—oh, you must see that the situation is altogether different, my lord."

"No, I don't," said Julius. "To be sure, I'm not a marquess, but I have a title of sorts, and sufficient private means of my own. I don't *need* to marry a fortune."

He looked at Elizabeth, but she did not answer. Julius went on, his voice growing softer as he looked down at her. "What's more, I've known you longer than Steinbridge has. I've had a chance to see you in situations he hasn't, and to appreciate the character that makes you unique. Why should not I have had quite as much reason to fall in love with you as any other man?"

Again Elizabeth did not immediately answer. She only went on looking at him, as though trying to read his thoughts. "What you say may be true," she said at last, "but it seems strange you never mentioned it before now, my lord. Why wait until you hear Lord Steinbridge proposing to me before you tell me that you—that you care for me?"

"That I love you," corrected Julius. "I am telling you now because if I wait any longer, it may be too late. Like any sensible man, I would have rather waited until I felt sure you returned my feelings before taking the risk of being rejected. But now that Steinbridge has forced my hand, I cannot afford any longer to behave like a sensible man. I have no choice but to lay my cards on the table and reveal to you frankly how matters stand with me."

"Indeed," said Elizabeth, a trifle breathlessly. "I must agree that your conduct is hardly that of a sensible man, my lord!"

"No, I know it is not. You've never given me any reason to suppose you cared a fig for me," agreed Julius. "But I care for *you*, Elizabeth. And I thought you ought to know it."

"Why?" said Elizabeth. Her eyes still searched his face intently.

"Why?" repeated Julius. "God knows! I'm well aware I've no chance against a man like Steinbridge. But if you'd prefer a different sort of man—a man who wants you unprovisionally, and doesn't need to ask permission from his mother to publish the banns—well, here I am."

An electric sort of silence followed these words. "You are being insulting, my lord," said Elizabeth. But her voice sounded a little uncertain.

"Am I? I thought I was merely being truthful," said Julius. "What kind of man proposes marriage by prating of provisions and conditions?" He looked down at Elizabeth. "If it were I who was wooing you, I would make no provisions at all. I'd merely tell you that I loved you and make sure you knew I was speaking the truth."

"Yes?" said Elizabeth. "And just how would you go about doing that, my lord?"

Her tone of voice was ironic, yet her expression was strangely intent and—it seemed to Julius—challenging. He could not have said what there was in it to inspire him to kiss her again, but that was exactly what he did. Folding her in his arms, he lowered his lips to hers.

It was a longer kiss than the other, but Elizabeth neither struggled nor protested. When at last Julius released her, she only went on looking at him with that same intent expression. Julius looked back at her. "I love you, Elizabeth Watson," he said. "And if you require more proof than that, I'll be glad to supply it."

Elizabeth said nothing. She put a hand to her lips, drew a deep breath, then abruptly turned and left the room.

Julius supposed he had offended her. That was not sur-

prising, of course, for he was obliged to admit he had behaved in a singularly high-handed manner. No doubt he
had destroyed any chance he had ever had of winning her.
But of course she meant to marry Steinbridge in any case,
and he had never had any chance of winning her to begin
with. That being the case, perhaps it was as well he had
declared his feelings for her. The last few weeks had been
a fearful strain, trying to pretend that he was disinterested
where she was concerned. Now she knew otherwise.

Julius felt he would not mind very much if all of London knew otherwise, too. He was seized by a sudden
desire to act naturally on his emotions rather than maintain his air of disinterest. Even if it meant he was acting
like a fool, he thought he would prefer it. He laughed
aloud suddenly as he recalled Elizabeth's remark about
his not being a sensible man.

"After all, why should I be sensible?" he mused aloud.
"Steinbridge is the most sensible of sensible men, so
there's no use my competing on that turf. Better I should
act the fool as I did today. Especially since it gives me
the pleasure of kissing her! I don't like the idea that I
offended her, but at least I gave her something to think
about besides Steinbridge."

He would have been amazed if he had known how
much he had given Elizabeth to think about. From the
drawing room, she had hurried up the stairs to her room,
feeling as though she might burst into tears at any moment. Yet why should she weep? There was no reason for
tears. She had just received two offers of marriage from
two eligible gentlemen in a single afternoon, and most
women would consider that cause for jubilation.

Of course she had never been like most women. The
idea of marriage had never greatly appealed to her. Even
now, when she had received the honor of a proposal from

one of the supreme *partis* of London society, she was far from sure she wished to be married.

"And as for the idea of marrying Julius Atwater, it's completely ridiculous," she said aloud. "If I marry any man, it must be Lord Steinbridge. Only I'm not sure—not entirely sure—I want to be married at all."

In truth, Elizabeth had never expected to get an offer of marriage from the marquess. Despite his increasingly particular attentions and Mrs. Reese-Whittington's hints, Elizabeth was too used to being thought a plain, socially awkward bluestocking to believe it possible that a man like Lord Steinbridge would ever want to marry her. As a result, his proposal had caught her off guard, and she had been forced to ask him for time in which to consider it.

Fortunately, the marquess had taken her pleas for time like a gentleman, assuring her he was not seeking more than an informal understanding at present. Only was that on her account or his own? Elizabeth frowned. He had seemed to take it for granted that it was the difference in their stations that was giving her pause. But in fact this was the least of her concerns. She was not worried about whether she was fit to become a marchioness; she was worried about whether she would be happy as one. There was no necessity at all for her to marry unless it contributed to her happiness.

The difficulty was deciding whether it would. There could be no doubt that the marquess's proposal encompassed all of what most women would consider earthly happiness. A handsome husband who cared for her, an exalted financial and social position, a companion who could enter into her interests—all these might be hers if she married the marquess. Likely she would be one of the most envied women in England.

Elizabeth told herself that such considerations were unworthy, but they had their weight with her nonetheless.

Besides, as she assured herself, she had a real regard for the marquess even apart from his wealth and title. He was a good man, a moral man, a scholarly man—a man such as was rare indeed to find in these degenerate days. If she accepted his offer, she need never doubt his motives in marrying her. For was he not abasing himself to propose to her, a woman whose birth was not aristocratic like his own? He must care for her most truly if he could bring himself to overlook the difference in their stations.

Yet much as Elizabeth tried to convince herself that this was so, there was an undercurrent of uneasiness in her thoughts. She supposed it must be because of what Julius had said. She had been trying very hard not to think of the things he had said that afternoon, but they had to be considered sooner or later, and Elizabeth decided she had better consider them now as calmly and rationally as she could and try to put them into context.

Why had Julius been so savage against the marquess, criticizing his actions and ridiculing his proposal as conditional? The answer was easy—because he did not want her to accept the marquess's offer. If she married Lord Steinbridge, Lucius Atwater's fortune would legally belong to the marquess, and neither Julius nor Gilbert would have any chance of recovering it.

Well, then, why had Julius thought it necessary to kiss her? That was easy, too. Of course it was not because he loved her, as he claimed. It was nonsense to say he loved her when his enmity was such a well-established fact. No, he had kissed her for the same reason he had criticized the marquess: because he wished to marry her himself and so secure her fortune for his own use. Any other motives he had given she might dismiss out of hand.

But having dismissed Julius's claims of love for her, Elizabeth was brought up against the most perplexing question of all. It was all very well to say that Julius had kissed her in order to supplant the marquess in her thoughts, but why had she allowed him to do it? For try as she might to deny it, Elizabeth knew perfectly well that she *had* allowed it. She might have been caught off guard the first time, but when he had bent to kiss her the second time she had known perfectly well what he was about. Yet she had not lifted a finger to stop him.

"*Why* didn't I stop him?" Elizabeth asked herself. "Why didn't I?" She shut her eyes, recalling once more that moment in which Julius had bent to kiss her. The recollection made her shiver as though with an ague. She tried to tell herself it was merely the experience of being kissed by a man—an experience with which she was little acquainted. But her own honest nature would not allow this to pass, and when she really examined her feelings, she discovered the situation was more complicated than she was trying to make herself believe.

The fact was that she felt something for Julius Atwater besides the antagonism she should have felt for him as her sworn enemy. She had been aware of it as far back as their first interview together, but had tried to rigidly repress the feeling. Now she realized she had only repressed the expression of it. She could force herself to avoid Julius's company. She could force herself to treat him coolly and talk to him no more than civility allowed when she did find herself in his company. She could even force herself to speak slightingly of him to others. But she could not help feeling a distinct partiality for him, and she could not help being stirred by the memory of his kiss. It was a lowering admission, but there it was.

"What a fool I am," said Elizabeth aloud. With a final effort, she tore aside the veil of self-deception with which she had so long shrouded her thoughts and feelings. The facts stared her uncompromisingly in the face. She had fallen in love with Julius Atwater, and there did not appear to be a thing she could do about it.

Thirteen

Having admitted her feelings for Julius, Elizabeth now had to consider what she was going to do about them.

Of course she could not give in to them. That went without saying. There could be no worse fate than to succumb to the blandishments of an unprincipled man, even if he did claim to love her and had kissed her as though he meant it. She reminded herself that Gilbert had been showering her with the most extravagant avowals of devotion for the past few weeks. Yet she had never been tempted to take Gilbert's words seriously. Well, she must not take Julius's seriously either. Undoubtedly the avowals of one meant no more than the other. It was merely because Julius was both more clever and more unprincipled than his cousin that he had managed somehow to trick her heart into betraying her against her own better judgment.

But even if her heart had turned traitor, Elizabeth was resolved not to give way to its urgings. She reminded herself that she had been fairly successful in controlling her feelings up till that afternoon. It was only being alone with Julius and having him kiss her that had tempted her beyond her power. She must avoid such situations in the future, and then there would be no danger of her giving way to her feelings a second time. In the meantime, she must be doing all she could to choke off those feelings.

It was intolerable that she, Elizabeth Watson, an intelligent, self-possessed woman, should be made to care for a man against her own will. And such a man, too—an unprincipled man who was her greatest enemy! She told herself scathingly that she was as bad as the silly girls who imagined corsairs and banditti to be romantic heroes.

But I won't give way to such folly, she told herself. *Lord Steinbridge is twice the man Julius Atwater is. If I marry anybody, it must be he.*

On thinking the situation over, she decided that the marquess was probably her best line of defense against the present threat. He was respectable, moral, scholarly— all the things Julius Atwater was not. What was more, he was sincerely in love with her. She must spend as much time as possible in his company and try to divert her romantic feelings into this more suitable channel if she could not choke them off altogether.

With this resolution strong in her mind, Elizabeth rose and went downstairs. Halfway down she encountered Sophia. There was an unhappy look on her sister's face that served to distract Elizabeth from her own problems. "What's the matter, Sophy?" she asked.

Sophia made a despairing gesture. "It's Mama," she said. "She's been after me to marry Mr. Alton again. She says that after you and Lord Steinbridge are wed, you won't want me on your hands, and that I ought to be glad of an opportunity to establish myself so credibly."

"Nonsense!" scoffed Elizabeth. "Mama is just talking through her hat, as usual."

"I don't think she is," said Sophia. "At least not regarding you and Lord Steinbridge. I think he does mean to make you an offer, Elizabeth. I've seen the way he looks at you."

Elizabeth flushed. "As a matter of fact, Lord Steinbridge already *has* made me an offer," she said. "He was here not much more than an hour ago and asked me to marry him—at least that's what it amounts to. He prefers that I visit his home and meet his mother before the engagement is announced." She frowned at the recollection.

Sophia, however, reacted very differently. "Oh, Elizabeth, truly?" she said. "I am very happy for you, Sister—very, very happy. Only I can't help fearing that it is as Mama says, and I will be in you and Lord Steinbridge's way after you are married."

"Nonsense," said Elizabeth firmly. "I'm not married to Lord Steinbridge yet. And if I do marry him, I will undertake that you shall be welcome in our home as long as you like."

She spoke with such certainty that Sophia looked relieved. Still, having had her mind set to rest on this issue, she seemed inclined to explore a little further the subject of the marquess's proposal.

"And so Lord Steinbridge has asked you to marry him," she marveled. "Of course we have all been expecting it, yet it still seems unbelievable. To think you will be a marchioness, Elizabeth! My, won't Miss Mathers back in Cheltenham stare when she hears!"

"But it is not settled that I shall marry Lord Steinbridge, Sophy," said Elizabeth quickly. "Indeed, I have not made up my mind whether I mean to accept him."

Sophia looked at her in wonderment. "Oh, Elizabeth, I don't know how you can be so cool about it. I'm sure I would be in transports if a marquess asked me to marry him."

"No, you wouldn't," said Elizabeth, laughing. "You would turn the poor man down flat because you are in love with Philip Arthur!"

Sophia smiled self-consciously. "Yes, I suppose I would. But what I meant was that I would be in transports if I were *you*. Because you are not in love with anybody else—and you do care for Lord Steinbridge, don't you? I know you do, Sister," she said, answering her own question. "You would not have been encouraging him the way you have been doing these last few weeks if you did not care for him."

"No-o-o," said Elizabeth. It was, she assured herself, quite true that she cared for the marquess. Even if she suspected she cared about somebody else more, that did not make it wrong to encourage Lord Steinbridge. She was merely trying to do the prudent thing rather than letting her wayward heart lead her to perdition. That being the case, there was no reason why Sophia's words should make her feel guilty.

Sophia smiled and squeezed her arm. "Then I am doubly happy for you, Sister," she said. Her face fell. "Won't Mama be wild when she hears! She will be twice as urgent about my marrying Mr. Alton when she learns about you and the marquess."

"Perhaps not," said Elizabeth mysteriously. "I have an idea about that, Sophia. Come up to my room, and we'll talk it over."

Elizabeth led the way back up to her room, shut the door, and sat down at the foot of her bed. Sophia sat down beside her. "You know," said Elizabeth, "despite what Mama may say, Mr. Arthur is a perfectly respectable suitor. He comes of a good family, and he is as industrious as he is clever. He may be only a curate now, but he is practically certain to get a living soon, and then he will be very well able to support you."

"Yes, of course," said Sophia. "I've said the same thing to Mama, many times. But she thinks I would do better to marry a man who can support me now, and one who has a title as well."

"Yes, that is the crux of the issue. She thinks you can do *better*," said Elizabeth. "What we must show her is that you could also do *worse*."

Sophia looked at Elizabeth uncomprehendingly. "I don't understand," she said.

"Why, I merely mean that if some really ineligible gentleman was paying you addresses, Mr. Arthur would begin to look very good by comparison."

"Yes," admitted Sophia. "That is true. But unfortunately all the gentlemen who have paid me addresses since coming to London are *more* eligible than Philip, not less."

"Well, that's where my plan comes in. You remember how Mama was complaining the other day about letting Sir Connor O'Connor take me to Vauxhall Gardens? She said it was unfitting for me to encourage an Irish half-pay officer to dangle after me when I had a marquess on the string."

Sophia nodded. "Yes, I remember," she said. "But what has that to do with me?"

"Well, you remember that I told Mama on that occasion that I am very fond of Sir Connor and would let him take me to Vauxhall if I wanted to. And in fact I *am* very fond of him—as a friend. And I believe he feels the same way about me. And I think he would be quite willing to do me a favor, if I asked him."

Seeing that Sophia still looked uncomprehending, Elizabeth reached out and squeezed her arm. "Sophy, you goose! Don't you see? I'll ask him to call on you, and take you places, and act as though he is falling in love with you. And you must act as though you are considering marrying him. And then we'll see if Mama won't accept Mr. Arthur as an excellent substitute."

"Oh!" said Sophia. Her face was a study in conflicting emotions. "That is a very clever plan, Elizabeth. But I don't think I would feel comfortable asking such a thing of Sir Connor—and I'm not sure I could act as though I cared about him, even to marry Philip. Because it's Philip I really care for, and it doesn't seem quite decent to pretend I am in love with another man."

"But you wouldn't have to pretend you were in love

with him," said Elizabeth. "You would merely have to act as though you like him better than any other man you have met in London. And indeed, I think you would find that quite easy, for Sir Connor is excellent company."

Sophia nodded dubiously. "But won't you feel odd, making such a request of Sir Connor?" she asked. "I mean, the whole point is that he is ineligible as a suitor. You can hardly come out and say that is why you need his help."

Elizabeth smiled. "Can't I? You don't know Sir Connor. He is refreshingly free of pretense."

Sophia nodded again, doubtfully. "I suppose you ought to know," she said. "But I'm sure I shall blush to look Sir Connor in the face, knowing you have asked such a favor of him."

"That will only make it look like you are the more smitten with him," said Elizabeth, laughing. "Soon Mama will be begging you to marry Mr. Arthur—see if I'm not right!"

Matters were easily arranged with Sir Connor. Encountering him at the park the following afternoon, Elizabeth explained the situation concerning Sophia and the plan she had in mind to resolve it. Sir Connor laughed and said he was very glad to serve her and her sister any way he could. He refused Elizabeth's delicate offer to recompense him for his trouble, but after a certain amount of persuasion was brought to accept a loan of fifty pounds, to be paid back at some indefinite time. He and Elizabeth then shook hands and parted, Sir Connor promising to appear in Grosvenor Square the following afternoon to begin the campaign to make Mrs. Watson embrace Philip Arthur as a son-in-law.

This campaign was an almost immediate success. Within a week, Mrs. Watson was fretting because Sophia seemed suddenly smitten with Sir Connor. Characteristically, she blamed Elizabeth for this state of affairs, saying such a dangerous character would never have dared approach Sophia if Elizabeth had not first encouraged him. Elizabeth merely shrugged and told her mother she could not see why she was so upset.

"You told Sophy just the other day that she would be throwing herself away if she did not marry a man with a title," she pointed out. "Well, Sir Connor has a title, doesn't he? I should think you would be very pleased that Sophia seems inclined to like him."

"An *Irish* title! And with nothing behind it but debts. That is not at all the kind of match I want for Sophia," said Mrs. Watson coldly.

"You are hard to please, Mama," remarked Elizabeth with affected surprise. "I remember your saying not so long ago that you would rather Sophia married any man but Philip Arthur."

Mrs. Watson admitted that she might have said this, but told Elizabeth it was nothing to the point. "Of course I did not mean for her to marry a man like Sir Connor," she said. "Why, that would be as bad as her marrying Philip Arthur. In fact, it would be worse. At least Mr. Arthur is not in *debt.*"

Elizabeth said cheerfully that she could probably give Sophia enough of a dowry so that she and Sir Connor could contrive to rub along, notwithstanding his debts. "I understand living in Ireland is cheaper than it is here, so they would probably have to live on Sir Connor's estate all or most of the year," she told her mother. "But if Sophia really loves him, I'm sure she would not mind. Of course it would be hard for us, being separated from her, but I have no doubt we would soon grow reconciled."

Mrs. Watson said tearfully she would rather see Sophia dead than condemned to a life of penury in Ireland. "Well, perhaps you had better encourage her to marry Mr. Arthur, then," said Elizabeth. "I think she does still care for him. At any rate, it would be worth trying if you object so strongly to Sir Connor."

Mrs. Watson was not quite ready to go as far as this, but her face bore a thoughtful look as she took leave of her elder daughter. On the whole, Elizabeth was encouraged to believe her plan was working very well, and she looked forward to seeing Sophia united to the man she loved at no very remote date.

Her other plans were progressing satisfactorily, too. So at least she assured herself, for she had resolutely avoided Julius Atwater in the weeks that had passed since he had kissed her. True, she had been unable to avoid seeing him at the park and the opera and various other public functions, but she had taken care that there were no opportunities for private conversation on these occasions and certainly no opportunities for kissing. Not that Julius had appeared to seek any such opportunities. On the contrary, he seemed to understand and acquiesce in her desire to avoid him. He gave her a brief formal greeting whenever they met, made no attempts to get her apart from others, and had otherwise behaved like a perfect gentleman.

Elizabeth told herself this was just as it ought to be. She could hardly admit even to herself that she found it disappointing.

After all, why should she care about Julius Atwater when she had the premier *parti* of London society at her feet? Or if not at her feet, at least by her side on an almost daily basis. In keeping with her resolution, she had made a point of accepting all Lord Steinbridge's invitations— all of his invitations except one, that is. For despite his continual urgings to visit Gantley, his country seat, and meet his mother the dowager marchioness, Elizabeth could not quite bring herself to take this decisive step. She did not mind if the greater part of her acquaintances believed her already as good as engaged to Lord Steinbridge; she did not even mind if Lord Steinbridge believed it himself. But she would not make the engagement official until she was sure of her own mind, and at present there was still a part of her that shrank from the idea of marrying the marquess.

"I wonder sometimes if I was ever intended to marry," she told Sophia one evening when she was feeling particularly despondent. "I do believe nature intended me for an old maid."

Sophia looked at her in alarm. "Elizabeth, you and Lord Steinbridge have not quarreled, have you?" she asked

"No, nothing like that," said Elizabeth. She could hardly bring herself to say what was her real concern. The plain fact was that the marquess had kissed her that evening for the first time, and the experience had been curiously disturbing.

It had not been a particularly intimate kiss. In truth, it had been a rather abortive one, for at the last moment Elizabeth had been overcome by a strange revulsion that had caused her to turn away before the marquess's lips had more than touched hers. He had not seemed to mind her shrinking from him; in fact, he had praised her maidenly modesty in refusing to relinquish her lips to him before marriage. Yet Elizabeth, remembering how freely she had relinquished her lips to Julius Atwater a few weeks before, was made very uncomfortable by his words. They made her feel guilty and deceitful, the same way she felt when Sophia took it for granted she was in love with Lord Steinbridge.

"I don't—" she began, then stopped.

"You don't what?" said Sophia, looking at her inquiringly.

Elizabeth knew she could not tell her sister the truth. Sophia would be shocked to learn how debased was her character. She must fight her own battles and vanquish her own private demons, the chief demon appearing in the person of Julius, Lord Atwater.

In an effort to distract her mind from the subject of Julius, she began speaking on a related subject, the subject of his cousin Gilbert. "I don't think Gilbert is ever going to give over trying to convince me to marry him," she told Sophia. "He proposed three times last week in spite my giving him no encouragement at all. He's getting to be quite a nuisance."

"Well, he's sure to stop when your engagement to Lord Steinbridge is announced," said Sophia cheerfully. "Even Gilbert would not be ninny enough to persevere after that!"

Elizabeth frowned. As always, the assumption that she was bound to marry the marquess made her uncomfortable. "Perhaps," she said. "But I begin to think Gilbert is ninny enough to persevere even then. He and Mrs. Atwater are so determined to get Lucius Atwater's fortune back in the family that they seem blind to every other consideration."

Just then there was a scratching at Elizabeth's bedchamber door. "Come in," called Elizabeth, glad of this distraction. She imagined the visitor must be her mother or cousin, but instead it proved to be Charles Bray. There was a perturbed look on his face.

"Beg your pardon, miss," he said. "Maria's here, and she's got something that you ought to hear about right away."

"Maria is here?" repeated Elizabeth in amazement. "Oh, but she should not have come, Charles! She should have sent a message in the usual way. You know if Mrs. Atwater ever learns she was here, she would know right away how we have been getting word of her plans."

Charles nodded. "Aye, I told Maria the same thing, miss. But she's got a particular reason for coming herself, and when you hear it, I think you'll agree the matter's an urgent one. Not to put too fine a point on it, there's dirty work afoot."

Sophia, looking frightened, begged Elizabeth to hear at once what Maria had to say. "Of course I shall," said Elizabeth, and bade Charles bring Maria in at once.

He returned a moment later accompanied by a slim young woman clad in a black cloak and a heavily veiled bonnet. Pushing the veil back from her face, Maria was revealed as a dark-haired girl in her early twenties with a countenance as intelligent as it was attractive.

"I do beg your pardon for coming to you this way, miss," she said, addressing Elizabeth with a mixture of assurance and contrition. "I know it's contrary to your instructions, but this seemed a matter of some urgency, and I didn't think I ought to delay in getting word to you."

"Yes, so Charles says," said Elizabeth with a nod. "What have you to tell me?"

"Well, I overheard Mrs. Atwater and Mr. Gilbert talking after dinner this evening, miss. You know they're both set on your marrying Mr. Gilbert." She glanced at Elizabeth, who nodded again, signifying she should go on. "Well, up till now it doesn't seem to have entered their heads that you might marry anybody else. But lately there's been a deal of talk about your marrying Lord Steinbridge, him who's in the papers all the time about the Royal Society and such things. And now the two of them are getting worried. Mrs. Atwater told Gilbert he'd have to do something to cut Lord Steinbridge out, or he'd lose any chance at getting Mr. Lucius's fortune. And Gilbert said he didn't see how he was supposed to cut out a fellow like Lord Steinbridge, who has a handle to his name and was rich as Croesus to boot."

Again Maria paused, then went on dramatically, "And Mrs. Atwater said, 'I don't care if he *is* rich and has a title. You marry her, Gilbert, if you have to carry her off to Gretna Green.' And to make a long story short, miss, that's just what he's decided to do."

Sophia gave a gasp, but Elizabeth laughed aloud. "How ridiculous," she said. "You don't mean to say that Gilbert really thinks he can marry me against my will?"

Maria shook her head. "I don't know if he thinks so, miss, but I know he's going to try. Indeed, it's no laughing matter. You may not have heard of Miss Elliot last year, but she was an heiress just like you, and she was abducted and taken off to Gretna by a man she hardly knew. Her family had a terrible time getting the marriage set aside. They ended up having to pay thousands and thousands of pounds, and even then they couldn't undo the damage to her reputation. They did their best to hush it up, but there'll always be whispers about her now, and yet the whole matter was none of her doing."

Elizabeth was looking sober now. "I see," she said. "I did not know such things still happened in this day and age. How perfectly barbarous!"

"It's dreadful!" said Sophia, looking horrified. "Dreadful!"

"Aye, that it is, miss," said Maria emphatically. "So when I heard Mrs. Atwater and Mr. Gilbert arguing about the best way to get you into Mr. Gilbert's carriage, I decided I'd better lose no time coming over here and letting you know what was afoot."

Elizabeth nodded. "Yes, and I thank you for it, Maria. So they mean to get me into Gilbert's carriage, do they? And then carry me off to Gretna Green? Hardly an original plan, and one fraught with difficulties, I should think. But I suppose I should know better than expect anything original from those two. In any case, it should be easy enough to forestall their intentions, now that I am on my guard. Unless . . ."

A thoughtful expression had stolen into Elizabeth's eyes. Charles and Maria regarded her with interest, and

Sophia with downright apprehension. "Elizabeth, what are you thinking?" she demanded. "You know you mustn't take any chance of letting Gilbert get you in his power. Only think how dreadful it would be if he succeeded in carrying you off to Gretna Green and marrying you!"

"Dreadful," agreed Elizabeth. "I certainly shan't take any chance of *that* happening. But at the same time I don't like the idea of having to remain on my guard for twenty-four hours a day until Gilbert and Mrs. Atwater give up this ridiculous plan. It seems to me it might be better to let it succeed—up to a point—and then have it recoil upon them so badly they won't be tempted to meddle with me again."

Maria was regarding Elizabeth with interest. "It'd be a neat trick if you could pull it off, miss," she said. "How was you thinking to go about it?"

"First, I must set up an opportunity for Gilbert to abduct me. I think I had better take to going on solitary walks in the evenings around the square. I'll mention next time I see him how much I like taking walks alone in the nighttime—no, I had better say I only like walking on nights when the moon is full. That will narrow it down to a particular night, and it just so happens the moon is full this coming Friday."

"But won't he suspect something if you make it as particular as that?" questioned Sophia. "It seems to me he might wonder to see you playing so completely into his hands."

"Anyone with ordinary intelligence might wonder, but not Gilbert," said Elizabeth with satisfaction. "If I know him and his mother, they'll swallow the bait in one gulp and never look for a hook. At any rate, we'll have Maria to tell us if they do." She looked at Maria. "You would know if Gilbert were making plans for a journey, wouldn't you?"

"Aye, I'd know," said Maria promptly. "I could find out from his valet if he asked to have his bags packed and ask his groom if he'd ordered his carriage round."

"Very good, then. We'll know beforehand if he really means to abduct me and take precautions accordingly."

"But Elizabeth," said Sophia, who had been looking more and more concerned. "I cannot like you to put yourself in Gilbert's power, even for a minute. If something were to go wrong with your plan—"

"But you see, I won't be in Gilbert's power, not even for a minute," said Elizabeth, her eyes dancing. "He may think he is abducting me, but in fact it will be somebody quite different he is abducting."

"But who, Elizabeth?" said Sophia, looking confused. "You would not want to risk sending one of the maids in your place—or indeed any decent woman. You know Gilbert's reputation."

Elizabeth laughed. "Yes, I do. And that is one of the reasons why I think it would be better if Sir Connor O'Connor were to go in my place instead of another woman."

"Sir Connor O'Connor!" exclaimed Sophia disbelievingly. "But Gilbert would never take *him* for you!"

"I think he would if Sir Connor were wearing my cloak and bonnet. We're much the same height, although Sir Connor's a little broader in the shoulders. I do hate to ask him to do any more favors, seeing how many he has already done for us, but I think he would find this one amusing."

Charles and Maria began to laugh, and after a minute Sophia joined in. "Oh, Elizabeth!" she said. "Can you imagine Gilbert's face, when he finds he has abducted Sir Connor instead of you? He will feel the most perfect fool!"

"Yes, and he will be the most perfect laughingstock if word of it ever gets out," said Elizabeth. "We can use that as a threat to hold over his head to keep him from ever trying such a trick again."

Everyone agreed this would be a powerful weapon against future transgressions on the part of the Atwaters, and Elizabeth went to bed that night fully determined to speak to Sir Connor on the morrow. As she lay there waiting for sleep to come, however, she found her mind drifting from the subject of Gilbert to Gilbert's cousin. Was Julius privy to the plan to abduct her? Had he consented to lend his assistance to such a diabolical scheme?

"Never!" Elizabeth told herself. She was certain that if Julius were to abduct her, he would go about it much more intelligently. She spent a little time speculating on just how he might go about it, but becoming belatedly aware that she was taking altogether too much interest in the subject, she resolutely turned her thoughts in a different direction. Still, as she drifted off to sleep, it was to reflect with comfortable certainty that if Julius ever carried her off, it would be by use of finesse rather than force.

Fourteen

Sir Connor proved very willing to participate in Elizabeth's plan. Indeed, he declared he wouldn't miss it for the world.

"Yes, but you know the whole business may come to nothing," cautioned Elizabeth. "The more I think about it, the more certain I feel that even Gilbert could not be foolish enough to attempt such a scheme. Likely all that will happen is that you will get to make an evening promenade around Grosvenor Square in my bonnet and cloak."

"Sure, and I don't mind doing that," said Sir Connor, grinning. "Only I hope you won't go telling the fellows of me regiment about it. I'd never hear the end of it, not if I lived to be a hundred."

Being assured of Sir Connor's cooperation, Elizabeth's next step was to offer the bait to Gilbert. As she had expected, the opportunity to do this was not long delayed. She encountered him that very evening at a rout given by a mutual acquaintance. As soon as he saw her, he came hurrying over full of insincere smiles and compliments. Contrary to her usual custom, Elizabeth encouraged him to remain with her and listened closely to all he said. Before long, she felt assured that Maria's fears were justified. He did seem unusually eager to get her into his carriage, urging her to go driving with him the following day and, failing that, to attend a ridotto al fresco Friday evening. This was the opportunity Elizabeth had been waiting for.

"You are very kind, Mr. Atwater, but I think I must decline your invitation," she said. "The ridotto sounds delightful, but I have been keeping such late hours these past few weeks that I am starting to feel rather pulled down. I believe I shall have to spend Friday resting quietly at home if I do not wish to fall ill."

Gilbert immediately made strenuous efforts to urge her to take a drive in the country with him Friday afternoon. "Nothing like fresh air to set you up," he urged. "I'll wager you'd be right as a trivet after spending the day in the country."

Elizabeth, however, declined this invitation firmly. "Thank you, but I would rather stay home Friday," she said. "I shall rest quietly in my room and see no one at all, and if I am very careful to avoid all noise and excitement, perhaps I will feel well enough to take a walk around the square in the evening. You know there will be a full moon that night, and I dote upon full moons. There is nothing I like better than to steal out of the house after dark and take a walk in the moonlight, all by myself."

Gilbert's eyes glistened at these words. "You do, do you?" he said.

"Yes, whenever I get the chance," said Elizabeth innocently. "Of course it hasn't often been possible since coming to London. We have been so busy, and Mrs. Reese-Whittington tells me it is not at all the thing for young ladies to walk alone after dark. But I don't see why that should be, as long as I do not go out of the square. You don't think it would be unsafe, do you, Mr. Atwater?"

She could hardly conceal a smile as Gilbert fell all over himself to assure her it would be perfectly safe. "Mind you, I wouldn't say anything to your cousin about it," he said earnestly. "Just you slip out and go for your walk, and don't give her a chance to kick up a dust. You know older ladies always have fussy notions about what's safe and what isn't."

"Indeed," agreed Elizabeth dryly. She observed with amusement that as soon as Gilbert had gained the information he sought, he was as eager to leave her as he had been to get to her in the first place. It was only a few minutes later that he excused himself, and she observed him leaving the party soon after.

Elizabeth was certain he had gone to confer with his mother and make arrangements to abduct her Friday. She felt satisfied that he had no inkling of the trap that had been laid for him. But her satisfaction was short-lived, for hardly had Gilbert taken himself off than Julius came strolling over.

"Good evening, my lord," said Elizabeth. She glanced at him, then looked away, wondering if she would ever be able to see him without remembering those kisses.

"Good evening, Miss Watson," said Julius. He made one or two commonplace remarks about the party, then asked abruptly, "What's my cousin been saying to you?"

Taken off guard by this question, Elizabeth found herself stalling for time. "What has Gilbert been saying?" she repeated. "I don't understand, my lord."

"Don't you?" said Julius. "Perhaps it is my imagination. But I caught him and my aunt whispering together the other day, and though I didn't hear what they were talking about, I thought I heard your name mentioned."

"Indeed?" said Elizabeth, trying to sound unconcerned.

"Indeed, yes. And just now I saw Gilbert take leave of you, looking like the cat that got into the cream pitcher. And I couldn't help wondering what was in the wind."

"Oh?" said Elizabeth, opening her eyes very wide. "What *should* be in the wind?"

"I don't know," said Julius. "That's what I'm asking you. Did Gilbert say anything in particular to you?"

"No, not really," said Elizabeth, reflecting with satisfaction that this was the simple truth. It was she who had done most of the talking, not Gilbert. "He asked me to drive with him, and to attend a ridotto Friday night, but I declined. Not that it's any of your business," she added pointedly.

Julius considered, then nodded. "No, I suppose not. Nevertheless, you will understand that feeling as I do, I cannot help taking an interest in your welfare."

It was the first reference he had made to his feelings since the day he had kissed her. In spite of herself, Elizabeth felt her color rising. "If Gilbert makes a nuisance of himself, you'll let me know, won't you?" continued Julius, fixing his eyes on hers. "I flatter myself I have some small authority over him, though not so much as I would like." He paused, still looking into her eyes.

Elizabeth was aware of the strangest urge to confide in him. It was very odd, for she had never felt an urge to reveal the details of her plans to any outsider—not even the marquess, who would have been the natural choice if she had wanted a confidant. But somehow she had been certain Lord Steinbridge would not approve of her plan for countering Gilbert's villainy. He would think she ought to call in a constable, or take other, similarly conventional measures.

Julius, she felt instinctively, would react differently. He would appreciate and applaud her plan, much as Sir Connor had done. But though in general she trusted her instincts, on this occasion she felt they could hardly have been more astray. It would be insanity to reveal her plan to Julius Atwater. Not only was he a member of the family who was planning to abduct her, he might even be the plan's moving spirit for all she knew to the contrary. He was a deep and subtle man, and the fact that he could make her think even momentarily of confiding her secrets to him was merely a further proof of his depth and subtlety.

So she said coolly, "Thank you, my lord, but I don't believe you need trouble yourself in the matter. I am quite capable of handling Gilbert myself."

"I don't doubt it," he said gravely. "But I would spare you the trouble if I could."

Another short silence ensued. "You are very kind," said Elizabeth at last. She felt she had to say something, for the silence was becoming embarrassing.

"Kind?" repeated Julius. "No, I don't think I am particularly kind. But I would welcome the chance to serve you in some way. One's feelings require a vent, you know, and I have no vent worth speaking of—at least, none that is available to me at the moment."

His eyes lingered on Elizabeth's face as he spoke. She felt sure he was referring to those kisses again. After a moment, Julius went on, his voice still sober. "May I extract one promise from you, Miss Watson?" he asked.

"That depends on the promise," said Elizabeth, eyeing him warily.

"Oh, it is nothing very much. Only if there is ever anything I can do for you—anything you *want* me to do for you—will you please let me know of it?"

Elizabeth was relieved by this request, yet oddly disappointed by it, too. Somehow she had expected he would ask something more of her, even if it was something she had to refuse.

To her horror, Julius seemed to discern these thoughts. "That wasn't what you were expecting, was it?" he said. "I suppose you thought I was going to ask you to marry me again. Well, and why not?" A reckless smile suddenly lit up his face. "I will, if you like. In fact, I would be very glad to go down on my knees right here and now, and—"

"Don't!" said Elizabeth, for he really showed signs of going down on his knees then and there. In her haste to stop him, she spoke more loudly than she had meant to, causing several people nearby to turn and stare. Elizabeth flushed with embarrassment.

"Of course I won't, if you don't want me to," said Julius, straightening obligingly. "I only wanted to show what lengths I am willing to go to in order to please you. If there is something you would rather have me do—"

"I don't want you to do anything!" said Elizabeth. She did not speak so loudly as before, but still her voice held great emphasis. "I don't want you to do anything at all."

Julius shook his head. "Well, that is no difficult task. I have been doing nothing, or next to nothing, most of my life. But it happens that of late I have been trying to turn over a new leaf, and I sometimes flatter myself I might really amount to something, especially if you were willing to take me in hand. Just give me a task—a quest, if you will—and see if I do not make good on it. No knight of the Round Table would ever strive more manfully to serve his lady than I would you."

"I think you are quite ridiculous," said Elizabeth. She tried to speak coldly, but something was interfering with her voice. For an instant she had seen a vision—a vision of Julius kneeling before her, her hand outstretched to him, with the two of them surrounded by a halo of light in an idealized image of love and romance.

It was ridiculous, of course—fully as ridiculous as the foolish dreams of her girlhood. This was no storybook lover come to rescue her from her tower, but an unprincipled man of the world, seeking to cheat her out of her own legitimately won fortune. Even if he were not an unprincipled man, she was a strong, independent, modern woman who had no need of rescuing. It was therefore very annoying to hear a quaver in her voice as she added,

"I wish you would not tease me like this, my lord. Indeed, I have no need of a knight."

He nodded soberly. "Very well. But you will remember your promise, will you not?"

Elizabeth hesitated. "I don't think—" she began.

"But yes, you must promise," he insisted. "You must let me know if I can ever do anything for you. You *must*, Elizabeth—Miss Watson. Will you do this for me, even if you can do nothing else?"

His eyes were on hers, and something in their expression compelled Elizabeth to assent. "Yes," she said. "I will, since you ask."

As she spoke, she had the sensation that she had lost ground somehow. Yet she could not see that her position was in any way weakened by the half promise she had just given. On the contrary, it had been merely a convenient way to end the conversation. Still, as Julius bowed and wished her a good evening, she had the sense that he had got the better of her in some manner.

This sense lingered with her in the days that followed. She thought incessantly of Julius and of the promise he had extracted from her. She also found herself pondering that vision she had seen—a vision of romance in which he had played an integral role. But so soon as these thoughts would creep into her mind, she quickly pushed them out again. Julius was, as she assured herself, unprincipled and an enemy. It was nonsensical to imagine him in any other wise, and in any case she had more important things to think about just then.

Friday was drawing near, the day appointed for her "abduction." It was apparent that Gilbert had decided to act upon the hint Elizabeth had dropped. Maria reported that he had told his valet he was going out of town Friday and instructed him to pack garments suitable for the Scottish climate. He had also given instructions to have his lightest chaise and fastest horses ready for his use Friday evening. So there was abundant reason to believe that he would be attempting to abduct Elizabeth that evening, and Elizabeth was resolved to see that he was thwarted.

"How do I look?" asked Sir Connor. Fits of giggles were his only answer. He turned to regard himself in the glass, and an involuntary chuckle broke from his own lips. "Why, it's pretty as a picture I look, don't I? A fine strapping lass, upon my word!"

"You *are* a bit larger than I am," admitted Elizabeth. "But I don't think it will be noticeable when you are alone on the street. Gilbert will be expecting me, not you, and as long as there is nothing in your appearance too noticeably amiss, I don't think it will ever occur to him that you are anybody else."

"Anyway, he knows that is Elizabeth's bonnet you are wearing," put in Sophia. "I took care to point it out to him when she was wearing it in the park the other day and ask him if he did not think it pretty."

"A tasty piece of headgear," agreed Sir Connor, critically appraising the confection of lace, plumes, and silk butterflies upon his head. "I'll take care to keep the veil pulled well down about me face, however. If Mr. Gilbert sees you've grown mustachios, even he's like to figure something's amiss!"

This elicited more giggling from the girls. "Yes, and you must remember to take short steps and not let your boots show," instructed Elizabeth. "It's a pity you can't fit into my slippers, but I suppose it can't be helped."

"Nay, it can't," agreed Sir Connor, glancing down at his gleaming Hessians. "But the cloak hides 'em well enough, and to speak truth I'd rather not be hampered by slippers, nor skirts neither. Mr. Gilbert will probably be a trifle put out when he discovers his bride isn't who he supposes, and it's likely I may have to defend meself against his wrath."

He did not look as though this prospect particularly dismayed him. Elizabeth, however, gave him a worried look. "I must say, I have been a trifle concerned about that myself," she said. "Do you think you had better take along a pistol?"

"Nay, there's no need for pistols," scoffed Sir Connor. "I can settle Mr. Gilbert easily enough with only me fists. Indeed, I'll be much disappointed if I don't have the chance to at least darken his daylights. When I think of the nerve of him, trying to abduct a young lady like yourself! He deserves a good thrashing by all that's holy, and I intend to see that he gets it."

"*If* he actually does try to abduct me," said Elizabeth scrupulously. "We still do not know for certain that he will. He may well lose his nerve when it comes to the point and decide to abandon the idea."

"Well, we'll soon know one way or the other," said Sir Connor. "D'you suppose it's dark enough now for me to be showing me face outside? Or should I be waiting a little longer?"

Elizabeth thought they ought to wait a little longer, but Sophia, who was very nervous now the plan was being put into execution, felt the sooner Sir Connor embarked on his walk, the sooner the whole adventure would be over. "Yes, but there is no point sending out Sir Connor if Gilbert isn't here yet," pointed out Elizabeth. "And I haven't seen any sign that he *is* here."

Even as she spoke, however, a carriage turned into the square and drew to a stop in front of one of the neighboring houses. Elizabeth and the others gathered around the window to watch. The carriage was a light chaise drawn by four horses, and though they waited and watched a considerable time, nobody either entered or got out of it. "I expect that's Gilbert," said Elizabeth with satisfaction. "Sir Connor, I think it's time you made your appearance."

Sophia escorted Sir Connor downstairs and let him out the side door, while Elizabeth remained watching from above between a crack in the curtains. Presently she saw Sir Connor appear, cloaked and bonneted, on the walk below. Elizabeth watched him, smiling a little at the affectedly feminine swing of his hips and his mincing stride. Although she felt he was overdoing his attempts to appear female, she was reasonably sure no one would have suspected him of being anything else.

Sophia joined her at the window a second later, breathless from having run upstairs. "Can you see Sir Connor?" she panted. "Is he still in sight?"

"Yes, he is just coming up opposite the carriage now," said Elizabeth. "Oh, look!" Even as she had spoken, the carriage door had swung open, and a great-coated figure had stepped down from its interior.

Sir Connor, on the sidewalk, paused. The great-coated figure advanced toward him and seemed to put to him some question. They saw Sir Connor's bonneted head shake in negation. Again the great-coated figure advanced and this time took him by the arm. Sir Connor seemed to protest and made an ineffectual attempt to break away, but the great-coated figure hustled him toward the carriage, shoved him bodily inside, and leaped in after him. The door slammed shut; then the driver immediately whipped up the horses, and the chaise shot out of the square at a pace that would have done justice to the Watsons' own John.

Sophia was wringing her hands. "Oh, Elizabeth!" she wailed. "What if Gilbert hurts Sir Connor? What if he kills him?"

Elizabeth felt a little uneasy on this score herself. Even though the plan had been hers and had worked just as she had intended, there had still been something disturbing in seeing Sir Connor pulled into Gilbert's chaise. "But why should Gilbert hurt Sir Connor?" she said, arguing as much to herself as Sophia. "Once he learns his mistake, he will quickly release him, I have no doubt. There would be no point in his carrying Sir Connor all the way to Gretna Green!"

"But he will be so angry when he learns what has happened! Oh, I do wish Sir Connor had taken a pistol with him as you suggested. At least then he might be able to defend himself if worst came to worst."

Elizabeth said that Sir Connor could no doubt defend himself even without a pistol, but she continued uneasy until a half-hour later, when a hackney chaise pulled up in front of the town house. It disgorged a slightly disheveled but very much alive Sir Connor O'Connor. He was stripped of his feminine finery, which he carried in a bundle beneath his arm, but even from the upstairs window it was possible to see that he was grinning broadly.

"It's him!" cried Sophia ungrammatically. With one accord she and Elizabeth rushed from the window and ran downstairs to admit the conquering hero.

At close range, Sir Connor's handsome countenance was seen to have suffered some slight damages in the form of an incipient black eye and a trace of blood on his lip. But his eyes were dancing, and it was evident there was nothing wrong with his spirits. "What a lark!" he said. "I haven't had that much fun since I went to Will O'Flynn's wake. Would it be possible for me to get something to drink, Miss Watson? Milling's thirsty work, and I wouldn't say 'no' to a pint of beer."

The girls took him into the parlor, and Elizabeth ordered beer for Sir Connor and tea for her and Sophia. "But you are hurt, Sir Connor," cried Sophia, catching sight of the blood on his lip for the first time. "How dreadful!"

"Not a bit of it," Sir Connor assured her. " 'Tis but a

scratch, Miss Sophia. Mr. Gilbert, now—'twas rather more than a scratch with *him.*" He chuckled. "I doubt you'll be seeing much of him in society these next few weeks. At least not till he's had a chance to recover from the worst of his injuries!"

"What happened?" said Elizabeth. "Was Gilbert very angry when he found out it was you rather than me he had abducted?"

Sir Connor burst out laughing. "Ah, that's the beauty of it, Miss Watson! He doesn't know it *wasn't* you! Listen, and I'll be telling you the way of it."

Between draughts of beer, Sir Connor described how Gilbert had leaped out of the chaise, confronted him, and suggested they take a drive together. "I told him no, I couldn't be doing that, but he was very insistent. In the end, he just grabbed me and pushed me into the chaise by force. I could have shook him off easily enough, of course, but I didn't think it was the thing to fight him too much—at least not *then.* So I let him put me in the chaise and waited to see what he'd do. He told the driver to make straight for Gretna, then turned to me and said we were off to be married and there wasn't a thing I could do about it. 'Oh, you think not, do you?' said I. Then I just waded into him with both fists." Sir Connor pantomimed this action with great gusto. "And the upshot is, I proceeded to wallop him properly."

Both Sophia and Elizabeth heartily approved this action, and Sophia said militantly that it served Gilbert right. "He deserved that and more besides, for trying to play such a dirty trick on Elizabeth," she said.

"Aye, that he did, Miss Sophia. But the best joke is, I don't think he ever realized it wasn't your sister here who was walloping him! He'll be treating you a bit more respectful after this, Miss Watson, I'm thinking!"

Sophia and Elizabeth both dissolved into helpless laughter, and it was some time before they were able to attend to the rest of Sir Connor's account. According to him, Gilbert had been largely senseless by the time he had finished administering what he considered a sufficient punishment. "So I just called to the driver to stop, got out, and caught the first hackney I saw back here. I took off me cloak and bonnet in the hackney and made meself as respectable as I could, and the driver wasn't half surprised when he got here and found his fare'd turned from a lady to a man along the way!"

Elizabeth declared that Sir Connor had acted with the utmost intrepidity and deserved a reward for his masterly handling of the situation. "Indeed, I owe you a great deal," she told him earnestly. "If you wouldn't be offended, I'd like to make you some compensation for your time and trouble."

"Nay, I couldn't be accepting any compensation," said Sir Connor grandly. " 'Twas all me pleasure." Under pressure, however, he did admit that another loan of fifty pounds would come in uncommon handy just then, certain creditors of his having become rather pressing. Elizabeth promptly gave him the fifty pounds and thanked him again for his service on her behalf. Sir Connor repeated that it was his pleasure, promised to pay back the money as soon as he was able, and took himself off with the air of a man well pleased with his night's work.

Fifteen

The immediate result of Gilbert's misadventure was to rid Elizabeth of his company for the rest of the Season. She knew it was for the rest of the Season because she received a note from him the following day, informing her that he was going into the country on a repairing lease.

Scanning through this missive with incredulous eyes, Elizabeth thought at first Gilbert was going to pass over all mention of his actions the previous night. But toward the end she came to a few sentences in which a small measure of apology was mingled with a great deal of self-justification.

"You observe, he is still trying to convince me that it is my feminine charms that attract him rather than my money," said Elizabeth in disgust, as she read this letter aloud to her sister. "He says he was so overwhelmed by my beauty that he felt he must win me by fair means or foul."

"Well, there's no doubt which of the two he chose," said Sophia. "Indeed, I wonder he cares to refer to the incident at all. But there, he's probably afraid that if he doesn't make you an apology, you will seek him out and administer another dose of what Sir Connor calls 'home brew!' "

She laughed merrily, and Elizabeth joined in her laughter. "Yes, I suppose that's possible," she said. "Although I suspect myself that Gilbert's apology has more to do with his still wanting to gain my fortune. There seems no end to the importunity of the Atwater family. The minute you think you are done with them, they pop up again in another form."

It was at this moment that Charles scratched on the door and informed Elizabeth that Lord Atwater was waiting below.

"Lord Atwater!" said Sophia.

"Lord Atwater!" echoed Elizabeth. "Whatever does *he* want?"

She looked at Charles, but he shook his head. "Couldn't say, miss. Lord Atwater merely asked if you was home, and I told him I'd look to see. Do you want me to tell him you're indisposed?"

"Yes!" urged Sophia.

"No," said Elizabeth, after a moment's consideration. "I will see Lord Atwater."

In her heart, she knew she was doing a reckless thing. If Julius had learned of her activities the night before, he might well be calling to wreak some form of revenge on behalf of his cousin. Even setting that possibility aside, there were cogent reasons why she ought to avoid him. She already knew she was vulnerable where he was concerned and inclined to cherish foolish, romantic feelings in spite of all she knew to his discredit. Yet despite this knowledge, she could not resist the urge to see him. She told herself it was merely curiosity to see how he was taking his cousin's discomfiture, but it was not curiosity alone that made her breath come quickly as she went downstairs to the drawing room.

Julius was seated on the sofa. He rose to his feet as she came in, and it struck her that his face was unusually grave. Without even waiting to exchange the usual social pleasantries, he addressed her directly. "Miss Watson, I have come to make you an apology," he said.

Elizabeth looked at him blankly. She had been so busy trying to stifle the feelings that the sight of him inspired in her breast that she honestly could not think what he might have to apologize for. "Apology?" she repeated.

"About last night," he said, "I would like to apologize for my cousin's behavior. Miss Watson, I am deeply chagrined that Gilbert should have attempted such a thing. If I had had any idea he would try anything so outrageous, so asinine, so completely inexcusable—"

"Oh, *that,*" said Elizabeth, enlightened.

"Yes, *that,*" said Julius, with bitter emphasis. "Indeed, I own myself amazed you were even willing to see me this morning. I would think that after what happened, you would regard the whole Atwater family with disgust."

Elizabeth regarded him closely. "But you had nothing to do with trying to abduct me, did you, my lord?" she asked. "I had supposed it was all Gilbert's doing—Gilbert's, and perhaps your aunt's."

She was not conscious of speaking an untruth. In fact she was not really speaking one, for though she had formerly been inclined to suspect Julius was involved in Gilbert's plot, she was suddenly certain he was not. His voice, his manner, the look in his eye—all carried sufficient assurance that his cousin's intentions had come as a shock to him. Her conscious mind might still argue that he was merely acting a part, but Elizabeth dismissed such doubts as unworthy. She *felt* he was innocent, with a conviction so strong that it amounted to certainty.

Her certainty was increased by the heat of Julius's reaction. "I? Good Lord, no!" he said. "I don't have that upon my conscience, at least. But still I am guilty in a sense, Miss Watson." He looked at her unhappily. "I knew something was in the wind. Don't you remember my mentioning it to you the other night? I could see Gilbert and my aunt were plotting something, and yet I made no attempt to discover what it was. It was not until this morning that I learned what an infamous business had been perpetrated."

He seemed so distressed that Elizabeth found herself trying to comfort him. "Ah, well, you couldn't know, my lord," she said. "It wasn't your fault."

"But I tell you I did know!" said Julius. "Or at least I suspected. I should have made it my business to investigate my cousin's affairs thoroughly as soon as my suspicions were aroused. God knows I am well enough acquainted with him, and with my aunt, too—I ought to know they are capable of any folly. When I think what you were forced to endure, it makes me almost wild."

The truth of these words was borne out by his appearance. He did indeed appear "almost wild." In an effort to soothe him, Elizabeth drew nearer and laid a hand on his arm. "But indeed, you have nothing to blame yourself for, my lord," she said. "As you say, you did warn me the other night that your cousin was planning something against me. And that, together with certain other information I received, was sufficient to put me on my guard."

Julius looked down at her searchingly. "Was it?" he said. "Well, I am very glad if I was able to help at all. But I would rather have spared you the ordeal, if I could have."

"As it happens, I *was* spared," said Elizabeth, smiling. "If you have spoken with your cousin, then you must know that he did not succeed in carrying me off to Gretna Green."

"Yes, but only because you were able to escape him," said Julius bitterly. "And it's God's own mercy that you did. Because if you hadn't, I'd have been forced to kill Gilbert instead of merely raking him over the coals."

All the while he was speaking, Elizabeth had been trying to make a decision. By the end of his speech, she found her mind was made up. "Indeed, it is not so bad as you think, my lord," she said. "Gilbert did behave very badly, but I believe he has already been sufficiently punished for his actions. Your words and some other information I received concerning his plans were enough to put me on my guard, and Gilbert did not find his would-be bride so compliant as he expected."

Julius did not actually smile, but the stern expression on his face abated a trifle at these words. "Well, if the appearance of his physiognomy this morning is anything to go by, I should say not indeed," he said. "He looked as though he had been fighting Jackson with the gloves off! I confess, I have been dying to ask how you did it. Of course Gilbert isn't the largest gentleman around, and he's hardly in fighting trim, but still I would not have expected a lady like yourself to have—er—reduced him to such straits. Do you number pugilism among your other talents?"

Elizabeth laughed. "Alas, no, though I begin to think I would do well to study the art! But it happens it was not really I who chastised your cousin last night, my lord. He only thought it was I." With these words, she set about explaining the deception that had resulted in Gilbert's carrying off Sir Connor O'Connor in her place.

By the time she was done, there were tears of laughter running down Julius's face. It was several minutes before he could get breath enough to speak. "Lord!" he said between gasps of laughter. "If only I had been there! I'd have given a thousand pounds to have seen Gilbert's face when his intended laid him out flat."

"Yes, so would I," said Elizabeth. "Sir Connor says it was very droll." She, too, was laughing, infected by Julius's hilarity and by her own retelling of the tale. He smiled down at her.

"Droll! It must have been priceless," he said. Then he leaned down and kissed her on the lips.

"Why did you do that?" demanded Elizabeth. Her laughter had died instantly at the touch of his lips. She told herself that she was very angry, but in truth her emotions were rather confused. "You had no right to kiss me!" she charged.

"I know it," said Julius. "I was merely following an impulse."

"You have these impulses far too often, my lord," said Elizabeth sternly.

A smile touched his lips. "Only when I am with you," he said. In a wistful voice he added, "Do you dislike my kissing you as much as that, Elizabeth?"

Much as Elizabeth wanted to give a strong affirmative, she could not quite bring herself to lie. She had not disliked his kissing her at all, but on the contrary had liked it very much. At that very moment, in fact, she was conscious of a strong desire to be kissed again.

But of course she could hardly admit this to Julius, any more than she could lie and say she had disliked his kissing her. Elizabeth sought to temporize. "I neither liked nor disliked it," she said primly. "I merely thought it improper."

"Yes, of course," agreed Julius. "But that is beside the point. If you do not actually dislike my kissing you—"

"I did not say I liked it, either," said Elizabeth sharply. "In fact, your kisses mean nothing to me one way or another, my lord!"

"No? Well, they mean a great deal to *me*," said Julius. There was a brief pause, during which Elizabeth found it hard to meet his eyes. Julius went on looking down at her. "I wish they meant as much to you as they do to me," he said in a quieter voice. "You know how I feel about you, Elizabeth."

"Yes," said Elizabeth, then added quickly, "At least, I know what you *say* you feel."

To her consternation, Julius pounced on this statement

at once. "What I *say* I feel," he repeated. "Do you doubt that my feelings are sincere? You doubt that I love you and want to marry you?"

His eyes were fixed on hers. For the life of her Elizabeth could not say yes, even though she did doubt his feelings or felt she ought to. Still, she found herself saying meekly, "No, I don't doubt it, my lord."

"That's good," Julius said. There was another silence, while he eyed her reflectively.

Elizabeth was unnerved by his gaze. She felt he might be going to kiss her again, or do something else equally discomfiting. In a voice she sought to make cool and calm, she said, "Indeed, I am very honored by your feelings, my lord. But it would be better that you not speak of them again. You will understand when I say there is no hope of my ever returning them."

"Indeed?" said Julius, looking at her very hard. "No hope at all?"

"None," said Elizabeth. She strove to speak the words firmly and meet his eyes squarely, but neither endeavor was a complete success. She felt instinctively that Julius was not going to take her answer as final. In desperation, she spoke the only words she could think of that would carry sufficient conviction. "There is no hope of my returning your feelings, my lord, because as it happens, my feelings are already engaged elsewhere."

Julius looked at her again very hard. "Indeed," he said. "I suppose I know what that means. Lord Steinbridge is to be the lucky man, is he?"

"Yes, he is," said Elizabeth defiantly. "I intend to marry Lord Steinbridge."

"And he is very glad to hear it," came a jubilant voice from behind her.

Elizabeth wondered with deep dismay if the butler took malicious amusement in admitting one suitor when she was being proposed to by another. She swung round to see the marquess standing in the doorway. There was a broad smile on his face as he came forward to take her hand. "Miss Watson! Do you mean it?" he asked. "You will marry me?"

There was nothing for Elizabeth to say but "yes," so she said it, but she avoided looking at Julius as she spoke. Still, she could not help glancing at him out of the corner of her eye.

There was a sardonic smile on his face as he contemplated her and the marquess. "You have my congratulations, Steinbridge," he said. "Or should I wait to congratulate you until your mother has approved the match?"

"I have no doubt Mother will approve once she has met Miss Watson," said Lord Steinbridge, sublimely unconscious of the mockery. "Have you plans for the week after the King's birthday, Miss Watson? I would like to take you to Gantley as soon as possible, so the arrangements may be made final."

Elizabeth felt as though the jaws of a trap were closing around her. "I don't know," she said weakly. "I shall have to speak to my mother and cousin and sister, and see what engagements we have for that week."

"Of course," agreed the marquess. "But even if they have engagements, I will be much surprised if they are not willing to set them aside. Few other engagements could be as important as this one, I think!"

He spoke with a pompous air that made Elizabeth avoid Julius's eye all the more. "Perhaps," she said. "But I will ask them just the same. For how long were you wishing to have me—us—visit? I know you had spoken of giving a house party at Gantley during that time, so I suppose it will be a matter of some weeks."

The marquess rubbed his chin. "I *had* spoken of giving a party," he said, "but it seems to me now that is hardly necessary. In the beginning, you know, I had thought that having other guests around would make you feel more comfortable at Gantley while you and Mother were getting to know each other. But on further reflection I have come to believe that would be unnecessary and perhaps even undesirable. I am quite certain Mother will be delighted with you, and that being the case, I would naturally prefer not to be distracted with social obligations while you are visiting."

"But I should prefer there to be a party while I am at Gantley," said Elizabeth breathlessly. "Could you not invite at least a few other people besides me and my family?"

She was conscious that Julius was looking at her fixedly, but she kept her eyes on Lord Steinbridge's face. He frowned. "I can, of course, if you really desire it," he said. "But I hardly see that it is necessary."

"Not necessary, but I *do* desire it," said Elizabeth. She could not have said how the presence of other people would make the situation any better, but instinctively she felt that to be mewed up alone at Gantley with only the marquess and his mother was a state of affairs to be avoided.

The marquess shrugged. "Very well," he said. "Of course I am willing to do anything within reason to make you happy." His tone implied that her wish to have a house party during her visit was not strictly reasonable, but that he was willing to humor it nonetheless.

Elizabeth was too relieved at having won her point to resent the marquess's tone. Her relief turned to consternation at his next words, however. "I hope you'll agree to be one of the party, Atwater," he said, turning to Julius and clasping him by the hand in turn. "In a sense all this is your doing, for you must know that up till now Miss Watson has been rather chary about committing to an engagement." He threw a smiling look at Elizabeth. "Why, if I hadn't walked in on the two of you just now and heard her declaring with her own lips she meant to marry me, I might have been tempted to think she was going to put me off indefinitely."

"Indeed," said Julius dryly.

"Indeed, yes! I assure you she has been amazingly coy. Perhaps you will recall that afternoon you walked in on us a few weeks ago, when she was telling me she needed time to make up her mind."

"Yes, I recall," said Julius, more dryly still.

"Amazing how you keep getting tangled up in our affairs," said the marquess. He laughed jovially. "But since that's the case, the least we can do is invite you to be one of the party at Gantley. You'll come, won't you?"

There was a pause before Julius said, very deliberately, "Why, surely, my lord. I wouldn't miss your party for the world."

Sixteen

In the days that followed, Elizabeth found herself far removed from that happy state of mind that should, by rights, have belonged to Lord Steinbridge's bride-to-be.

To be sure, her engagement had not yet been made official. With an apologetic air, the marquess had explained that though he considered them already as good as betrothed, he felt it would be improper to put any notice in the newspapers until his mother had given formal consent to the match. Elizabeth agreed with this. She was happy to grasp at any straw that would delay a formal publication of her engagement. It was not that she was sorry to be engaged, she assured herself. The marquess was the perfect man for her, insofar as any man could be. It was merely that the notion of being engaged to anyone was new to her, and she needed time to grow adjusted to the idea.

Yet though she was glad for the delay in having her engagement announced, she could not help being irked by the reason for the delay. It was annoying to have the marquess so deferential to his mother. Of course he was the scion of a noble family, and a man in his position had naturally to consult his relatives' opinions more than a man from a humbler walk of life, but still it was annoying. Elizabeth found herself remembering now and then how Julius had said he personally would be ashamed to have to wait to marry because he had to obtain his mother's permission.

But of course she was going to marry the marquess, not Julius Atwater. That being the case, she, too, must learn to respect the dowager marchioness's opinions. Elizabeth made up her mind to do so, but she could not help having an occasional misgiving on the subject. From various things the marquess had let slip, she had gained the impression that her ladyship had an opinion on nearly every subject, and that those opinions tended to be as decided as they were inflexible.

But that was only Elizabeth's impression, and she told herself she might well be mistaken. In spite of these self-assurances, however, she found more comfort in reflecting that the engagement had not been yet been formally announced. If worst came to worst, the whole business might yet be called off with no real harm done to anybody.

So Elizabeth thought, at least. But as the date for her visit to Gantley drew nearer, it became clear that news of her engagement had somehow leaked out in spite of her own efforts at discretion.

In her darker moods, she was inclined to blame Julius for this. She already considered him an unprincipled fortune hunter, and to imagine him a malicious gossip as well was no great stretch of the imagination. But in her heart she suspected that the news had probably been spread by her mother and Mrs. Reese-Whittington. Originally Elizabeth had hoped to keep her engagement secret from these two along with the rest of the world, but the marquess had pooh-poohed her caution, saying the need for secrecy did not extend to her own family. He had then put an end to further discussion of the subject by calling Sophia, Mrs. Watson, and Mrs. Reese-Whittington into the drawing room and telling them about the engagement himself.

Sophia had said very little, merely staring at Elizabeth wide-eyed as though she could already see a coronet on her head. The two elder ladies, however, had been volubly delighted. Elizabeth had tried with all her might to stress how important it was that the engagement be kept secret for the present, but even at the time she had suspected she was wasting her breath. Mrs. Watson and Mrs. Reese-Whittington's idea of keeping a secret was to tell it to not more than a dozen of their closest friends, after first swearing them to silence and in the process making disclosure inevitable.

"Well, why should you care?" said Sophia reasonably, when Elizabeth bewailed this state of affairs. "I have told no one myself, but I really don't see what harm it will do if Mama and Cousin Amelia have told a few people. Everyone is bound to learn sooner or later that you are to marry Lord Steinbridge. What harm can it do?"

Elizabeth could not say what harm it would do. She only knew she would rather have kept the whole matter swathed in darkest secrecy. "Lady Steinbridge has not yet given formal approval to the match," she offered weakly.

"She soon will, though, won't she?" said Sophia. "When it comes right down to it, she'll *have* to. Lord Steinbridge is over the age of consent and can marry without her approval if he so chooses. Besides, it would be infamous of her to try to stop your marrying now. Considering what has already passed between you and Lord Steinbridge—"

"Nothing has passed between us!" said Elizabeth. She blushed as Sophia looked at her in surprise. "Well, of course Lord Steinbridge and I have *spoken* of marriage," she amended. "But indeed, I should not be surprised if it came to nothing, even at this late date."

Sophia bent a penetrating look upon her. "Elizabeth,

that doesn't sound like you," she said. "Do you not *want* to marry Lord Steinbridge?"

"I do," protested Elizabeth feebly. "I do want to marry him. But not if his mother doesn't approve of my doing so, of course."

"Well, that does not sound like you either! Why should you care whether his mother approves or not? It makes me quite impatient to hear the way you go on about Lady Steinbridge and her having the final say about everything. She sounds a right harridan to me, for all she is a marchioness."

Since Elizabeth secretly shared this opinion, she could hardly dispute it. She contented herself with saying defensively, "Well, *you* won't marry without *Mama's* consent."

Sophia shook her head. "Yes, but the cases are not the same, Elizabeth," she said. "Of course we both know most of Mama's objections are nonsensical, but she does have a point in saying that Philip would have difficulty in supporting a wife in his present position. However, I think she is starting to change that opinion." Sophia's lips curved into a smile. "She asked me the other day if I still wrote to Philip. That was after I danced three times with Sir Connor at the Newberrys' party. And when I told her that of course I still wrote to Philip, that I considered myself engaged to him, she said she might be brought to think of the match if only he could get some kind of preferment."

"That's wonderful news, Sophia!" said Elizabeth. "It sounds as though we have almost won *that* battle. Why, if all else fails, I can purchase an estate that has a living attached, set Philip up as the local clergyman, and have you married with all speed."

Sophia eyed her curiously. "But surely that is unnecessary, Elizabeth," she said. "Lord Steinbridge must have a number of livings at his disposal. Not that I mean to hint at such a thing, only it would be strange if you had to buy an estate merely to give Philip employment."

"Yes, of course," said Elizabeth, covered with confusion once more. She wondered why this solution had never occurred to her. Of course a wealthy nobleman like Lord Steinbridge would have any number of livings in his possession. No doubt he could easily obtain preferment for an up-and-coming young clergyman.

Yet somehow the idea had never crossed her mind. Elizabeth told herself it was because she had been so long the head of the Watson household that she was unused to relying on anyone else. But she could not help feeling that it was a trifle unnatural, in her position, not to look to her betrothed for help and support.

Of course Lord Steinbridge would be glad to provide help and support if she asked for it. Elizabeth felt assured on this score, and she told herself it was yet another good reason why she ought to marry him. Not that she needed another reason, of course. *And in any case, I'm already engaged to him,* Elizabeth told herself. *It's too late to back out now.* But this consideration did strangely little to ease her state of mind.

Betrothed she was, however, at least unofficially. Seeing that this was the case, Elizabeth sought to look on the bright side. Once she was married to the marquess, she would be able to help Sophia and Mr. Arthur to be married also. She would be able to turn her present house in town over to her mother and Mrs. Reese-Whittington, an arrangement that both ladies had hinted would be very acceptable to them. She would be able to do a great deal of good as a leader in society and the co-owner of virtually unlimited wealth. And she would be free once and for all of Julius Atwater, who had been a thorn in her side ever since she had come to town and who was still performing that function admirably in spite of the fact that her engagement to the Marquess of Steinbridge was now common knowledge.

Elizabeth had supposed Julius would avoid her once he knew her to be affianced to Lord Steinbridge. Certainly she did not imagine he really meant to accept the marquess's invitation to make up one of the house party at Gantley. She reasoned that if he were truly in love with her as he claimed, then nothing could have been more painful than attending such an affair. But a few casual questions put to the marquess elicited the information that Julius had reinforced his verbal consent with a written one, saying he would be pleased to make up one of the party at Gantley. It only went to prove, as Elizabeth reflected bitterly to herself, that all his talk about love was mere whitewashing. He was merely after her money, and love had nothing to do with it.

In truth, Elizabeth was feeling particularly bitter on this score. She had just had something very like a quarrel with the marquess on the subject of money. They had gone out driving together one afternoon the week before she was to leave for Gantley, and their talk had turned to a recently announced engagement between the middle-aged widow of a wealthy brewer and a young viscount known to be embarrassed as to finances.

"Surely Mrs. Tigg cannot imagine Lord Ogilvie is in love with her," said Elizabeth scornfully. "Oh, I know he makes a great pretence of devotion, but it's perfectly obvious where the real attraction lies. It's cream-pot love, pure and simple. If she were suddenly penniless, I'll wager he would soon find a way to wriggle out of the engagement."

The marquess regarded her reprovingly. "I think you are unnecessarily harsh in your judgment, my dear," he said. "In my opinion, Lord Ogilvie is quite justified in looking after his worldly estate. He is a viscount, you know, and a member of one of our oldest families. A man in such a position has a responsibility not only to himself but to future generations."

"But that cannot excuse his marrying for money alone," argued Elizabeth. "Surely you do not think a title and family position excuse greed?"

The marquess smiled indulgently. "Certainly not! But I think it is necessary in this case to make a distinction between greed and prudence. Perhaps there is nothing like love between Lord Ogilvie and Mrs. Tigg, but I have no doubt he has a just appreciation of her merits."

"Yes, her chief merit being her sixty thousand pounds," said Elizabeth tartly.

The marquess looked displeased at this interjection, but answered patiently, "Yes, certainly that is a merit. Mrs. Tigg could hardly expect to make such a match if she had no fortune. To my mind, there is nothing wrong in Lord Ogilvie wishing his bride to come to her marriage with a substantial portion. It is no more than any prudent and reasonable man would expect."

Elizabeth regarded him a moment before she finally spoke. "Indeed," she said. "And that being the case, I suppose *my* fortune was a consideration when you made up your mind to propose to me?"

The marquess looked surprised at this question. "Well, of course it was," he said. "Although naturally it was not my *main* consideration. You know my financial situation is rather different from Lord Ogilvie's!"

He laughed jovially at this, but Elizabeth did not join in his laughter. "You may be a wealthier man than Lord Ogilvie, but still it seems you expect your bride to come accompanied by a substantial portion," she said, "Tell me, my lord: if I were suddenly deprived of my money, would you still wish to marry me?"

The marquess looked annoyed. "I do not see what that question has to do with anything," he said shortly. "You have not been deprived of your fortune, so what I would do in such a case is entirely beside the point."

Elizabeth made no reply to this, but the marquess seemed to feel there was something critical in her silence. He embarked on a long, involved speech in which he sought to justify the prudence of a man wishing his future wife to be endowed with a comfortable portion. "Of course I am not condoning fortune hunting, or anything like it," he assured Elizabeth. "Indeed, it gives me great pain to see such persons as Sir Connor O'Connor permitted in decent society."

"And what exception have you to take with Sir Connor O'Connor?" inquired Elizabeth in a silky voice. "He is no worse a man than Lord Ogilvie, whom you were defending only a short time before. Indeed, to my mind, he is infinitely superior."

The marquess looked amused. "That only shows you are still unfamiliar with the ways of London society," he told Elizabeth. "There can be no comparison between the two men. Indeed, my dear, I have often thought of giving you a hint about your—well, I can only call it your predilection for Sir Connor's society. I meet him at your house nearly every time I come there, and I notice you danced with him twice at the Beckers' masquerade last night. It does not look well, your spending so much time in his company."

"No?" said Elizabeth, her voice silkier than ever.

Lord Steinbridge shook his head gravely. "No, indeed! I have tolerated it these many weeks only because I felt I had no right to do anything else. But now that we are engaged, I trust I have some rights in the matter. Please do me the favor of breaking off the acquaintance immediately. As I say, it does not look well, your spending so much time in his company, and if word of such a thing were to reach Mother's ears it might prejudice her against you."

Elizabeth had to count to ten before she felt it safe to

respond to this speech. "Indeed," she said through clenched teeth. "Well, I am afraid I shall have to risk your mother's prejudice, my lord. Sir Connor is a friend of mine, and I could not think of cutting his acquaintance for no better reasons than you are able to give me."

The marquess regarded her openmouthed for a full minute before he could find his voice. "You refuse to obey my wishes?" he said in a dumbfounded voice.

"I do," said Elizabeth, her own voice uncompromising. "Your objections don't seem reasonable to me, my lord."

"But I tell you the fellow's nothing but a fortune hunter!"

"Because he would like to marry a rich wife? But that only makes him prudent, according to your own words, my lord. Indeed, in that respect it seems to me that there is little to choose from between you, Sir Connor, and every other gentleman I have met since coming to London."

There was a long silence after this. When at last the marquess spoke again, he sounded as though he were having difficulty keeping his temper. "You are pleased to make game of me," he said. "Of course I know you do not mean what you say. We will speak no more of it at present."

He had then changed the subject and begun speaking of the King's latest bout of illness. Elizabeth had willingly allowed the subject of Sir Connor to drop, but the argument had put her in a bad mood. Her mood was not improved when she reached home and was informed by the butler that Julius was waiting for her in the drawing room.

"For heaven's sake!" she said. "Tell him that I—" She stopped. "No, on second thought, perhaps I'd better see him."

It had just occurred to her that it would be a relief to give someone a piece of her mind. And who could be a better recipient for that purpose than Julius Atwater? She had been wanting to tell him her opinion of him ever since coming to London. For some reason or other she had never gotten around to doing it, but the present occasion seemed perfect. Eyes flashing, Elizabeth strode toward the drawing room, already anticipating what she would say.

Julius was, as usual, seated on the sofa. He rose to his feet as she came in, a smile on his lips, but Elizabeth was not going to be sidetracked by civilities. "Why are *you* here?" she demanded without preamble.

Julius seemed a trifle surprised by this unconventional greeting, but responded equably, "Why is a moth drawn to a flame?"

Elizabeth glared at him. "That is not answering my question," she said. "Indeed, there is no point in your coming here, my lord."

"You must let me be the judge of that," he said gravely. "Just to see and talk to you is point enough as far as I am concerned."

He was looking at her as he spoke, with a tenderness in his eyes that only further inflamed Elizabeth's temper. Of course it was not real tenderness. It was all pretense, as she knew very well. She drew a deep, uneven breath. "Gammon," she said. "I am not quite seven, you know, my lord. Let us drop this nonsense once and for all."

He looked at her with what appeared to be genuine puzzlement. "I don't think I quite understand," he said. "What nonsense are you talking about?"

"This nonsense about your being in love with me," said Elizabeth. It felt wonderful to speak the words aloud, and she went on, her voice growing louder as she vented her pent-up spleen. "I know perfectly well you don't care a fig for me. I knew it from the start. It is only my fortune that interests you—the money I inherited from your uncle. If I were still penniless and living in Cheltenham, you would never have thought of falling in love with me or of asking me to marry you."

Julius said nothing. He only looked at her so long and hard that, in spite of herself, her eyes finally dropped to the floor. "Do you really believe that?" he asked.

"I do," said Elizabeth. She tried to say it defiantly, but her voice came out a little shaky.

"No wonder you seemed to despise me," he said. "If you could believe that . . ." His voice trailed off, and he seemed to be thinking deeply.

"I'm sorry," said Elizabeth in a whisper. She *was* sorry, though she could not have said what she was sorry about. It was merely the truth she had spoken, as she assured herself, and it was better for both of them that she had spoken it. Julius must learn he was wasting his time in pursuing her. It was intolerable that he should pretend to love her, when his real feelings were more akin to hatred.

Yet in spite of these assurances, Elizabeth felt a hint of doubt creeping in. There was something in Julius's face that gave her grave misgivings. It was not so much that he looked hurt and shocked; she had expected that, knowing his abilities as an actor. But this was something deeper than mere looks. It was something Elizabeth could *feel*—a sense of anguish that emanated from him like a physical ache. "Julius?" she said uncertainly.

His eyes met hers with an impact that made her wince. "Elizabeth," he said, "you can't believe all I care about is your money. Do you?"

His voice was low and tense. Elizabeth felt the absurdest desire to say that of course she didn't believe it. But her doubts were real, and she found herself voicing them as though it were a perfectly natural thing to do. "How can I know what you feel?" she cried. "How can I know what anyone really feels for me? Ever since I inherited your uncle's money, I have been courted and feted and flattered by gentlemen who would never have looked at me twice if I were still plain Miss Watson without a sou to my name. They say they want to marry me, but all they really want is my money. And because English law gives my property to my husband the instant the marriage vows are pronounced, I have no means of telling who may be sincere and who may not be."

Julius had listened to this diatribe in absorbed silence. At its conclusion he nodded slowly. "No doubt," he said. "I have often thought the English marriage laws unjust in their treatment of the wife's property. But Elizabeth, if you suspect my sincerity in this regard, I can very easily prove your suspicions unfounded. Only get rid of your property, and see if I do not show myself as eager as ever to marry you."

"Get rid of my property?" repeated Elizabeth blankly.

"Yes, get rid of it. Settle it on your mother or your sister—found an orphanage or a home for retired sailors—lose it all at faro or *rouge-et-noir.* It makes no difference to me. Just get rid of it, so you can see how sincere I am when I say it is you and you alone that I want."

"But I can't get rid of my property!" said Elizabeth in a rising voice. "Besides, I wouldn't want to. Why should I have to get rid of it merely to satisfy myself that you—that *someone*—really cares for me?"

Julius nodded sympathetically. "It does seem rather hard," he said. "Perhaps there is some legal way of tying up the money so that only you may have access to it after your marriage. At any rate, I'm sure it could be arranged so that you receive pin money out of my estate equal to the income you receive now, while your own income was settled wholly on any future children you might have. That would amount to the same thing and leave you quite independent."

Elizabeth looked at him for a long moment. He appeared to be perfectly serious. "I see," she said. "You seem to have thought of everything, my lord—or almost everything. But there is one thing you seem to be forgetting."

"And what is that?"

"That I am engaged to marry Lord Steinbridge."

Julius smiled wryly. "No, I haven't forgotten that," he said. "But I am taking heart in remembering that your engagement is only provisional." He looked steadily at Elizabeth. "I can't hope to offer you all that Steinbridge has. I'll never have his title, or his station, or the half of his wealth. But there is one thing I do have that I'll wager he doesn't, and that is a heart that is wholly yours. I'd be willing to sacrifice every earthly consideration in order to win you."

Elizabeth was silent. Julius took her hand in his. "You're an intelligent woman, Elizabeth," he said softly. "The most intelligent woman it's ever been my fortune to know. I don't expect you to break your engagement merely because of what I have said today. All I want is for you to think about it, and consider what both Steinbridge and I have to offer you. In the end, I feel sure you will arrive at a just valuation of our respective merits."

Elizabeth felt tears pricking behind her eyes. Making an effort to show spirit, she responded, "And what if I should decide I value Lord Steinbridge's merits above your own?"

Julius smiled. "If you can honestly decide that, then I'll be quite content to see you marry him," he said. He turned as though to go, then turned around again.

"In case you're wondering, I'm not going to kiss you," he said. "Not as long as you are engaged to Steinbridge— even if it is only a *provisional* engagement." With these words, he turned and left the room. And though there were a dozen cutting things Elizabeth might have said in reply, not one of them occurred to her until it was much too late.

Seventeen

Elizabeth was in a defiant mood when she set off for Gantley on the tenth of June.

She had been in a defiant mood ever since her conversation with Julius a week before. "What right has he to give me an ultimatum?" she demanded of herself, and reflected that it was typical Atwater presumption for him to suppose she would even consider breaking her engagement with the marquess in order to marry a reprobate like him. Of course she was not going to marry Julius Atwater. Lord Steinbridge was a good, principled, intelligent man whose tastes were perfectly in accord with hers. Julius was a superficial, mercenary wretch—well, perhaps not a *mercenary* wretch—and perhaps he *had* written an intelligent and well-reasoned speech or two, which would show he was not strictly superficial, either.

In fact, as Elizabeth discovered, the matter was not so strictly black and white as she was trying to make it. The longer she looked at it, the more it seemed to blur into shades of gray. The marquess had spoken of her fortune as a factor in his choosing her as wife, while Julius had signified he was willing to take her without a penny. That seemed to mean something—*if* Julius were speaking the truth—but was he? And after all, was it so very bad to have an eye to worldly advantage in choosing one's future spouse? She herself might well have been influenced by the marquess's wealth and station as much as by his morals and manners in choosing him as her future husband.

Elizabeth argued these questions back and forth for a time without coming to any satisfactory conclusion. She kept remembering the autocratic way the marquess had instructed her to break off her friendship with Sir Connor. Of course he was in no position to insist on it now, but what would happen after they were married? Would he think he could order her personal affairs as if she were a slave? The very thought made Elizabeth's anger rise.

But of course he does not know how much Sir Connor has done for me, she reasoned with herself. *If he knew, he might take a different view of the friendship.* Yet when she tried to imagine telling the marquess what role Sir Connor had played in her personal affairs, she found she shrank from the idea. She felt instinctively certain he would disapprove of what she had done. He would not laugh as Julius had done and say he would have given a thousand pounds to have witnessed Gilbert's discomfiture.

But even so, that did not mean Julius was the better man. Certainly it did not give him the right to make ultimatums, or to sneer at her engagement with Lord Steinbridge as conditional. Elizabeth clung firmly to this idea amid the turmoil of her thoughts. Thus it was that her mood was decidedly defiant when she finally stepped out of the carriage in front of the looming Baroque bulk of Gantley.

Sophia, who had preceded her out of the carriage, was regarding the vast building with wide eyes. "My, but it's big," she said. "It didn't look so big in the guidebook."

"No," agreed Elizabeth. She found her defiance giving way to nervousness in the face of this evidence of the marquess's wealth and position. Still, mere worldly wealth and position did not make him one ounce better than any other man, as Elizabeth assured herself. Gathering the shreds of her defiance about her once more, she remarked with affected composure, "It *is* very large, but you know the guidebook said it is not so big as Blenheim or Chatsworth. I daresay it is not so intimidating inside as out."

This proved to be mere wishful thinking, however. The entrance hall into which she and her relations were presently ushered was large, lofty, and oppressively grand. Mrs. Watson gazed upon all the gilt and splendor without saying a word, and even the normally chatty Mrs. Reese-Whittington seemed ill at ease as the butler ushered them into a reception room chilly with marble and adorned with a bewildering array of classical statuary. It was a sumptuous room, but there seemed nowhere to sit unless one were willing to perch on a windowsill or share a pedestal with a statue. Elizabeth found herself wondering where the marquess and his mother were. Surely they must appear soon to make their guests welcome. But the minutes ticked by without anyone appearing, while the Watsons and Mrs. Reese-Whittington stood uncomfortably about, making halfhearted conversation about the events of their recent journey.

At last, nearly a full hour after their arrival, the marquess appeared in the doorway. He was alone, and there was an apologetic smile on his face. "Do forgive me," he said. "I just received word that you were here. Mother has been rather unwell, and what with one thing and another our household has been rather disordered."

Mrs. Watson and Mrs. Reese-Whittington made understanding murmurs, and Sophia said sympathetically that she hoped the Dowager Lady Steinbridge was not very ill. Elizabeth alone said nothing. She was glad to see the marquess, and sorry to hear his mother was ill, but her internment in the reception room had depressed her. She wanted nothing so much as to flee the whole cold, formal, inhospitable house.

She did manage to summon up a smile as Lord Steinbridge came forward to take her hand, but when he raised it to his lips she found herself thinking of how Julius had refused to kiss her the last time they met. As soon as she decently could, she snatched back her hand, fighting an urge to blush.

Mrs. Reese-Whittington, meanwhile, was asking in a voice of concern whether the dowager marchioness would be well enough to appear at dinner. "Indeed, I hope so," said the marquess, looking anxious. "But yes, I am sure she will be. I know she is most eager to meet all of you." He spoke generally to all the ladies, but his eyes rested on Elizabeth with a meaningful expression.

Elizabeth summoned up another feeble smile. She was relieved when the marquess's steward appeared and informed them their rooms were ready. *I will feel better once I have washed and changed,* she told herself, hoping with all her might it would be so.

She did feel better after she had washed and changed into an *eau-de-Nil* lutestring dinner dress with a lace tucker. She still felt a trifle nervous, but that might have been attributable to the decor of her room. The windows were hung with heavy draperies of plum-colored velvet that seemed to soak up what little sunlight they admitted, and the bed was adorned with matching draperies and crowned with clusters of funereal-looking plumes. The maid who had helped her dress had lighted a fire to drive off the worst of the room's chill, but the chimney smoked so badly that she had been forced to extinguish it immediately, and altogether the room had an inhospitable atmosphere. Elizabeth drew her shawl about her shoulders with a shiver. She could not help wondering if the dowager marchioness, in assigning her this particular room, had been aware of its shortcomings.

But of course there must be thirty or forty bedchambers in this house, she reminded herself. *Her ladyship cannot be expected to remember all the ones that have smoking chimneys.*

Still, as Elizabeth readied herself to go down and meet her future mother-in-law, she found herself feeling distinctly apprehensive. It did not help to remember that Julius might be a witness to their meeting. She wished she had asked to meet the dowager marchioness privately before they had to encounter each other in company. But it was already arranged that the party was to meet in the statuary room before going in to dinner, and there was something about the atmosphere of Gantley that made Elizabeth reluctant to meddle with its arrangements.

Still, that's nonsense, she told herself. *If I marry Lord Steinbridge, then this will be my house, too, and I would expect to have some say in its arrangements. I'll send a message to him right now and see if it can be managed.*

Accordingly, she sat down at her dressing table and dashed off a hasty note to the marquess, asking if a private meeting between her and the dowager might be arranged before dinner. A passing maidservant agreed to carry it to Lord Steinbridge and returned within a few minutes, saying his lordship would be pleased to meet Miss Watson at the dowager's rooms if she would be so kind as to follow.

"I do hope Lord Steinbridge was not much put out by my message," said Elizabeth, as she followed the maid along the corridor. Once more her defiance was dwindling away, and she was beginning to feel she had done a reckless thing in meddling with the Steinbridges' affairs.

"Oh, no, miss, his lordship wasn't put out at all by your note," the girl assured her. "In fact, he seemed kind of relieved." Elizabeth was inclined to doubt this, but when she finally reached the doorway where the marquess stood waiting, his first words reassured her.

"Your message was most opportune, my dear," he told

Elizabeth. "It happens that Mother is feeling too unwell to go down to dinner this evening. It will suit her much better to meet you here in her rooms. Just a brief meeting, of course, since she is still feeling indisposed."

"Oh," said Elizabeth faintly. "If her ladyship is unwell, perhaps it would be better if we postponed the meeting altogether. I would not want to discommode her."

The marquess's jaw took on a very firm look. "I'm sure it will not discommode her if we stay only a few minutes. I'll just slip in first and tell her you're here." Not giving Elizabeth time to argue, he opened the door and went inside, pulling it shut behind him.

Even with the door shut, however, Elizabeth could not help hearing a good part of the conversation that ensued.

"It's you, is it, Gilfroy?" said a querulous voice that Elizabeth supposed to be the dowager marchioness's. "I hope you haven't come to argue with me any more about going downstairs tonight. It's absolutely out of the question. I'm feeling very poorly."

"Of course you must not get up if you are feeling unwell, Mama," was the marquess's soothing answer. "But I knew you were eager to meet Miss Watson, and so I have brought her up to talk with you a few minutes before we go downstairs."

"Well, you needn't have done so on my account," was the dowager's ungracious reply. "You know I still don't half approve of the match, Gilfroy. There's not a gel in the kingdom you couldn't have married if you wanted to. It would be much more suitable if you offered for Lady Madeleine Rivers, or one of Lord Tarlington's daughters—"

"You know we have been into all that before, Mother," said the marquess with a note of iron in his voice. "It is Miss Watson I wish to marry. Of course her family is not so illustrious as Lady Madeleine's, but still it is quite respectable."

The marchioness made a sound like a snort. "She's rich," she said. "That's all I can see in her favor. And even then I can't see that heiresses are so scarce but what you had to choose one who's a virtual nobody. I suppose she's a beauty, eh? If a gel's a beauty, it never fails but you men lose your heads completely over her. But beauty ain't everything, and I still think you might have considered what was due your position before you went proposing to a Miss Watson nobody's ever heard of."

Here the marquess lowered his voice, so that Elizabeth was unable to hear his reply. But it was easy to guess the gist of it, for the marchioness said irritably, "Don't be a fool, Gilfroy. She may have written a book, but it's not a book *I* ever heard of. Besides, writing books isn't a proper business for a woman. Look at Caro Lamb and what a scandal she made with that *Glenarvon* business."

Again, the marquess's reply to this speech was inaudible. But it seemed to reconcile the dowager to the idea of meeting Elizabeth, for she said ungraciously, "Very well. If you insist, Gilfroy. Bring her in, and let's get it over with."

When the marquess presently emerged from the bedroom, he found Elizabeth standing with her arms folded across her chest, her eyes dangerously bright. He paid no mind to these warning signals, however, being intent on other things. "Mother is ready to receive you now," he told her. "Come in, and I'll introduce you."

Elizabeth felt a strong urge to resist as the marquess took her arm and drew her into the room. Even before coming to Gantley she had suspected that she and her future mother-in-law were not going to hit it off, and the conversation she had just overheard had made her certain of it. But was it the marquess's fault if his mother would have preferred him to offer for another woman? Elizabeth acknowledged to herself that it was not. She also reminded herself that the marquess had defended her in the teeth of his mother's objections. The least she could do was to humor his wishes now. Nevertheless, it was with extreme reluctance that she accompanied the marquess into his mother's bedchamber.

The dowager marchioness was ensconced in a great four-poster bed, propped up by a dozen lace-covered pillows. Her face was thin and wrinkled and bore a notably spiteful expression in spite of the fact her eyes were closed. She opened them as Elizabeth approached the bed and surveyed her without enthusiasm. "So you're Miss Watson, eh?" she said.

"Yes," said Elizabeth, curtsying politely. "I am very pleased to meet you, ma'am."

The marchioness eyed her a moment longer, then shut her eyes again. *"Not* a beauty," she said distinctly. "Gilfroy, I feel one of my spells coming on. Send one of the servants after Dr. Havilland, and have Susan bring me some hartshorn and water."

"Of course, Mother," said the marquess. He hastened to ring the bell and relay his mother's instructions to the servant. Elizabeth did not linger to watch this business, however. She was already halfway down the hall when the marquess finally caught up with her.

"There you are," he said. "Why did you not wait for me, Miss Watson? I only had to attend to Mother's needs, and then I would have been with you."

"I saw no point in lingering where I was not wanted," said Elizabeth, not pausing in her progress down the hall.

The marquess fell into pace beside her. "I am sorry if Mother was not so hospitable as could have been desired," he said. "When one of her spells is upon her, she tends to be rather—ahem—short in her speech."

"So I gathered," said Elizabeth. "Still, what speech she had was very much to the point."

The marquess walked on a step or two in silence. "Mother prides herself on her frankness," he said at last.

"I hope—I do hope you weren't offended by her saying what she did."

"That I wasn't a beauty?" said Elizabeth. "Or that she would rather you married Lady Madeleine Rivers or one of Lord Tarlington's daughters? I'm afraid I couldn't help overhearing your conversation beforehand, my lord."

The marquess reddened slightly. "You mustn't let that offend you," he said. "As I said, Mother prides herself on her frankness. Of course she would rather I had married one of the ladies you mention."

"Why 'of course?' " inquired Elizabeth.

The marquess looked surprised. "Well, because they are of high and noble birth," he said. "I should think that went without saying."

"Does it?" said Elizabeth. She stopped abruptly, turning to face the marquess. "It seems to me that we have been letting a number of things go without saying these past few weeks, my lord. All of a sudden I have a desire to say them and get them out in the open."

"Of course, if you wish," said the marquess, looking harried. "But cannot it wait until after dinner? It's only a few minutes of seven now, and—"

"This will take only a few minutes. Let us have it out now, please, and then we can both be easy."

"But we can't discuss our personal affairs here in the hallway," protested the marquess. "Really, it would be better if we waited until after dinner."

"If you don't want to discuss our affairs in the hall, then let us go into the library. There doesn't appear to be anyone here." Elizabeth stepped into the large paneled room with its rows of glass-covered bookcases. The marquess followed her reluctantly and took care to shut the door behind them.

"Now what was it you wanted to discuss?" he said, glancing at his watch in a pointed manner. "I do hope you will hurry. I dislike keeping my guests waiting."

"You did not mind keeping at least four of your guests waiting this afternoon," reminded Elizabeth.

The marquess frowned. "That was unavoidable," he said. "Mother had one of her spells right after the servants brought word that you had arrived. I had to get her to her rooms and call her maid before I could leave her."

Elizabeth smiled ironically. "I'll wager I know what brought on her spell," she said. "But never mind that. The first thing I'd like to discuss is this business of my not being of high and noble birth. It seems to me that if you feel as you do, my lord, you would do better to choose a bride whose birth suits you and your mother better than mine."

The marquess, who had been looking wary, smiled condescendingly at these words. "Oh, my dear," he said, "I can understand that Mother's remark would rankle. But you really mustn't let it disturb you. You know a woman always takes her husband's station when she marries, whether it be higher or lower than that she is born to. In this case, you will take mine, and I flatter myself that once you have become Lady Steinbridge there will be none who dare criticize you, whatever your own birth may have been."

Elizabeth looked at him steadily. "But why did you choose *me* to become Lady Steinbridge?" she said. "You concede that my birth is not what you would prefer."

The marquess sighed. "Must we go into this again?" he said. "I chose you because you are a lovely, talented, well-principled young woman who will, in my opinion, make me a most admirable wife."

"Only because of those things?" said Elizabeth, still regarding him steadily. "You say nothing about love, I notice."

The marquess smiled. "Is that it?" he said. "Of course women are romantic creatures, but I had supposed you were above that kind of thing. However, if you insist on my spelling it out—yes, of course I love you. Indeed, it would not be too much to say that I am 'in love with you,' as the expression commonly goes. The very fact of my proposing to you in the face of Mother's wishes should show you that."

"It would seem to," agreed Elizabeth. "But still I can't help wondering if there might be other factors involved as well. Tell me, would you consent to marry me if I had no fortune?"

The marquess looked exasperated. "We discussed all this the other day," he said.

"No, we did not discuss it the other day," said Elizabeth. "I brought the subject up, but you refused to discuss it."

"Well, I can only say to you what I said then, that the question has no bearing on the present situation."

"But it does have a bearing," said Elizabeth. "You know I have had several other proposals besides yours, my lord. One of the gentlemen who proposed to me said he would be willing to settle all my personal fortune on my future children, and to give me pin money equal to my present income out of his own estate as part of the marriage settlements. And I wondered if you were willing to do the same."

The marquess stared at her, his mouth open. "Ridiculous," he said at last. "You must be joking. No man would consent to such a settlement—no man who was in his right senses, at any rate."

"I don't believe this man was joking," said Elizabeth. "And I believe he was perfectly in his senses at the time—at least as much in his senses as a man who was really in love with me could ever be."

"Ridiculous," said the marquess again. "In any case, your theoretical gentleman's sanity and motivation are beside the point. You surely did not expect I would consent to such a settlement myself?"

"No, I didn't expect it, my lord. In fact, I was pretty sure you would say just what you have said. That being the case, I am afraid I have no choice but to break our engagement."

Again the marquess stared at her openmouthed. "You are overwrought," he said. "Of course you cannot mean what you say. Why, Mother has given her consent to our marrying!"

"Not a very enthusiastic consent," said Elizabeth. "I am sure she would not be heartbroken if I were to call the whole business off."

"But you cannot do that! Why, the engagement is to be announced at dinner this evening. I have it all arranged."

"What a mercy I insisted on talking to you before dinner, then," said Elizabeth affably. "You will be spared the trouble of contradicting yourself."

The marquess's jaw tightened. "This is all nonsense," he said. "Of course you will marry me, my dear. I have already had the marriage settlements drawn up, and the notice is ready to go out to the newspapers. This is merely nerves—nerves and hysteria."

Elizabeth eyed him coldly. "I have never been less hysterical in my life," she said. "I am speaking the simple truth, my lord. I—will—not—marry—you. Do you understand? I don't know how I can make it any more clear than that."

"What's clear to me is that you are hysterical," retorted the marquess. "It is as I have already told you. The engagement is to be announced tonight at dinner, and it's too late for you to change your mind."

"I am sorry to spoil your arrangements, but the engagement is *not* going to be announced tonight," said Elizabeth. "If you dare tell people we are engaged in spite of what I have just said, I will deny it."

"No, you won't," said the marquess. He had clearly

gotten over the shock of Elizabeth's refusal, and he even managed to smile as he went on speaking. "I know very well you have no intention of really breaking our engagement. This is merely hysteria, as I said before. Just you come downstairs with me, and eat your dinner, and—"

"I won't!" said Elizabeth, now truly nettled by his manner. "Have the goodness to ring for my carriage immediately. If you insist on making a fool of yourself, it shall not be with my connivance. I don't intend to stay here any longer and argue with you."

Grim-lipped, the marquess reached for the bell rope. When a servant arrived in response to the summons, however, the orders he gave were the very reverse of what Elizabeth expected. "Ned, I want you to carry word to the stables that no horses or carriages are to leave tonight," he told the servant. "None, do you hear? If any of the guests request their carriages, the men are to tell them politely that they cannot have them. And tell the men they have my authority to use force, if necessary, to keep any carriage from being taken out tonight."

"Yes, my lord," said the servant. He cast a wondering look at Elizabeth, then bowed and left the room.

"You see, my dear," said the marquess, as soon as the servant had gone, "I do not intend to have my plans spoiled by a childish fit of nerves. I have no doubt you will be glad later that I have acted as I have, when you have recovered your tone of mind."

Elizabeth said nothing but merely stared at him. He smiled at her indulgently. "You will forgive me for being a trifle peremptory," he said. "But it's as well you should know from the beginning that I'm not a man to brook any nonsense."

"How dare you?" said Elizabeth, in a voice choked with anger. "How *dare* you prevent me from leaving?"

"Now, my dear, don't be melodramatic. You really must see this is for the best. Just come down with me and have your dinner, and when you have eaten you will feel better." He tried to take Elizabeth's arm, but she jerked it away from him. He drew away from her with an offended air. "Very well," he said. "If you don't come down with me now, you can stay here until you've got the better of your fit of temper. It makes no difference to me. I'll tell the servants to put dinner back half an hour, and I'll come back then to see if you're in a more reasonable frame of mind." Removing the key from the door, he left the room and shut it behind him. Before Elizabeth could divine his intention, she heard the key grating as he locked the door from the outside.

Elizabeth was so angry that for a moment she could do nothing but think what a satisfaction it would have been to hit the marquess over the head with some heavy object. Her thoughts soon took a more practical turn, however. *I must think what is best to do,* she told herself. *It may be I cannot prevent Lord Steinbridge from announcing our engagement, but I'm damned if I'm going to let him lock me up like a naughty child.*

When she began to examine her prison, however, she realized it was more secure than she had anticipated. The door was a solid oak-paneled affair that seemed calculated to withstand the assault of an army, while the windows gave on a sheer drop of some thirty feet onto a stone-flagged terrace. Going to the bell rope, Elizabeth jerked it several times in quick succession. Alas, it brought no response. The marquess had apparently given orders to his servants not to answer it. It appeared her only hope was to pound on the door and shout for help.

With luck Mama or Sophia or Cousin Amelia will hear me and come to investigate, Elizabeth told herself. *What a tyrannical, conceited ass Lord Steinbridge is! He must be mad to think he can treat me this way.*

But though Elizabeth pounded on the door until her fists were sore and shouted until she was hoarse, no one came. With sinking heart, she concluded that the other guests were already assembled for dinner in the statuary room, which was not only on a lower floor than the library but in another wing of the house altogether. She gained some comfort in recalling that Lord Steinbridge could not actually compel her to marry him; he could only keep her here while he announced their engagement and then force her to undergo the annoyance of having to contradict him. But her ire was up, and it went against the grain to let him think he had scored even this small victory over her.

"Bloody tyrant," Elizabeth swore aloud. "I may not be able to get out, but I'm damned if I'll sit here calmly waiting for him to unlock the door." Taking up a bust of Socrates that stood beside the sofa, she heaved it through the nearest window.

It made a satisfying crash. Elizabeth picked up another bust and prepared to send it after the first one. But before she could do so, she heard a voice from the terrace below exclaim, "What the hell?" in tones of considerable astonishment.

Elizabeth rushed to the window. Peering out, she saw a gentleman standing on the terrace below. He was staring up at the library window with a lighted cigar in his hand, and even in the deepening twilight she could see he was the man of all others she would have wished to see. "Julius!" she exclaimed.

"Elizabeth?" said Julius in a dumbfounded voice. "Is that you?"

"Yes, it's I," said Elizabeth. "Oh, Julius, I *am* glad to see you."

There was a silence while Julius considered this. "That's why you just tried to brain me with a bust of Plato, no doubt," he remarked at last, in a conversational tone.

Elizabeth gave a weak giggle. "Actually it was a bust

of Socrates," she said. "And I wasn't trying to brain you, Julius. I didn't know anybody was out there."

"I see," said Julius politely.

"No, you don't," contradicted Elizabeth. "But I've no time to explain it now. Julius, would you please come up and let me out? I'm locked in the library."

Julius started to speak, then stopped. "Of course," he said. Grinding out his cigar upon the terrace railing, he disappeared into the house.

It seemed an age to Elizabeth before she heard steps in the hall outside and the sound of the key turning in the lock. "Thank God," she said, as the door swung open. Julius peeped cautiously around the edge of the door, an apprehensive expression on his face.

"Any more busts in evidence?" he asked

"No, of course not. Don't be silly, my lord," said Elizabeth. Wrapping her shawl around her shoulders, she brushed past him and started down the stairs. Midway down, however, she paused to look back at him. "I can't thank you enough, my lord," she said. "If I had time, I would try to tell you how grateful I am. But I haven't a minute to lose. It's essential I get away from Gantley immediately, before Lord Steinbridge discovers I am gone."

Julius's eyebrows rose. "Indeed?" he said. "Well, I shan't hinder you, then. Only—is there anything I can do, Elizabeth? I'll be happy to order your carriage if you like."

Elizabeth laughed shortly. "Much good that would do," she said. "Lord Steinbridge has given orders that no carriages or horses are to be allowed to leave the stables tonight. The stable hands have been authorized to use force, if necessary, to prevent it."

Julius's eyebrows rose higher still, but he only said mildly, "That seems rather high-handed."

"It is *extremely* high-handed," said Elizabeth. "But if

Lord Steinbridge thinks that will keep me from leaving, he is quite mistaken. I'd sooner walk every step of the way back to London than remain a second longer in this abominable house."

Julius regarded her a moment with an inscrutable expression. "I see," he said. "But I don't believe you will be obliged to walk if you are really determined to get back to London tonight. There's an evening coach that leaves from the inn in the village here, and you should be able to catch it easily, even if you have to walk there."

"I am much obliged to you, my lord," said Elizabeth warmly. She turned and began to hurry down the stairs.

"Elizabeth, wait," said Julius. Elizabeth paused again, looking back at him. "Elizabeth, is there any other way I can assist you?" he said. "I would be happy to go along with you to the village, or all the way to London for that matter."

Elizabeth lifted her head proudly. "You are very kind, my lord," she said. "But I am quite capable of getting back to London by myself."

"I don't doubt it," said Julius. "I am sure you can manage admirably on your own. But I thought perhaps you might like some company. Being all on one's own— it's a lonely business sometimes."

Elizabeth had the strangest sense that he had just said something very profound. She stood looking at him a moment, then smiled and extended her hand to him. "Since you mention it, some company would indeed be very welcome," she said. "Come along then, my lord, and let us be on our way."

Eighteen

In the end, the escape from Gantley was accomplished with only a few small hitches.

Elizabeth was so eager to get out of the house before Lord Steinbridge returned that at first she gave no thought to any other consideration. But as soon as she and Julius had found a side door that opened into the garden with freedom beckoning just beyond it, he turned to her. "It's a warm night, thank heaven," he said. "But still I fancy you will want something warmer than that shawl. Shall I fetch your cloak for you?"

Elizabeth opened her mouth to demur, then was struck by a picture of herself boarding a stagecoach in full evening dress without even a hat on her head. "Yes, thank you," she said formally. "If you would be so kind, my lord, I would appreciate that very much." As he turned to go, she added, "My lord?"

"Yes?" he said, turning back.

"Thank you," she said, and flashed a smile at him. He smiled back, then turned and hastened up the stairs.

When he returned a moment later, he was bearing her cloak in one hand and his own hat and topcoat in the other. Elizabeth took the cloak from him with a word of thanks. "My lord, I've been thinking," she said. "I believe I'd better leave a note for Lord Steinbridge. It may not keep him from doing something rash, but then again it might."

Julius looked as though he badly wanted to ask a question, but all he said was, "I saw a writing desk in that room just off the stairs. Step in and write your note, and I'll stand guard to see no one interrupts you."

Elizabeth thanked him with another smile, then stepped into the room and hastily scribbled the following note:

> *My Lord:*
>
> *You will understand on receiving this note that I have elected to refuse further example of your hospitality. I also take this opportunity to restate, in writing, that our engagement is irrevocably dissolved. If you choose to announce otherwise in defiance of my wishes, you will shortly find your announcement contradicted in a manner that I believe you will find extremely embarrassing.*
>
> Yours sincerely,
Elizabeth Watson

Having hastily sealed this missive, she gave it to Julius. He ran up the stairs and returned a moment later to say he had left it prominently displayed on the library mantelpiece. "Now we'd better make good our escape before Steinbridge decides to take any more high-handed measures," he said.

"Indeed," said Elizabeth with fervor. Together they hurried through the side door and set off down the drive. When they reached the gates, however, they found them locked and the gatekeeper nowhere in evidence. "I'll wager this is another of Lord Steinbridge's stratagems," said Elizabeth, scowling. "What an officious man!"

"Never mind," said Julius. "The gates may be locked,

but the wall here isn't high. I'll climb over it, then help you over."

This he did, assisting Elizabeth so adroitly that she suffered no more worse injury than a scuff or two on her satin slippers. As they set off down the lane toward the village, she began to laugh. "What an adventure!" she said. "I wonder if Steinbridge has found my note yet?" She cast a smile at Julius. "Thank heaven you were on the terrace!"

"Believe me, I am thanking heaven for that, too," said Julius. "It's purest luck that I was. I was downstairs with the others when Steinbridge came in to tell us that dinner would be delayed a half hour. Well, I didn't feel like standing around for another half hour in that damned drafty room. It was dashed uncomfortable, for one thing, and for another I didn't care for the company. Which is to say, *you* weren't there." He cast a sidelong look at Elizabeth. "So I thought I'd just step outside and smoke a cheroot. And the next thing I knew, a bust of Socrates came crashing down at my feet, and when I looked up, there you were!"

Elizabeth smiled, but there was embarrassment in her eyes. "I suppose you are wondering how I came to be shut in the library," she said.

"Yes, I am perishing to know," said Julius frankly. "But please don't feel obliged to tell me if you don't want to. I can see the matter is one of some delicacy."

"That's one way to put it," said Elizabeth, and she began to laugh once more. "But I don't believe I mind telling you, my lord. Indeed, I think you will appreciate the humor of the situation as much as I do."

She described her meeting with the dowager marchioness, and how it had led to the breaking of her engagement with Lord Steinbridge. "So you see, my lord, my imprisonment was not to be of long duration. Only until I had time to recover from my fit of feminine hysterics."

Julius was laughing helplessly now. "I don't believe it," he said. "Not even Steinbridge could be obtuse enough to think you a hysterical female!"

"But he did, my lord! To him, there was no other possible explanation. I would not marry him, and so naturally I must be hysterical."

"Well, I always thought he was a bit of a slow top, for all he did take double firsts at Oxford," said Julius. "But I suppose there's more than one type of intelligence." He walked on in silence a moment. "And so you have definitely decided not to marry Steinbridge?" he asked.

Elizabeth smiled wryly. "I would hardly be here now if I had not," she said. "You must own that in coming away with you, my lord, I have burned my bridges most effectually!"

Julius smiled, too, but it was a rather abstracted smile. Elizabeth was puzzled by it. She had expected he would be happy to hear her engagement was broken—that he might, perhaps, even try to kiss her now she was free. He had said last time they met that he would not kiss her as long as she was engaged to the marquess, and it did not seem unreasonable to suppose he would take advantage of her newly liberated state to make up for his former reticence. But Julius made no attempt to kiss her. He merely walked silently by her side until they reached the posting house where the London night coach took its departure.

At the posting house, Elizabeth found more to occupy her thoughts than disappointment at not being kissed. When she inquired about being placed on the waybill, she discovered to her dismay that all the places were taken. "But I must get back to London tonight," she exclaimed. "I must!"

"All the places are taken," repeated the clerk. "All the inside ones, that is. And of course a lady like you wouldn't care to ride outside." Despite the plain dark cloak she had draped over her dinner dress, it was evident he had singled her out as a lady of quality.

"Nonsense," said Elizabeth briskly. "If there are no inside places to be had, then of course I must ride outside."

She glanced defiantly at Julius, expecting him to make some protest. But he merely smiled and told the clerk, "The lady is quite equal to riding outside for such a short journey as this will be. And so, I trust, will I be. Two outside places, if you please."

Having purchased the tickets, he helped Elizabeth mount to the roof and seated himself beside her. The only other outside passenger was an elderly man swathed in mufflers who eyed them both with distrust. Elizabeth smiled at him, and after a moment he gave her a grudging smile in return, but she still could feel his eyes flicking from her to Julius with a mistrustful air. As soon as the coachman whipped up the horses, however, he fell instantly asleep and gave them no further trouble.

Elizabeth's main preoccupation throughout the journey was to keep from falling off the coach roof. This was not an easy proceeding, considering they were bowling along at the giddy rate of nine miles per hour. There was, to be sure, a railing, but it was very low and to Elizabeth's eyes quite insubstantial-looking. Fortunately, before they had gone more than a mile or two, Julius put his arm about her shoulders. Elizabeth felt this to be an improper proceeding, but since it added materially to her sense of security, she allowed the arm to remain. Perhaps she supposed it might be a prelude to further intimacies. The situation was not ill-suited to them, for their only possible witness was not merely asleep but snoring loudly. Julius, however, showed no inclination to presume on his position. He seemed content merely to sit with his arm around Elizabeth, and so she had perforce to be content with that, too.

When they reached London, Julius helped her to dismount from the roof, then respectfully begged permission to accompany her to her home. Elizabeth consented, feeling quite certain that he would kiss her when they reached her own door. On the doorstep, she looked up at him shyly. "I don't know how to thank you for all you have done, my lord," she said.

"No thanks are necessary," he said. "Knowing you, I am sure you would have managed perfectly well without me." Raising her hand to his lips, he kissed it, then reentered the waiting hackney. Elizabeth, watching him drive off, found herself feeling oddly cheated.

But he did kiss my hand, she reminded herself. That was something, but not the something she had expected. *Perhaps he will call tomorrow. Yes, I daresay that is it. He will come tomorrow, and then he will ask me to marry him.*

Elizabeth wondered what she would say when he did. She had been thinking of him as her enemy so long that it seemed strange to consider him now in the light of a future husband. Yet there was a certain rightness in the idea that had never been there when she had considered marrying Lord Steinbridge. It had something to do with Julius's attitude toward her money, and something more with her own response to him as a man, but the thing that chiefly struck her when she considered the matter was his chance remark earlier that evening. "I am sure you can manage admirably on your own. But I thought perhaps you might like some company."

There was no doubt that Julius was entertaining, sympathetic, and congenial company. It seemed to Elizabeth that she would not mind having that kind of company for the rest of her life.

But Julius did not come the following day, as Elizabeth had expected. He sent a bouquet of beautiful roses, but there was not so much as a note accompanying them. Try as she might, Elizabeth could not feel certain they presaged more than a friendly concern for her welfare. She was mooning about the drawing room late that afternoon when she heard voices in the hall outside. A moment later her mother and Mrs. Reese-Whittington burst into the room, followed a moment later by Sophia. All three ladies were dusty and travel-stained and full of questions about her abrupt departure from Gantley.

"My dear, whatever possessed you?" demanded Mrs. Watson, plumping down in a chair. "Lord Steinbridge would only say you were called away suddenly. We could not imagine what had happened, especially when we found you did not take so much as your dressing case with you! It seems a strangely irregular business, to say no worse of it."

"If my departure was irregular, lay that to Lord Steinbridge's account, not mine," said Elizabeth coldly. "You may as well know that I have broken our engagement— our *provisional* engagement. In the future, I wish nothing further to do with the man."

This provoked a terrible outcry from Mrs. Watson and Mrs. Reese-Whittington. But Sophia drew near to whisper, "Elizabeth, I don't blame you a bit for breaking your engagement. I have wondered all along whether Lord Steinbridge was really the man to make you happy. Now I have seen him in his own home, I am perfectly sure he would not be. His mother, too, is very disagreeable. She came downstairs just as we were leaving, and I must say I thought her very offensive."

Elizabeth smiled at Sophia, but she had no chance to say more just then, for her mother was loudly bewailing her elder daughter's folly in giving up the chance of marrying a marquess. "It would have been such a wonderful thing for you! Mistress of Gantley, and rich enough to buy any number of abbeys! And now I daresay you will dwindle into an old maid and never marry at all. If Lord

Steinbridge is not good enough for you, I am sure I cannot think of any man who will be."

Elizabeth colored at this, but made no reply. All the rest of that day she silently bore her mother's rebukes, and when, at bedtime, Mrs. Watson tapped on the door of her room and asked if she might come in for a few minutes, Elizabeth was sure it was only to rebuke her some more. But it appeared Mrs. Watson had something else on her mind. She fidgeted about the bedroom, hemming and hawing, and after clearing her throat a few times she finally got down to the issue that was troubling her.

"My dear, I believe I shall have to give permission for Sophia to marry Mr. Arthur after all," she told Elizabeth. "Goodness knows it's not the match I would like for her, but at least it's better than her marrying that dreadful Sir Connor. And it will be a comfort to have *one* of you married and settled in life."

Elizabeth forbore to respond to this jab against herself. She said only that she thought her mother was being very wise. "I don't know about *wise*," said Mrs. Watson disconsolately. "Mr. Arthur is only a curate, after all, and how he and Sophia are to live after they're married I cannot imagine. If only you had married Lord Steinbridge! In his position, and with all his property, he surely might have helped Mr. Arthur to a good living. But your running away from Gantley as you did means there's no chance of that now, I suppose."

"I'm afraid not," said Elizabeth meekly. "But you mustn't despair, Mama. I am sure some kind of preferment will turn up for Mr. Arthur if only we are patient."

She could not help thinking of Julius as she spoke. He might not be as wealthy as Lord Steinbridge, but it seemed possible that he, too, might have a living or two at his disposal. Whether he would be willing to bestow one of those livings at Elizabeth's request began to seem

more and more a moot point, however. An
passed, and then another without his coming to
her, though each day brought a bouquet of flowe
him and on several occasions some other small
well. Elizabeth did not know what to make of it.
Julius possibly have changed his mind about mar.
her? But if so, why the constant gifts?

When, on the fifth day after her return to Lond
Charles Bray brought her word that Lord Atwater w.
below and wished to see her, Elizabeth did not wait t
hear any more. She dismissed the maid who had just
begun arranging her hair, twisted it into a hasty knot, and
tore downstairs like a whirlwind, only slowing her pace
as she approached the drawing room door.

Julius was seated on the sofa in his usual position. On
his lap lay another sheaf of roses. When he saw Elizabeth,
he rose to his feet and extended the bouquet toward her.
"You have changed your hair," he said, scrutinizing her
face. "I like that way of dressing it. It suits you very
well."

Elizabeth laughed shakily. "If it does, it is merest
chance! I am sure I put it up in the most helter-skelter
manner." She accepted the roses, glancing shyly up at
Julius. "More roses! You have been very generous, my
lord. This is five days in a row you have sent me flowers."

"Ah, you noticed! I wondered if you would."

"Well, of course I noticed!" said Elizabeth. "And of
course I appreciated them. But I wondered why you did
not come yourself."

Again she looked shyly at Julius. His face was solemn,
but there was a telltale twinkle in his eye. "Why, I should
think that you, being a military historian, should have
guessed the reason for that," he said.

"I cannot in the *least* guess," said Elizabeth with as-
perity. "But I do not mean to reproach you for not calling

lord. You were under no obligation to do so,
"

but I wanted to call sooner. The truth is that my
was by way of being a strategic withdrawal."

Elizabeth opened her mouth, then shut it again. Julius
on, not seeming to notice her reaction. "The flow-
of course, were a bombardment to soften your de-
ses. I only hope they have worked. Have they?"

Once more Elizabeth opened her mouth, then shut it
again. "My lord!" was all she could think to say.

"I should prefer you to call me Julius," he said. "You
have already called me that once, you know, on that
memorable evening when I helped you escape Steinbridge's somewhat oppressive hospitality."

Elizabeth gave him a quick smile. "I remember," she
said.

"I thought then it was a favorable sign. But I didn't
want to take anything for granted, and I still don't." Julius
looked down at Elizabeth. "I love you, Elizabeth Watson.
I believe I've loved you from the first moment I saw you.
It's my dearest wish that you might see your way clear
to marrying me someday. But I don't want you as my
wife unless you love me, too."

Once more Elizabeth opened her mouth, then closed
it again. Julius went on, his voice and manner very grave.
"You've complained once or twice of being pursued by
men who only wanted your fortune. Well, not all fortune
hunters are male, you know. I've been pursued by a few
of the female variety in my time, and it's an experience
that tends to make one cynical in regard to love and romance. Yet I've never been so cynical that I've entirely
lost hope that someday I'd meet a woman who would love
me for myself, rather than merely for my title and fortune."

Still Elizabeth was silent. Julius went on looking down
at her. "Somehow, from the first time I met you, I thought

you might be that woman. I don't know why, f
never given me any encouragement. On the c
you've let me know on more than one occasion t
had a very poor opinion of me—"

Elizabeth's tongue was suddenly loosened. "That
true," she said. "I felt I *ought* to have a poor opinio
you, Julius, but that was only because I thought y
shared your aunt and cousin's opinion of me. I suppos
you thought me an unprincipled adventuress who ha
tricked your uncle into leaving me his fortune."

"Truly?" said Julius, giving her a searching look.

"Truly," said Elizabeth, meeting the look and then
dropping her eyes again. "I was an unmitigated fool to
imagine you were like your relations."

"Not at all," said Julius. "I can see how you might
reasonably assume I shared my relatives' opinions. I am
only glad if you have learned to believe otherwise."

"Yes, I have," said Elizabeth, her eyes still downcast.
"I believe I have a just appreciation of your merits now,
Julius."

"But a just appreciation of my merits is not what I
want, my love," he said gently. He put his hand under
her chin and tilted her face until she was forced to look
into his eyes. "You must know I am fool enough—or
romantic enough—to want your whole heart. In fact, it's
a matter of all or nothing with me. That's why I've held
off coming to you these past few days, in spite of the
fact that I wanted to in the worst way."

Elizabeth smiled a little. "And is that also why you
didn't kiss me the other night on the stagecoach?" she
asked.

"Yes, though that was partly chivalry, too. You were
in a vulnerable position, and I didn't want to take advantage of it. The situation was equivocal enough as it was.
If someone we knew happened to see us kissing on top
of a stagecoach, the word would have gotten around like

and your reputation would have suffered. In the ⸻ might have felt obligated to marry me just to ⸻ scandal. And I don't want you to marry me be⸻ ⸻ ruined you, or because you feel obligated to me, ⸻ en because you like and esteem me. I only want you ⸻ y wife if you love me as I love you." Julius looked ⸻ her eyes. "You do believe now that I love you, don't ⸻ u, Elizabeth? That it isn't your money I am after at ⸻l?"

"I do believe it, Julius," Elizabeth said in a low voice.

"Then do you think you could come to care for me, too? Please understand that I'm not trying to rush you into anything. I know you were engaged to Steinbridge less than a week ago."

"You forget," said Elizabeth demurely. "My engagement to Lord Steinbridge was a *provisional* one."

"No, I don't forget that," said Julius. He regarded her closely. "All the same, it's pretty commonly supposed among our friends and acquaintances that you're going to marry Steinbridge. When word gets out that you're not, it's bound to make a deal of talk. I wouldn't want to make the situation worse by asking you to formally engage yourself to me anytime soon. All I want is to know whether you might be willing to look on me someday as more than a friend."

He paused, looking at Elizabeth anxiously. Her color was high, but she was smiling. "Do you know, Julius, I don't believe I have any objection to causing talk," she said. "I have always suspected I am not a very conventional woman. If I really wanted to do a thing, I don't believe the fact that it was likely to cause talk would in any way deter me."

There was a look of dawning hope on Julius's face. "We share a common trait, then," he said. "I, too, have been accused in the past of a certain disregard for convention. Indeed, there are those around town who call me downright eccentric. If you intend to marry me, you may as well know it now as later."

"I don't object to a touch of eccentricity," said Elizabeth, looking him steadily in the eye. "I have been called eccentric myself."

Julius took her hand in his. "My love, you fill me with encouragement," he said. "But before you encourage me too far, remember who I am—and more to the point, who my relations are. After everything that has happened, I can hardly expect you would look kindly upon the idea of allying yourself with my abominable aunt and cousin."

Elizabeth laughed. "At that, I don't think it would be any worse than allying myself with the Dowager Marchioness of Steinbridge!" she said. "Honestly, Julius, I don't see your aunt and cousin as any obstacle to our marrying. It's true I don't have the fondest of feelings for them, but so long as they don't make any further attempts to abduct me, I think I can contrive to rub along with them." She smiled up at Julius. "Besides, if I marry you, then your Uncle Lucius's money will be back in the family again, and that was the sum total of their grievance against me."

"My dear," said Julius. "My dear! Does this mean you think you can care for me?"

"It means that I already do," said Elizabeth.

Julius's response was to take her in his arms and kiss her soundly. "Zama," murmured Elizabeth with a sigh.

"What did you say?" asked Julius, drawing back to look at her quizzically.

"Nothing," said Elizabeth. She reflected with satisfaction that there could be no connection between the present moment and Hannibal's last battle. His surrender at Zama had been an undoubted loss, whereas her surrender to Julius had gained her not only a lifelong friend and companion but the romantic lover of her dreams.

* * *

It was some time later that Mrs. Watson, hearing voices inside the drawing room, came to investigate. Great was her shock to find her elder daughter in the arms of Lord Atwater. "Elizabeth!" she gasped. "What on earth does this mean?"

"It means I am going to marry Lord Atwater, Mama," said Elizabeth joyfully. Mrs. Watson observed with disapproval that she looked and sounded not one whit discomposed. "I hope you will wish us both happy."

Mrs. Watson opened her mouth to say she would do nothing of the kind. Then she reflected that Julius Atwater, for all his demerits, was an eligible baron and a well-respected member of the *ton,* while her elder daughter was a singularly cross-grained girl whom she had despaired of ever marrying anyone. "I see," she said cautiously. "Well, my dear, this is all very sudden. But I am sure I am pleased if you are."

Elizabeth kissed her, and Julius followed suit, telling Mrs. Watson that he felt deeply honored at the prospect of becoming a member of her family. This pleased Mrs. Watson so much that she was able to listen patiently while the two of them babbled on about their plans. These seemed to include an extended wedding trip to Italy, where Elizabeth hoped to make certain researches concerning the First Punic War. "For you know, having accepted your Uncle Lucius's fortune, the least I can do is obey the wishes he expressed in connection with it," she explained to Julius. "I only hope you will not find it tedious, trailing around looking at ruins and battle sites."

"My dear, I will warrant not to find anyplace tedious so long as you are there," he said tenderly. "I ask nothing better than to look at ruins and battle sites in your company."

Mrs. Watson held her tongue during this exchange, but

later, after Julius had gone, she ventured to remonstrate with her daughter. "Elizabeth, I cannot think what has come over you. The last I heard, you detested Lord Atwater and claimed he was your enemy. And now you say you are going to marry him!"

Elizabeth looked rueful. "Yes, I did say some dreadful things about him, but that was because I did not know him. Now that I do know him, I can think of no man I would rather marry."

"If you say so," said Mrs. Watson dubiously. "Of course he's not a bad catch, all things considered. I must say, however, that I still regret that your engagement with Lord Steinbridge fell through. He was such a pleasant gentleman, and I am quite sure he would have been willing to do something for Sophia and Mr. Arthur—"

"But Julius is willing to do something for Sophia and Mr. Arthur, too," said Elizabeth, smiling. "Julius has a seat near Reading, and the rector of the parish there is planning to retire this fall. Julius is quite willing that the living should go to Mr. Arthur. You must see that nothing could be better, Mama. Not only will Sophia and I be able to see each other when Julius and I are staying there, but it's close enough to London that we can visit back and forth whenever we like."

Mrs. Watson was so pleased by this news that she could summon up only one further objection to her daughter's proposed marriage. "I won't deny that Lord Atwater is an eligible gentleman, and not a bad-looking one, either, as far as that goes," she told Elizabeth. "But it has often struck me that there is something a little *eccentric* about him."

Elizabeth laughed. "Yes, but you know I am eccentric myself, Mama," she said. "You've told me so yourself, countless times."

"That's so," said Mrs. Watson, looking struck. "Do

you know, my dear, I shouldn't wonder if you and Lord Atwater wouldn't deal very well together!"

"I shouldn't wonder if you're right," said Elizabeth.

ABOUT THE AUTHOR

JOY REED lives with her family in Michigan. She is cu rently working on her next Zebra Regency romance LORD DESMOND'S DESTINY, which will be published in July 2002. Joy loves hearing from readers and you may write to her c/o Zebra Books. Please include a self-addressed stamped envelope if you wish a reply.

The Queen of Romance

Cassie Edwards

__re's Blossom _217-6405-5	$5.99US/$7.99CAN
__xclusive Ecstasy _0-8217-6597-3	$5.99US/$7.99CAN
__Passion's Web 0-8217-5726-1	$5.99US/$7.50CAN
__Portrait of Desire 0-8217-5862-4	$5.99US/$7.50CAN
__Savage Obsession 0-8217-5554-4	$5.99US/$7.50CAN
__Silken Rapture 0-8217-5999-X	$5.99US/$7.50CAN
__Rapture's Rendezvous 0-8217-6115-3	$5.99US/$7.50CAN

More Zebra Re~~gency Romances~~

Call toll free **1-888-345-BOOK** to order by phone or use this
coupon to order by mail.

Name_____

Address_____

City_____ State_____ Zip_____

Please send me the books I have checked above.

I am enclosing $_____

Plus postage and handling* $_____

Sales tax (in New York and Tennessee only) $_____

Total amount enclosed $_____

*Add $2.50 for the first book and $.50 for each additional book.

Send check or money order (no cash or CODs) to:

Kensington Publishing Corp., 850 Third Avenue, New York, NY 10022

Prices and numbers subject to change without notice.

All orders subject to availability.

Check out our website at **www.kensingtonbooks.com**.